A Slave to the Darkness

Book 2 in the Black Rose Series

LAURA MORGAN

Second edition
Produced 2016 by Laura Morgan

For print copies:
ISBN: 1499321937
ISBN-13:978-1499321937

An important message from the author.

Before you read this book, please be ready to delve into a dark and taboo world of demons and angels who can and will do as they please. This series will immerse you in a world filled with dark places and even darker beings. They are not human, and do not act the way you and I act, or think the way you and I think. Please be ready for some controversial themes and for me to push the boundaries.

I tell you this not just because there are adult scenes or a few taboo subjects, but because I mean it, and would hate to give you any false expectations about happy endings and softly, softly romance. This series is not for everyone, and I know that, so please decide if you're ready before diving in.

If you're on the fence, or have heard the rumours of the depravities and darkness that await you, please assume they are all true. I can understand how some readers were upset and discouraged by the thought of some of the darker themes, but urge you to trust me…

If you're interested, I explain these points further on my blog, and would urge you to take a look before starting this book. Please be aware there are spoilers in the post, but that it might put your mind at ease before you dive in.

PLEASE NOTE

This story depicts explicit sexual relationships between consenting adults, including elements of coerced consent and intimidation, which may be a trigger for some readers.

This novel is absolutely not suitable for those under the age of 18.

Cover art by Laura Morgan
Cover photograph © Dundanim courtesy of Shutterstock.com

Praise for A Slave to the Darkness...

I was given this book to ARC for honest review.... well wasn't sure how this would compare to the first book but wow fell in love with this book straight away its awesome. Who doesn't love a fantastic love story with strong believable, charismatic characters and a story line which leaves you hanging at the end wanting more...
Really eager to read the rest of this series.
--Vicky

I was given this book as an ARC for an honest review. I had read the first instalment to this series and completely fell in love with it. Book 2 certainly did not let me down!! I was hooked from the first page! If I am honest I enjoyed this one more than the first but the first was giving you the history of the series.
I fell in love with Blake and Tilly's story from the very beginning. I'm a romantic at heart and high hopes that this love story would work out...
The story flowed and the characters are strong.
The story was left on a cliffhanger, which left me flabbergasted!! Can't wait to start book 3!! Thanks for this opportunity Laura!! I love this series!!--Sarah

Couldn't stop gasping! I totally fell into the story, felt for the characters and slightly drained at the end and picked up book 3 immediately.
Tilly and Blake provide such a great romance and all they achieve and overcome.
--Beckie

Dedication

For Brian, Jemma and Miranda. Your support and help in continuing my writing journey has been invaluable, I could not have done any of this without any of you.

And, to my wonderful readers, this is for you. I would love to say I am sorry for the sudden ending in the last book, and I'd like to promise not to do it again, but I would hate to lie to you now that we have a connection with one another, enjoy!

PROLOGUE

Fifty years had passed since Lottie, the child of both light and darkness, had left Earth forever and gone to Hell so that she could be with her long-lost mother, Cate Rose. A mother who had every reason to have been absent from her daughter for so long, and in knowing that, Lottie forgave her for all of it. Her mother had come back to her strong, commanding, and free of the ties that'd once bound her mind, body, heart and soul to her ex-husband, Lucifer. She had overthrown him and taken his place as the ruler of Hell, and then come to Earth to claim her secret daughter as the all-powerful, new Devil.

It was fifty years in which Lottie had also seen her adoptive father, Harry adapt to his new life as a demon following the willing transition from his human existence to becoming an immortal, dark being. As a human, Harry had given Cate his heart many years before Lottie was even born, and when she'd called upon him in her hour of need, he had taken on her burdens without any hesitation, fear, doubt, or care for his own safety. Harry had chosen to love his soulmate no matter what fate might befall him because of it, and when the time had come for Lottie to go home with her mother, Harry too had pledged his soul to the Dark Queen and performed a gory, ancient ritual that'd transformed him into a powerful demon so that they could finally be together for all eternity.

Cate's older children, twins Blake and Luna, had welcomed their new family with open arms and open hearts. They each followed their own paths, but they were paths that led to one another's sides, and which made them grow stronger and closer as the years passed them by.

The fifty short years had also given Cate the time to nurture her almighty prowess and embrace her powerful position as the fierce and almighty Dark Queen. She did so thanks to the warmth and love of her family, and she was now both loved and feared by all who served her. Hell's immortal royal family knew that their dark reign would last forever—that they were strong and whole at last—and yet the powerful beings remained ever grateful for every gift that they'd been given along the hard and grisly road. They grew, they lived, and they loved each other with every ounce of power that they possessed, and while their bodies remained unaffected by the passing of time, their minds adapted—each of them growing wiser and more commanding with every year that passed. They had all changed and adjusted to the new world around them, but most importantly, they'd stayed together, and knew that they always would.

Each member of the Rose family protected their Queen as their first and foremost priority, knowing that there would always be those who lived in the light who would rejoice in her demise if they ever let down those protective walls around her. Her ex-lover and Lottie's father, an angel named Uriel, wanted nothing more than to lure Cate out of hiding, but she was clever and cunning. Cate had the entire underworld at her command, an army of demons, and a formidable dark coven that constantly strengthened their portals and thresholds in order to keep her and her family safe.

And so, the bitter, unsatisfied angel watched from his heavenly home and waited, hoping one day that he would sense his long-lost daughter's presence on Earth again. When he did, he hoped to take her away from her mother at long last, but he was never satisfied in his search for her, and Cate knew she would give her life making sure that he never would be.

The wars raged on, and neither side would find peace until it chose to cease its plight for power and control over the other. And yet, with the lives of their children at stake, neither could safely yield.

It would continue forevermore, and Cate vowed she would never risk the lives of those she loved to appease her old master, or the High Council of Angels.

CHAPTER ONE

Matilda Mayfair—or Tilly as she was better known—and her two best friends, Renee and Gwen, took their seats a few minutes before the show began. She'd never been to the circus before, and had only gone along tonight on the assurance from Renee that this was going to be the most spectacular show she would ever see. The infamous *'Diablo Circus'* was performing tonight for their second night in Coventry, England and had been a hit all across the world, selling out in London, Paris, and even as far afield as Tokyo and New York as they'd toured over the past few years. The gloomily dressed performers were critically acclaimed and renowned for their skills and death-defying feats that wowed the crowds and kept the audiences coming back night after night, and their night was no exception from what Tilly could tell. She had to admit, she was intrigued to see what all the fuss was about.

The main performance hadn't even begun, but Tilly could already see what Renee had meant. It was fantastic inside the huge tent, and the air was thick with excitement and the expectation of what was to come. Some of the circus performers were out amongst the audience, wooing the crowd and going between the tightly packed benches, doing tricks and showing off for the eager public to small bursts of praise and applause.

As Tilly scanned the crowd, a tall juggler caught her attention right away. He was gorgeous, even behind his shadowy makeup and black clothes, and she watched him a moment. The juggler grinned and lapped up the attention from the women before him as he speedily flung their donated bracelets and watches up and down before them as they gasped and giggled excitedly. A real showman, he had them wowed without even breaking a sweat. Tilly guessed he was in his mid-twenties, far too old for her as she was only eighteen, but she couldn't help but window-shop for a few moments, watching him intently for a short while before Renee nudged her, breaking her reverie as she asked if Tilly wanted any popcorn.

"Yeah, go on then," she replied, paying and then thanking the vendor as she passed her a warm box of the sweet, fluffy corn. When she looked back towards the crowd again, Tilly jumped. The juggler she'd been watching was now standing right in front of her with a cheeky grin on his handsome face as he reached down and stole a handful of corn from her box. Without a word, he then plucked the black hat she'd been wearing from the top of her head. It was a warm summer's evening, and she'd almost forgotten she was still wearing her trilby from when they'd been stood in the bright sunshine waiting to be let into the huge tent earlier that evening—until that moment. She'd dressed comfortably for their night out in a floral printed maxi dress and denim jacket, and she couldn't help but feel as though she looked garishly casual before him in his all-black tuxedo. Tilly blushed as he watched her for a moment and ate his stolen popcorn, seemingly intrigued by her for some reason, and her friends giggled as they watched their moment from beside her on the bench. She assumed that the man would start tossing the hat like he'd just done with the other peoples' things, but for some reason he didn't. He simply looked down at her, smiled widely, and then popped her hat on his own head before he wandered off back to the centre of the large tent without a word, looking back at her from the stage with a wicked grin as he gathered up his juggling balls and began showing off to the crowd once again.

"Whoa, what was that?" Gwen asked from Renee's other side, bewildered at the gorgeous man's actions, but also excited by the attraction they'd all sensed pass between them. Tilly just shrugged; unsure herself what he was playing at, but she hoped she wasn't imagining things.

"I'm thinking he wants you to go and get it back later," Renee told Tilly, her blue eyes wide as a cheeky grin crossed her tanned face.

"Maybe," Tilly answered her thoughtfully, hoping she might just get the chance to find out whether Renee's theory was correct later on in their evening.

The show was amazing. Each of the various acts and performers had time in the spotlight to show off their personal talents, as well as some groups of them performing together, demonstrating their incredible skills and fearless routines before the gasping, elated crowd. The three girls sat silent and utterly mesmerised by the night's eye-opening entertainment, taking in every fantastic act, and applauding loudly along with the rest of the crowd when the impressive finale signified the end of that night's show.

Once the performers had taken their last bows and left the stage, Tilly and her friends hung around for a little while to try and find the gorgeous juggler who'd stolen her hat. He'd worn it throughout his entire performance and had even given her a cheeky wink during the big finish when he tossed it high up in the air and it'd then landed perfectly back on his head.

She'd been sure he was interested in seeing her again after their brief encounter earlier, but now she was having absolutely no luck in finding him. She didn't want to come across as some pathetic groupie or stalker, but couldn't resist hanging around the entrance to the huge tent for a little while with her friends, trying not to be too obvious about it. After a few more minutes, Tilly checked her watch. Her curfew was coming up, so she decided to call it a night and started to make her way over to Renee's car, disappointed that she hadn't gotten to meet the handsome juggler properly after all his flirting.

"Hey, aren't you forgetting something?" a voice called from behind the trio of girls after they had taken just a few steps away. They all turned back in an instant, and Tilly could see the voices owner clearly as he stood propped against a post just a few metres away from them. It was the juggler, and he was even more gorgeous now, having changed out of his carnival costume into black jeans and a t-shirt. His dark-blond hair was pulled back into a short ponytail and his light blue eyes stared over at the three of them as the girls approached. He spun her hat on his index finger playfully, before throwing it in the air as Tilly neared him. It landed on her head perfectly, and she couldn't help but giggle, mentally kicking herself for being so girly, but she was in awe of this gorgeous boy, and couldn't understand why he had chosen to flirt with her out of all the women there tonight.

She smiled coyly at him, not really knowing what to say. "I hope you didn't mind me borrowing it for a while?" he asked, putting out a hand to introduce himself as Tilly reached him. She shook it, swooning when he gave her another dazzling grin, while the bright lights of the circus around him illuminated his handsome face and eyes wonderfully.

"Tilly," she told him, before adding, "and no, I didn't mind at all."

"My name's Brent," he replied, keeping a firm grip of her hand as he took her in, and she could do nothing but smile back up at him.

He knew that Tilly must only be young, but there was something about this girl that he'd liked from the moment he'd caught her watching him from the audience. Her dark-blonde hair and blue eyes matched his own, but her features were innocent and beautiful, whereas he'd always looked older than he actually was. Brent knew his years of hard work at the hands of his father and circus master, Lucas McCulloch, had hardened and weathered his once so boyish looks. He was usually emotionally closed-off with the women he flirted with and, more often than not, went on to take home with him after the shows. He'd always made a habit of having one-night-stands and then kicking the women out the next morning, full of empty promises and fake excuses, and all the while telling himself he was too busy for a real relationship. Tonight though it was somehow, different. For some reason he looked at Tilly differently. He wasn't interested in the short-term, and even after such a small amount of time, he knew he wanted to get to know this girl.

Both Renee and Gwen's mouths dropped open in shock as they watched the pair of them in absolute amazement. Their spark was undeniable. They were hooked on the pairs every move, and neither said a word—not even the usually so chatty Renee.

"It's been lovely to meet you, but I'm afraid I have to go home now. It's almost past my curfew," Tilly told him. She blushed and looked down at her hands, feeling ashamed of her childish restrictions.

"It's okay," he said, smiling at her. "We're here for two more nights, so how do you fancy coming back tomorrow about noon?

You can help me practice? Bring your friends, too," he added, looking over to the two girls behind her and Tilly looked back up into his bright eyes and smiled.

"Yes, yes, yes!" cried Renee in response before she could even say another word. "We'll be here."

"Good, see you then." Brent replied, grabbing Tilly's hand and then planting a kiss on the back of it before letting her walk away with her friends.

The girls giggled quietly with each other as they made their way over to the car again. When they were inside, they all screamed with excitement. Even Tilly couldn't control herself, and she jumped up and down in her seat as she let the wonderful, warm feelings wash over her. It amazed her that after only a tiny bit of time with the incredible man, he'd gotten her all hot and bothered, and she could wait to come back again the next day.

CHAPTER TWO

The following afternoon, Tilly, Renee, and Gwen arrived outside the huge circus tent just before midday, as per Brent's instructions from the night before. It was strange to see the place during the day. The tent was so empty and quiet in comparison to the busy and hectic crowds there the night before, and it felt odd to the girls as they approached. Brent stood at the entrance waiting for them, and he beckoned the girls inside after they climbed out of Renee's car and wandered over towards the gigantic dome.

"Hi," he said, giving Tilly a smile and taking her hand in his before leading her into the huge arena.

"Hi," was all she could reply, feeling shy and quiet thanks to this gorgeous boy's affectionate gaze as it swept over her in the bright sunshine. She'd opted for black shorts and a red strapless bandeau top, suffering with both the heat from the summer sunshine and from her excited blush at seeing Brent again, so she'd dressed for comfort as well as coolness. Tilly also had her dark-blonde hair pulled up into a high ponytail, unable to bear the feel of it against her sweat-dusted skin.

Brent led the way, laughing when the girls gasped in awe as they took in the men and women that were practising their talents inside, each of them smiling welcomingly at the group when they passed by. Two more young men came over and joined them once they were inside, and Brent quickly made the introductions. They were his two younger brothers, David and Jackson, who both eagerly shook hands with the girls, and had broad and warm smiles on their faces. Renee had her sights already set, and soon wandered off with the eldest of Brent's two brothers, David, while Gwen took Jackson's offered hand and followed him over to the fire-breathing station where he'd been practising just a few minutes earlier.

Tilly followed Brent to the main stage, where she then met his father, Lucas, whom she guessed must be in his mid-forties. He too had dark-blond hair and deep blue eyes, just like Brent and his brothers, and he had a once thick Scottish accent that was now dulled down thanks to having moved around for so long, but was still clearly recognisable when he chatted to her for a few minutes.

"Welcome to our humble little enterprise," Lucas said modestly, taking in the two of them with a satisfied grin, while he wrapped his hands in bandages and powdered them with chalk in preparation for his acrobatic practice session.

"Thanks for having me. It's amazing to be allowed to come and see behind the scenes," she replied, and was genuinely excited to be there.

"No problem at all, but I do hope you're prepared to give Brent a good workout for me?" he asked, a sly smile curling at his lips. Tilly could do nothing but giggle in response, while Brent rolled his eyes and laughed to himself. "Well, I'll offer you one piece of advice either way. Don't watch the batons when he gets going, you'll get dizzy, keep your eyes locked on his and you'll be fine."

"I'll bear that in mind, thanks," she replied with a smile.

"Well, I'd better get practising, too. It was lovely to meet you, Tilly," he said, grinning down at her warmly. She had the sense that Lucas was a genuine gentleman, leading her to hope that Brent too had inherited the same qualities. She'd never felt so excited and optimistic about a boy before, and wanted to believe in the way he and everyone else at the circus was making her feel—safe, happy, welcome, and in Brent's case, hot under the collar.

"It was lovely to meet you too, Lucas," she replied politely, watching as he climbed the steps to the trapeze. It was Brent's rough hand in hers that eventually broke her gaze, and she followed his lead towards a smaller stage.

The pair of them then spent the next couple of hours messing around with the juggling balls, batons, and bowling pins she'd seen him use the night before. His skill and speed were truly amazing, and she watched in awe as he spun them around with ease, while he urged Tilly to throw more into the fray. She followed Lucas' advice and kept her eyes on Brent's as he practised, and his moves really were mesmerising—yet dizzying. Staring into his gorgeous blue eyes for so long soon made Tilly feel a little overwhelmed by her own giddiness though. She became genuinely flustered as he stared back into her eyes intensely, and all the while with a gorgeous, knowing grin curling at his lips.

By the time Brent finally let the batons crash to the floor, he was panting and dusted with a light layer of sweat. He welcomed Tilly's suggestion to take a break, needing both a drink and a moment away from her bewitching gaze, too.

They talked for a while as they sat with a can of cola on one of the now empty audience benches. Tilly told him all about her parents' farm where they lived in the rural quietness of the Warwickshire countryside, but how she enjoyed the liveliness and opportunities that having the cities close by gave her. She also told him all about how she loved to cook. Out of her school time she baked cakes and tarts to sell in the family farm shop that her mother ran, and where she worked on weekends and the odd afternoon if it was busy.

As she told him about herself, Tilly couldn't help but feel as though her quiet, simple life seemed so small in comparison to Brent's, and she was envious of him travelling the world. Part of her couldn't imagine that he thought her little existence on the farm was very interesting, and yet he listened intently as she spoke, smiling and asking her more about herself as she went, seeming genuinely interested. Tilly carried on, chatting away animatedly about her first memories of the farm, and she told him the story of how she'd helped her dad deliver a foal at the age of six, a horse she'd named Raven as he was jet-black, and who was now hers thanks to the kind nature of her father, Robert.

"And what about you? What do you do for fun?" she eventually asked him, aware that she'd been talking away for a while, and Brent actually had to think for a minute before answering her.

"Well, aside from the obvious," he said, indicating the circus. "I suppose I don't really get much down time, but when I do, I like to read. Boring I know, but when you travel around as much as I do, there's not much you can take with you as you go. But, a good book can always fit in your backpack, and a good imagination will take you anywhere, even small farms in the English countryside," he told her with a sheepish grin, and was surprised by his own honesty—he'd never told anyone that before.

Tilly smiled up at Brent with an understanding look, and he knew right away he was smitten with her. He wouldn't push her, knowing she was so young, but he was sure about one thing. This girl was going to leave her mark on him, but he didn't care. He wanted her and he had no doubt that she wanted him, too. Tilly was worth risking everything for, and for the first time in his otherwise shallow love life, Brent was finally ready to sacrifice the bachelor lifestyle he'd once had in preference of a place at someone like Tilly's side.

CHAPTER THREE

Tilly and her friends stayed with the McCulloch brothers at the circus site all afternoon, and she felt comfortable and happy there the entire time. Her connection with the gorgeous juggler was both thrilling and terrifying, and she quickly fell more and more under his sensuous spell.

She and Gwen sat together on one of the benches a few hours later, squealing excitedly as they watched Brent throwing Jackson around effortlessly as they practised their new routine. It was a combination of mixed acrobatics and thrilling displays of their strengths and perfectly honed skills, and was amazing. The two boys simply laughed together as the girls shrieked, using their reaction as an indication that the new routine was going to be a hit.

By the time the large group of performers had then eaten some delicious home cooked chilli—a huge bowl of which was given to each of the girls without them even having to ask—it was nearly time for the preparations to begin for that night's show. Tilly half expected them to ask the girls to leave, but Lucas wouldn't hear of it. He and his wife Lily already treated them like friends, and quickly enlisted Renee and Gwen to help out in the ticket booths for them while she handed out flyers by the doorway. Lily was an odd addition to their team. She was beautiful, warm and young. Much younger than she would've thought given the age of the three McCulloch boys. Tilly had liked her instantly, and as soon as she had promised free entrance to the three girls as a small thank you for their help, they'd happily agreed.

"Yes of course!" Renee cried, seemingly eager to stay as much as Tilly. She and David had shared a kiss behind the ticket booth already that afternoon, and she wanted to stick around in the hope she might get more from the handsome middle brother. Renee, with her long-blonde hair and tanned, pretty face, was the most promiscuous of their small group of friends, and she knew how to wrap any man she wanted around her little finger. David was nineteen years old, just a year older than she was, so it seemed like a good match as there was much less of an age gap than there was between Tilly and Brent.

Oddly, she felt like he was so much older than her, despite it only actually being a few years difference, and Brent seemed to feel the same way. He was being on his best behaviour with her, although Tilly knew he must have women throwing themselves at him every night, and was no stranger to the games men and women would play while vying for each other's attention. She could already sense that he was no novice in the bedroom, as well as him clearly knowing how to turn on the charm, but for some reason he wasn't doing that with her, or at least it felt that way.

He came to see her after she'd collected her flyers, and kissed her cheek before he turned to leave, needing to go and change his clothes and apply his dark makeup before the crowds arrived, but then turned back, staring down at Tilly for a moment longer. Her heart pounded in her ears as he reached down and grabbed her chin before then planting a deep, urgent kiss on her lips. She let herself get lost in that kiss, and knew she was already falling. As he pulled back, she was sure she heard an almost silent gasp come from his parted lips, but then he let her go and walked away, a cheeky, gorgeous smile on his face as he backed into the shadows.

The late summer evening then settled over the site as Tilly, Renee, and Gwen watched from beside the main stage while Brent and his extended family performed their well-rehearsed acts with ease and skill again. The crowds roared and called for more as they took their bows, so Jackson and David performed one last fire-breathing routine, taking everyone's breath away once again, before the audience finally dispersed and the tent became quiet once more. After the last of the cars had left the parking area, Tilly wandered off in search of Brent. When she helped tidy up some of the scattered leaflets from earlier on her way, she bumped into Lily as she made her way through the empty lot. The woman wasn't tall, but was somehow commanding. Powerful in her own way. Tilly had learned now how she wasn't Brent's mum, but his stepmother, but that he and his brothers loved her like they were her own, and how she felt the same way about them. They chatted for a couple of minutes before Lily directed her towards Brent's mobile home with a smile. Tilly thanked her and then went inside, feeling awkward despite Lily's encouragement, when she found herself coming face to face with a half naked, surprised, yet relaxed Brent, still wet from his shower with a towel wrapped around his waist. He dripped water onto the hard floor as he dried his hair with a second towel, and for a second she couldn't peel her eyes away.

"Hey," he said, calm and steady, while Tilly blushed and turned away.

"Oh my God, I'm so sorry! Lily said you would be in here and I just..." she tailed off, feeling both embarrassed and foolish. She'd never done anything more than kiss a boy before and didn't know where to even begin processing the half naked image of him that was now well and truly engrained in her skull, an image that made her body tingle at the memory, and she desperately wanted to see more.

Brent reached out and gently grabbed her arm, pulling her around to face him again, despite him still being just barely covered by the towel.

"It's okay, really," he said, laughing at her coyness. He was obviously much more used to women seeing him naked than Tilly was to seeing muscular, gorgeous men, dripping wet before her. "I know you're, how should I say this? *Inexperienced,* Tilly, but you don't need to be ashamed. I won't ever expect you to do anything you don't want to do, okay?" he added, looking her in the eye with a genuine smile.

"Okay," she managed to reply, and Tilly could feel herself relaxing already.

"Good," he said with a cheeky grin, before without another word, he leaned forward and planted another deep kiss on her lips.

Tilly relished in his soft, yet strong touch, and didn't hold back. She let her hands go up to his wet hair and then she ran them through his shoulder-length locks as she kissed him back passionately. He then pulled her up into his strong arms and sat down on the small sofa that was built into one of the walls of his small motor home, their mouths never once leaving each other's.

She straddled him on the chair, and could feel the hardness of his arousal pushing up from underneath the towel. Tilly couldn't help herself, and in a moment of hormone-fuelled confidence she reached down and grabbed it, pushing the towel aside and gripping his length tightly with her small hands. Brent gasped, but didn't stop her as she began pulling up and down, gently at first and then harder and faster as they continued to kiss each other intensely. He came quickly, the hot, thick, wetness bursting out onto the damp towel as she finished her pulls and finally let go, and she was surprised to have managed so well on her first try.

Tilly giggled as she planted one more kiss on his lips and then climbed off his lap, but Brent simply smiled as he stood, completely naked before her, wiping himself clean and then bunching up the dirty towel before throwing it into his hamper. Tilly blushed again as she found her eyes uncontrollably drawn to his glorious body, and Brent lapped up her attention for a moment before he padded over to his small chest of drawers and slipped on some black tracksuit trousers. He then returned to the sofa and grabbed her again for more kisses, not taking his lips off hers until it was eventually time for Tilly to head home, but he didn't make any more advances. Strangely for him, Brent didn't want to move too quickly, despite being more than ready for it. For her, he'd take it slowly. For her, he wanted to savour every moment.

CHAPTER FOUR

The girls were invited to spend the next day with Brent and his brothers again too, and they couldn't wait to get back to the site. Renee had reportedly had sex with David the night before, and Gwen had apparently shared a kiss with the younger brother, Jackson, so they too were completely besotted with the handsome McCulloch brothers.

Tilly had barely been able to sleep once she'd gone home the night before, and could feel her tiredness, but didn't care. She'd been so horny following her wonderful day with Brent and had needed to pleasure herself before her body would calm down and eventually let her drift off to sleep. Her hands had travelled down inside her knickers as she'd thought about him and his deep kisses. She imagined that long, thick, cock inside her as Tilly stroked her tender clit and slipped her fingers into her wet cleft, moving her hips up and down eagerly while imagining his mouth, those hands, and that glorious body on hers. It wasn't long until she'd reached her climax, the aftershocks reverberating throughout her entire body for a few minutes, and had then drifted off to a relaxed sleep at last.

The three young women all lied to their parents the next morning, saying they were sleeping over at one another's houses in order for them to all stay the entire night on the campsite for the circus' final show in their area. Tilly knew she was old enough to just tell her parents the truth about staying overnight with her new crush, but she'd always lived a sheltered life and couldn't bring herself to tell them. Her parents were strict, and she couldn't bear the conversation she knew they'd put her through if she told them she was planning on staying out all night with a boy. It was better to lie than die of embarrassment, or at least that was what she told herself.

The day brought with it a bittersweet anticipation for both her and Brent. Tilly already hated the thought of him leaving, and was even having wild ideas of running away with the circus, but knew she'd never actually have the guts to do anything quite so crazy. She hoped they would try and stay in contact once the circus moved on, but for now, the last few days had been the most wonderful of her life, and she wanted to enjoy her last bit of time with her gorgeous juggler without worrying about the future.

Brent welcomed her with a deep, desperate kiss the instant she climbed out of the car, and the pair quickly went off to his motor home to be alone while the other girls did the same with their suitors. Lucas had given Brent some time off to relax, rather than practice hard again that afternoon, and the two of them loved having some time to themselves. They kissed and chatted quietly for a while, opening up more about their hopes and dreams while they gazed into each other's eyes.

"I've never had to worry about leaving anywhere before, Tilly," Brent told her honestly as he made her a cup of tea. "But this time, I don't want to go. I want to stay here. I want to stay with you," he said, blushing slightly himself as he let his feelings show for the first time ever. Tilly smiled, basking in his attention, and she adored his sudden coyness.

"Me too, but you have to go, Brent. This is your life, and I can't take you away from it. I've got nothing to offer you here," she said, and accepted the tea he'd made but then looked down into the mug forlornly after she'd said the words. He reached across the small counter and grabbed her chin, pulling her gaze up to meet his.

"You have everything to offer me, Tilly. Don't you understand, that's the problem?" he asked, leaning closer and then kissing her gently. She didn't really understand in all honesty, and could not let herself hope that he felt the same way about her as she did him. She smiled up at Brent and kissed him back, allowing his loving words to wash over her, but wouldn't let herself dream they could be true.

The air between them changed, and he felt it too. Brent stared at her thoughtfully for a moment over his strong tea, and wondered how it was that he'd become so beguiled. His father had given him some advice that morning, urging him to follow his gut with Tilly and take the next step, but not lead her on, and he knew that Lucas was right. He wanted her with every fibre of his being, but couldn't bear the thought of hurting Tilly the way he was so accustomed to do so with other women. Then and there, he vowed to himself that he'd take care of this sweet, gorgeous girl. He was desperate not to hurt her.

There were only a few moments of tense silence before the tea was discarded and the pair resumed their position from the previous night on the sofa—Brent having pulled Tilly onto his lap while they kissed one another feverishly. She wanted him to be her first, but was scared and unsure of herself, still feeling self-conscious despite her conviction. He sensed it, and expertly guided her, knowing she could do with a helping hand, and someone to take the lead. He didn't say a word, and simply started by taking off her white t-shirt and bra. He then took the time to kiss her small breasts, sucking on each nipple gently as she groaned with pleasure atop him.

Brent then lifted her up in his strong arms and moved Tilly over to his double bed, and laying her down on the dark sheets before pulling off her denim skirt and knickers in one quick move. She blushed as he swept his smouldering eyes over her naked body. She was a curvy girl, neither short nor tall, but Tilly had always been self-conscious about her wide hips and small breasts that she prayed would grow some more, but didn't hold out too much hope of doing so now that she was already a woman. Despite her insecurities, she couldn't help but smile up at him when she saw his hard erection that was already threatening to burst out of his jeans.

"It's only fair," he said with a cheeky grin, leaning down on top of Tilly to kiss her again, his clothes staying on for now. "Seeing as you got to see me completely naked last night," he added, trailing soft kisses down her chest to kiss her nipples again. She groaned her affirmations as he kept going, reaching her navel and then expertly sinking his mouth into her wet nether lips, enveloping her clit and sucking on it as she writhed beneath him. Tilly arched her back, forgetting all about her shyness, and she felt ready and willing for him to take her further. Brent pushed open her thighs with his hands and then plunged two fingers inside her wetness, sensing her readiness for him.

She gasped and moaned loudly again, twitching when soon she came for him, her body hot and more than ready for what she hoped would come next. Brent then rose from between her thighs and pulled off his black t-shirt, followed quickly by his jeans and boxers. Tilly watched him with a smile, still buzzing from her orgasm and wanting him so much. She nodded, giving him that silent confirmation he craved, and then he grabbed a condom from a drawer to the side of the bed.

Once sheathed, he climbed on top of Tilly and pulled her hips up to greet his, sliding himself inside of her with ease and opening up her tender muscles as he pushed deeper inside of her gloriously inviting cleft. The pain she expected flared deep within her for a moment but she urged him to continue, relishing in his desire for her and wanting him to reach his climax, needing him to enjoy his own release, too. They thrust together wonderfully until Brent reached his own glorious end, gasping as he came, and all the while kissing her passionately.

Tilly lay in his arms afterwards, content and happy as she revelled in the afterglow of her first time. It was perfect. Brent was perfect, and although she was too sore to do anything more, she was glad she'd decided that today was the day. She was hardly experienced when it came to making love, but was certainly looking forward to doing more with Brent later that night after the show was over.

CHAPTER FIVE

The girls watched their lovers perform again later that evening for the third night in a row, relishing in the tantalising and thrilling feats of the show with even broader smiles after the wonderful second full day spent at the circus. Tilly watched Brent with an excited glint in her eye, catching his deep blue eyes on her many times over the evening. She laughed to herself as the other women in the crowd, both young and old, fawned over him and tried to get his attention. Tonight though, he wasn't interested in them, and his attention was reserved for her alone. The three best friends loved every minute of their last show, their shrieks and applause just as loud and genuine as they'd been on the first night. Renee and Gwen laughed raucously along with the crowd as David performed his hilarious one-man clown act before the big finale, and Tilly slipped away, heading outside the great big tent just as the encore began inside with a sly grin on her face.

Brent almost ran out of the tent once he'd finished his part of the finale, and had ducked inside his motor home before the show was even completely over. He'd hoped to find Tilly waiting for him inside, having noticed her sneak away, but was even more pleasantly surprised when he found her naked and soaking wet from having just helped herself to a hot shower in his motor home.

She smiled at his both shocked and impressed expression, towelling her hair for a moment before rubbing the soft cotton down her torso as Brent watched her hungrily. She then wrapped the damp cloth around herself, covering her body teasingly before folding it under her armpit, securing it with a simple knot.

"Oh no you don't," he told her with a cheeky grin, dropping to his knees in front of her. Brent tugged on the edge of the towel, which quickly dropped to the floor, exposing her naked body again. He then grabbed her hips and pulled Tilly towards his ready mouth, taking her throbbing nub between his lips before he then began sucking gently on it. Tilly reached down and ran her hands through his long hair, gripping onto Brent tightly as he pursued her climax effortlessly and with an expert touch. She came quickly, the glorious pulses resonating around her body as she stood woozily before her lover. Brent looked up, watching as she relished in the aftermath of her climax, his face still covered in his black and white makeup, some of which he had inadvertently shared with her freshly washed mound.

Tilly couldn't help but giggle as she took in the dark and sexy man that still kneeled before her, and Brent shrugged his shoulders and laughed along with her. He then stood up, pulling off his own clothes eagerly as she watched him, biting her lip in anticipation when his hard length sprung loose from its restraints. Brent pulled her back into the small bathroom with him, taking her hand and leading her under the hot shower as he washed off the makeup, sweat and dirt from himself, before gently rubbing the smeared and greying face paint from atop her thighs with a soap covered hand. Tilly groaned as he touched her sensitive nerve endings again, and then pushed herself up against Brent's muscular body under the hot water, pressing him into the tiled wall behind. They kissed passionately and eagerly, their desire and need for one another so very clear and unrestrained. His hard length stroked against the tender folds between Tilly's thighs as she rocked back and forth against him for a while longer, neither one ready to release their grip on each other until they were forced out of the shower by the quickly subsiding warm water thanks to the rapidly emptying hot water tank of the motor-home. The pair then grabbed two fresh towels and wrapped them around their trembling bodies as they dried themselves, but then Tilly quickly pushed Brent against the edge of the sofa. She knelt before him and he smiled down at her, gasping as she leaned forward and sucked the tip of his thick shaft before he could even finish drying it from his shower. She slid up and down, slowly at first, and then faster as she took more and more of him in her eager mouth. Brent muttered his approving groans as she went, urging her onwards until he eventually came into her mouth. She spat out the salty wetness, unable to swallow it down for him, but he didn't mind, laughing to himself as she tried to hide the deposit into one of the nearby towels. It was almost impossible to believe she hadn't done any of this before, and he had to smile at how eager she was to please him.

It wasn't long until Brent was ready for her again, and he was pleasantly surprised to find her ready, too. He lifted Tilly onto the bed, kissing and sheathing himself again in preparation for the rest of their night together. She then lifted her hips and wrapped her thighs around him tightly, urging his thick length inside her wet cleft, and this time she was able to enjoy his hard and heavy thrusts without the pains her inexperienced inner muscles had felt earlier that afternoon. She stared up into his deep blue eyes as he made love to her, relishing in his wonderful closeness and soft touch that drove her crazy, and didn't regret a moment of their time together.

Tilly then laid with her head on Brent's chest, listening to the thumping of his heart and the rhythmic sound of his breathing, her body still buzzing. She knew exactly how much she'd miss him after the circus moved on again, and cursed their short time together. Even after just a few days, their connection was so strong, and Brent wrapped his arms around her, thinking that their day had been a day of many firsts—and not only for her. Walking away was not going to be easy this time.

CHAPTER SIX

Tilly jolted awake in the early hours of the next morning, having heard a crash from somewhere in the camp, and then what sounded like Renee giggling from somewhere not too far away. She quickly assumed that David and her loose friend must be up to some kind of mischief somewhere, and decided she wasn't the least bit interested in leaving Brent's warm embrace in order to check it out. Annoyingly though, she soon found she couldn't fall back to sleep after being awoken so close to morning, and lay back down, snuggling into her lover's arms in an attempt to shut out the morning light, but it was no use. A quick glance at the clock on the bedside table told her it was five o'clock in the morning, but her body was already trying to persuade her it was breakfast time. Tilly's stomach rumbled loudly and she eventually gave in. She climbed up out of Brent's arms and slid on her skirt and blouse from the night before, and then she went looking in the small kitchenette for any sign of substantial food. There was nothing in the fridge but cola cans and beer bottles, while the cupboards held only dry pasta and stale cereal.

Tilly then decided to head out of Brent's mobile home for a quick dash to Renee's car, grabbing the car keys from her bag as she went. She knew there were some cereal bars in the back seat that she'd made and left there the day before, and was ready to eat at least two or three to appease her rumbling stomach.

Thanks to the summer sunrise, it was already light outside as Tilly made her way over to the small blue car and grabbed the bars from her backpack. She then unwrapped one and took a big bite, devouring it in seconds before putting another in her pocket, and locked the car door behind her, quickly heading back towards Brent's warm bed. She then heard another giggle as she neared the caravans again, her mouth full of chocolaty muesli, and Tilly looked over in the direction of the sound, catching the sight of Lily as she disappeared behind the huge main tent's entryway. She turned to follow her, intrigued as to what she might be up to, but quickly decided against it. It was no business of hers what Brent's stepmother was up to, and she didn't want to taint her wonderful experiences from the last few days by potentially finding her up to mischief, or worse. Instead, she took another step in the direction of her lover's warm beacon.

Curiosity soon got the better of her though when a second giggle broke the silence, followed quickly by another crash, and the sound of a man laughing. Tilly tiptoed forward, swallowing down the last of the bar before heading silently towards the circus entrance in search of an explanation of the early morning wakeup call.

She reached the big tent and looked around to check that no one was watching her before stepping inside the doorway, the dim light obscuring her vision for a moment until her eyes became accustomed to the darkness. She could see two figures on the stage, and could tell it was Lily and a man, and that she was bouncing up and down quickly on top of his hard cock as he lay beneath her, her mouth on the man's neck. Thankfully, Tilly soon realised that the man Lily was riding happened to be her husband, so she made to go, embarrassed to have caught them in the throes of passion, but she then stopped dead when Lily sat up and she saw her face properly in the dim light. Her once soft, pale features were now dark, and her eyes seemed almost black as she looked down at Lucas from atop his lap, continuing to thrust up and down on him eagerly. His hands were bound above his head with rope that was tied to one of the metal joints, and Tilly could see blood dripping down Lily's chin, as though she'd been drinking it from him. She then noticed a small cut on Lucas' collar, which told her that her suspicions were absolutely right.

She turned and crept away, hopeful that she hadn't been spotted, but as she rounded the doorway, Lily was somehow stood directly in front of her. Tilly looked back over her shoulder for a second and saw how Lucas still lying on the stage, his naked body and hard erection left exactly in the same place and position as they'd been just moments before, but his wife was now inexplicably over by Tilly in the doorway—stark naked and blocking her exit with a dark and menacing look on her pale face.

She was back to looking like the same woman Tilly had first met just a couple of days before, apart from the blood that still dripped down her chin, and she eyed the young girl for a moment as though unsure how best to proceed. Lily then stepped forward, closing the gap between them and pinning her to the heavy wooden beam behind, taking in her scared sight before her with a satisfied smirk. She then leaned closer and sniffed Tilly, smiling when she pulled up and peered into her blue eyes knowingly.

"You smell like sex, my dear. Tell me, did my stepson suitably sort out your little virginity problem?" she asked her with a bloody smile. Tilly couldn't answer. She was utterly disgusted and shocked by the woman's strangeness and filthy words and couldn't fathom as response. Lily continued to stare deep into her eyes as though waiting for a reply, but then reached down and grabbed her right wrist, pulling it up and twisting it slightly so that she could see the inside of Tilly's forearm.

"May I?" she then asked, and Tilly frowned but nodded, unsure what she was agreeing to as Lily then delicately traced an inverted cross in the soft flesh there with the tip of her index finger. The mark suddenly burned hot and flared red, before somehow sinking away as though it was never there. Wearing only a devilish smile, Lily then raised the same finger to her lips and bit down on it, drawing a tiny drop of blood to the surface, which she then deposited into Tilly's mouth without a word.

She couldn't fight her. Tilly was completely mesmerised and controlled by Lily within seconds of the blood touching her lips, and didn't know where to begin fighting back against her powerful ownership. As the dark drop of blood seeped down her throat, the memory of what Tilly had just seen and experienced magically drifted away, and she then wandered back to Brent's motor-home having completely forgotten the last few minutes of her strange morning, believing that she had just wandered back from Renee's car.

Tired and dazed, Tilly climbed back into bed with her lover and fell into a deep sleep, oblivious once again to the dark world all around her.

CHAPTER SEVEN

A year had passed since Tilly had last seen Brent, and he'd been on the road with the circus ever since those first few glorious days they'd spent together had come to an end. The two lovers had stayed in touch, talking almost every day on the phone and via web chats on Tilly's laptop, and she posted Brent books to read in his down-time while he sent her strange gifts and food from around the world, with postcards from all along the whistle-stop tour that Lucas had planned for the thriving performers.

The pair of them had agreed not to be exclusive to one another, neither one wanting to tie the other into a long-distance relationship. But still, neither had been seeing anyone else in the time since they'd first met. Tilly hadn't met a man since Brent that'd made her feel the way he had, and he too had stopped his womanising ways in preference to holding out until he could be with Tilly again—a fact that both surprised and brought happiness to the usually so casual lover.

During the past year, Tilly had enrolled at a local college, choosing to follow her dreams of being a chef rather than work full-time on the farm once her mandatory schooling was over, and she was enjoying every minute of it. Renee and Gwen were both studying different courses to Tilly at the college, but they all saw each other every day, and would go out drinking together in the bars and nightclubs in the city most weekends and during their end of term holidays.

When the circus finally finished their eastern European leg of the tour and came back to England, Tilly couldn't wait for them to be closer. She quickly set about arranging a road trip with Renee to see Brent and the others while she had a few days off from her studies before the summer break, and couldn't wait to see him. The two young women chatted excitedly as they drove down the motorway, off to spend a few days with him and the others in London while the circus performed at a huge indoor arena there—a very welcome upgrade from the huge tent.

The show had continued to be a huge success since they'd last seen it, and Brent had promised the girls VIP access into the arena. They felt like celebrities as they approached the security guarded doors, walking past hordes of queuing young girls and poster bearing fans, all of whom hoping for autographs and to have their picture taken with the performers. She and Renee gave their names to the bouncers and, after receiving their VIP all-access passes, were shown straight over to the backstage area by the darkly dressed guard.

Brent ran over as soon as he saw them walk in and he scooped Tilly up in his arms, embracing her tightly as they greeted one another. Neither of them could hold back and they kissed each other deeply, their desire and passion for one another obvious to all that were around them.

"Brent," his father and boss, Lucas, called over to him from the stage area after watching the besotted couple be re-united at long last, beckoning with his hand for his son to go and see him. "You're excused for today, take the night off son," he told him with a wide smile and a slap on his back when he reached him. Lucas then nodded to Tilly and waved, giving her a welcoming smile. She couldn't help but grin back at him over Jackson's shoulder while he too scooped her off of her feet and into a huge hug in welcome.

"Thanks, Dad," Brent replied. He was so grateful for the time to be with the woman he had missed so very much, and he made no effort to hide his affections for her now that she was back in his arms again.

Renee was only there as Tilly driver, but seemed happy to stick around. She and David hadn't bothered to stay in touch with each other during the circus' touring time, each of them having been perfectly happy with their short and sweet love affair the summer before, but they too sneaked away after the show that night. It was ideal, and left Tilly's conscience clear when she and Brent checked into a nearby hotel and holed up there for the next twenty-four hours straight, surviving on room service and the contents of the mini bar between their passionate lovemaking sessions.

The next few days passed by in a blur, and all far too quickly before the team had to pack up and move on to their next venue in Bournemouth on the south coast of England. Tilly hugged Brent goodbye, hating to have to let him go again, but was glad the circus was staying in England for a while now. Around college and work they would be able to see each other as much as they possibly could, and she knew they'd both make it work.

Renee drove the two of them home after the goodbyes were finally over, regaling Tilly with stories of hers and David's sexual exploits from the last few days, and demanding to know how hers and Brent's passionate reunion had gone. Tilly just laughed, but replied that her lips were firmly sealed and for Renee to keep her nose out. She couldn't help but give her nosy friend a sly grin though, letting her know just how wonderful it'd been being back in his arms after such a long time apart.

Tilly then travelled back and forth between various venues for the first few weeks of the circus' tour, but soon ran out of time and money once they'd moved on to perform in cities that were further away than she could travel to using the trains and buses so easily. She couldn't deny that she hated reverting back to their old, long-distance style relationship though. Both of them had known for a while that they were well and truly an item despite their previous resistance.

***

A couple of months later, a quiet knock at the door of her converted barn made Tilly jump as she relaxed on her sofa with a book. She'd recently turned the farm's guesthouse into her own private little home with the permission of her parents, as she was nearly twenty now, and had wanted some space of her own. It was a lovely little home, but she never had visitors, especially ones that knocked. Renee and Gwen would always just wander in unannounced when either of them stopped by.

She rounded the corner of the living room and pulled open the frosted glass door to find Brent was stood in the doorway, a huge smile on his face and a dozen red roses in one hand. She almost jumped for joy at the sight of him, but managed to stop herself, keeping her cool, and she opted instead for a passionate kiss to welcome him to her home.

"What're you doing here?" she asked excitedly, ushering him inside. He held up his right wrist, which was bandaged and in a splint.

"Accidents in the workplace," he explained with a smile, but winced slightly when he let it fall back down to his side. "It was

David's fault. He fell on me while we were trying to put together a new number, which obviously isn't gonna work anyway, and now I've ended up out of the show for a week or so while I rest my sprained wrist." Despite the pain he was clearly in, his smile told her that he was not all too upset by his brother's foolishness. "And, well...I figured, where better to come and rest than here with you? If you don't mind, that is?" he then asked, hoping she wasn't going to turn him down.

"Hmmm, now let me think," Tilly replied, tapping her chin with her index finger while trying to fool him into believing that she might not be up for it, but she failed miserably. "Okay, I suppose so," she added and Brent smiled, scooping her into his arms for another deep kiss, despite his sore wrist.

Inside the doorway, they finally released one another and Tilly took the flowers off to the kitchen to find a vase, while he put down his backpack and took a look around. The tiny home had her touch all over it, and Brent knew that Tilly must have decorated it all herself. The living room was only just about big enough for a television unit topped with a large flat-screen and one small sofa, but the stunning black and white damask covered walls were adorned with different sized black shelves that showed off her ornaments and photographs of her friends and family. He even saw one of her and Brent backstage at one of the London shows and had to smile. Each of them were smiling and staring in each other's eyes, so obviously in love, even if they hadn't known it themselves back then.

CHAPTER EIGHT

Tilly and Brent's week alone together was wonderful. The besotted pair made love for hours every night and talked until the small hours every morning. They acted like a real couple, and went out on dates for meals at Tilly's favourite restaurants, to watch movies at the local cinema, or they went out in the town for drinks with Tilly's friends. Brent seemed to enjoy wowing them all as he showed off some of his circus skills, being careful not to put any stress on his bad wrist. He even had time to get to know Tilly's parents while he was there, and the pair of them really responded to him. They seemed to like him instantly and quickly accepted Brent as being a big part of their daughter's life. She'd spoken with her mum, Bianca, about him many times, but she could now finally see what all the fuss was about, and couldn't deny having seen their strong connection for herself during his visit.

When his wrist was healed, Brent stayed one more day, not ready to leave her just yet. He couldn't risk longer, otherwise he knew he'd be in trouble, but the next morning Tilly was sad to say goodbye to him. At least it wasn't for long, though. She knew they would see each other again in a couple of months when the circus came back to Coventry, so didn't mind as much this time around.

She and Brent kissed each other deeply on the train station platform, and each of them finally said, "I love you," for the first time to one another before he boarded his train to Glasgow to meet up with his family there before the circus moved on to an arena in Edinburgh.

When she got home, Tilly sat staring sullenly at her photographs from the last few days, missing Brent terribly, when her mobile phone rang in her handbag. She reached for it and answered just in time before the voicemail kicked in.

"Hello?" she barked at the unknown caller as she lifted the receiver to her ear.

"Hi Tilly, it's Lily—Brent's stepmother," a soft voice on the other end replied.

"Oh, yes, hello Lily. How are you? Brent's on his way up to meet you guys now if that's what you were wondering?" she asked, unsure why Lily had called her out of the blue.

"Thanks, that's good to know, but no, that's not why I rang," she answered with a smile in her voice. "We're having a ceremony in Edinburgh on Halloween night to celebrate mine and Lucas' wedding anniversary, and I was calling to ask if you'd like to come up and join us, as a special surprise for Brent?" Lily asked her, and Tilly smiled, her face lighting up at the prospect of seeing Brent again so soon.

"What a lovely idea, thanks Lily. Yes, I'll definitely be there," she answered, pleased that Brent's parents considered her important enough to invite her along to such a big family event.

"Great, I'll send you your tickets and all the hotel information etcetera via email now, and don't forget, not a word to Brent about this okay? I want it to be a surprise," she added excitedly.

"Sure, my lips are sealed. Thanks Lily, see you in a few days."

They hung up the phone and within seconds, an email arrived confirming her train timings and telling her that a car would be waiting for her at the train station in Edinburgh to take her to the ceremony's venue, which was also their hotel. "Wow, she works fast," Tilly said to herself, printing off the information before heading over to her parents' house to tell them the exciting news.

Two days later, Tilly boarded her train and travelled first-class to Edinburgh. It was incredibly comfortable in the spacious car, and she loved the feeling of travelling in style. She'd picked a stunning red dress to wear for the occasion, assuming that there would be a party or something following the ceremony, and felt like a VIP travelling in style. Lily hadn't given many other details, so she also took a suitcase with plenty of outfit options along in case she changed her mind on the red dress.

A few hours later, she arrived at the station and found a driver in a black, crisp suit waiting for her, her name printed on a card that he held high. Tilly blushed and followed him out to a posh, black sports car that was parked just outside the station. She smiled and relished the admiring looks she received as he held open the door for her. Without a word, the man then climbed in the driver's seat, setting off towards Lucas and Lily's ceremony as the sun began to set over the old city.

Less than an hour later, they pulled up at a huge dark-bricked building. It looked like an ancient and ominous mansion, and it dominated the sparse skyline outside the city. There were no signs or directions outside the iron gates or on the huge wooden doors that led inside, but the driver seemed to know where he was going and took her up through the narrow driveway without a care. He then grabbed her bags and lead Tilly inside. It was a magnificent old castle, probably hundreds of years old, and it was decorated with stunning black and red motifs and drapes, adding to the theme, and Tilly admired them as she stood and took it all in.

"The ceremony's through there," the driver said, pointing to a closed set of doors a few feet away. He checked his watch, and added, "they've just started, but if you go in now you should be fine. I'll take your bags to your room, master Brent has the key."

Tilly nodded to the man, surprised by the way he had called Brent 'master,' and she made her way over to the huge wooden doors and hovered outside them for a moment, worrying that she might be going to barge in at exactly the wrong moment. She leaned close and listened, and heard lots of muffled voices, which indicated to her that there were no speeches or anything going on inside just yet, so she clicked open the door and quietly sneaked into the hall.

She looked around the large room on the other side, seeing many people in there, but all of them were dressed in black and it was so dimly lit that she couldn't make out who any of them were. There were no seats inside, just a large black altar in the centre of the room, in front of which kneeled Lucas. He had his head bowed and Lily was stood over him, and despite her petite frame she looked somehow tall and commanding. She was smiling down at her husband as the crowd encircled them, each of them talking quietly while the couple spoke in whispers to one another, ignoring the others nearby. Lily looked beautiful, dressed all in black with her dark-brown hair pinned back from her delicately featured face with hair-clips adorned with large black roses.

Tilly suddenly felt as if she'd made a huge mistake. She didn't understand what on earth was going on, and didn't like the way this strange ceremony made her feel. It was dark, ominous and she sensed evil all around her. She turned to leave, but then she saw the pair of wide, blue eyes that were watching her from across the room, just to the side of the altar. The scared gaze was from Brent, his face pale and his mouth open as he stared at her, fear very obvious on his usually so handsome face. He looked up to Lily, who peered down at her stepson with a wicked grin and eyes that seemed shrouded in black shadows, but Tilly had to assume it was just a trick in the dim light. Lily then looked through the crowd directly at her, a sinister look on her satisfied face as she took her in.

"Come here, dearest Tilly. You're just in time," she called to her, and the personal request made the entire group of dark followers turn to look at the new arrival. There must have been twenty or thirty faces now watching her, seemingly curious about the new girl, yet far from welcoming. Their grim gazes were unfriendly as their many eyes swept over Tilly and her bright dress.

She stepped forward without a word, feeling like she had no choice but to join them beside the altar, however she took a wide birth around the dark steps to join Brent at his side. He peered down at her; anger and fear very clear on his sullen face. The surprise for him, it seemed, had worked exactly as Lily had hoped.

"What are you doing here?" he asked Tilly a few seconds later, his voice an urgent whisper.

"Lily invited me, she paid for me to travel up here and everything. She said it would be a nice surprise for you," Tilly said, looking up at him. Like Brent, she was afraid now, and couldn't understand what was going on. She looked around at the strange gathering, realisation starting to dawn on her. "Are you in some sort of a cult, Brent?" she had to ask, her voice a whisper now too as she looked again at the other people all around them. David was by the altar with them, but Jackson was over by the back wall with some of the other younger members of the group, and she didn't know why they stood separately to the rest of the crowd, but assumed it might be that they either weren't initiated yet or were too young to participate in whatever ceremony was about to commence.

Brent didn't respond for a moment, looking up at his stepmother questioningly as his father stayed rooted to his spot at the base of the dark altar, his eyes still only either down at the floor or on his wife.

Tilly continued to look around for a few seconds, completely bemused by it all. The other attendees were no longer interested in her though, and she was glad the spotlight was off of her again. They were all gazing up towards the altar, watching Lucas with expectant, excited stares. Brent looked down at Tilly, not knowing where to start to explain it all to her and he took a deep breath.

"It's much, much, more than that, Tilly. I didn't want to tell you about it yet, but," he began.

"But I forced his hand," Lily interjected before he could finish, climbing down from the altar and flashing the pair of them an evil grin, stepping closer so that she was now just inches from Tilly's face. She reached up and brushed a lock of blonde hair out of the girl's eyes with intrigue and a satisfied look on her face that Tilly could just not understand. Lily then ran an index finger down her cheek, peering into Tilly's eyes as she the made contact. The strange woman's touch somehow made the inside of her right wrist suddenly burn red-hot, and she lifted it up, looking at it in confusion as it glowed red and a shape began to form there. Brent gasped beside her, seeing the inverted cross rise from underneath her skin.

"You marked her, Lilith?" he asked his stepmother, his voice only a gruff whisper but she could hear him clearly in the quiet room.

"Yes, she is mine, just as you all are. Be grateful, my son, for I have decided to let you keep her. For now," she told him with an air of frustration at having had to explain herself, but Brent just stared back at her angrily. Tilly couldn't understand what they were saying, their unusual wording and sinister meaning completely lost on her. Before she could ask them to explain, a sudden twinge of pain hit her temple, making Tilly wince for a moment before it disappeared again just as quickly. In its wake, the memory of what she'd seen that night in the tent came crashing back to her. She looked up again at the woman before her and trembled at the remembrance of Lily's actions that early morning the summer before, and then gasped as she saw her true dark face in the shadows again before Lilith then turned and wandered away, climbing back up the steps to her husband's side.

CHAPTER NINE

"Brent, what *is* going on?" Tilly demanded as Lily stood back atop the steps that were obviously the centre-point of whatever ceremony was due to start, and which was clearly going to include Lucas in some way. The scary woman looked out at her dark congregation as though she was about to begin a sermon, her smile firmly on her face as she took in the faces of her loyal subjects.

"I will explain everything later, Tilly, but for now stay close to me, keep your mouth shut, and your head down, do you understand?" he demanded in a harsh whisper, and Tilly nodded. "I mean it. This is no joke," he added, looking forlornly at his lover. She took his hand and held it tight, eager for all this to be over, but she somehow knew deep down that it was only the start.

The group soon hushed, and Lilith began to speak.

"Welcome to you all, my most loyal and devoted followers. Tonight we have gathered together to carry out the final challenge in my husband's demonic trials," she said, calling out as the group stared up at her, no one saying a word as they absorbed her speech. "We are in for a rare treat indeed my friends. His Royal Highness the Black Prince, Blake, has graciously agreed to come and be his adjudicator for the proceedings. Tonight is all Hallow's Eve after all," she added happily, and the followers all gasped. Mutters began among the crowd, whispers of excitement and frenzied admiration, and some even shouted their affirmations as they looked up at her lovingly.

"Who's Blake?" Tilly whispered to Brent, looking at his pale face as he stared up at Lilith deep in thought, and he inhaled sharply at her words, his face screwing up into a scared and pained wince as he peered down at her.

"That would be me," a deep and omnipotent voice boomed from across the room, but the sound seemed to come from inside her head as well as her hearing it in her ears. Tilly looked around behind her, but couldn't see where the voice had come from. She then turned back to look towards Lilith at the altar, afraid to say anything more, but was startled to come face to face with a man who had appeared to have come out of nowhere and was now standing just inches away from her.

He was tall, powerfully built, and droop-dead gorgeous. His dark-brown hair was short but curled slightly at the ends and he looked to be in his mid-twenties, however something about him made the man seem much, much older and wiser. Fear flared in her gut, and she could tell he wasn't only all-powerful, but also exceptionally evil. Tilly stared into his deep green eyes for a moment, and was utterly mesmerised by him. He stared back into her eyes too, seemingly deep in thought as he took in the sight of the foolish girl that stood before him.

In their moment of shared intrigue, Tilly had failed to notice that every other person in the room had dropped to their knees before this daunting new arrival. When she did notice them, she saw how some of those around her shook in fear while others buzzed with some kind of excited anticipation in his presence. Even Lilith had knelt before the young man, her head bowed in respect to him, but Tilly just stood there awkwardly for a moment.

She then started to kneel down, hoping to join the others in their respectful poses but he stopped her, grabbing her arm tightly, and pulling both Tilly's body and her gaze back up to meet his own. "Well, well, well," he said quietly, his voice deep and stern. "I see that Lilith has marked you, and that she's the one who invited you here tonight, yet she hasn't given you proper instructions on how to behave in the presence of royalty," he said, breaking his eye contact with Tilly for a moment to look scornfully at the woman at the altar, who bowed lower to her master in response to her admonishment. "I'll tell you what," he continued, staring back into Tilly's wide blue eyes. "I'll let you off this once, but the next time you see me, I suggest that you get on your knees and worship me, just like your friends here. Is that understood?" he asked her, gesturing to Brent and his brother along with the rest of the crowd, and Tilly nodded, too scared to speak. "And don't you ever say my name again, or else I'll have your tongue," he added, his eyes somehow speckling with black as he threatened her, sending Tilly's mind into overdrive. She whimpered slightly, trembling, and nodded again at his fierce order.

She hoped that her telling off was over with, but the Black Prince eyed her for a few moments longer, looking Tilly up and down with intrigue, and taking in the red dress that made her stand out so prominently in the otherwise black-filled room. He then lifted her wrist up so that he could inspect it for a moment, and covered the area where her red inverted cross had not long ago appeared showing Lilith's claim on her with his hand.

She felt it burn beneath his touch, but didn't dare pull her arm away, too afraid to move a muscle. "I'm sure she won't mind," he told her with a wink, and Tilly stared into his deep, suddenly all black eyes, mesmerised again by the powerful man before her. He let her arm drop back to her side, and then moved over to the altar without another word to her, speaking quietly with Lilith as she rose to greet him.

Tilly looked down at her arm, and saw that the inverted cross Lilith had previously drawn on her had now turned from red to black after his burning touch, but she still had no idea what it all meant.

"Whoa," David whispered from behind her, staring at the black mark as he climbed to his feet with the others. She wanted to know what he'd meant by it, but Brent gave him a stern look and David said nothing more to her. Her lover didn't say a word either, however Brent couldn't help looking clearly afraid as he stared into Tilly's eyes from beside her. She had to wonder whether this black mark meant something far worse than Lilith's red one, but knew nothing of what was going on or why they were here to understand its meaning. Perhaps she was to become a sacrificial lamb to the slaughter, or a slave to their strange cause. Tilly had no way of knowing until it was explained to her, and she also instinctively knew she had no hope of escape either. All she could do was stare into Brent's eyes and silently beg for answers, but received none.

CHAPTER TEN

The final trial Lilith had spoken of was soon ready to begin, and Tilly and Brent watched from the sidelines in fearful silence with David and the others as Blake addressed the crowd.

"This human has conquered all in order to win this demon's heart, as well as her hand in marriage, and now she seeks sponsorship in order for him to complete his demonic rite of passage," the Black Prince said to the members of Lilith's following, who each gazed up at him lovingly from the floor below. Tilly watched in awe, and could see his darkness, sense his power, and feel the almighty buzz in the air all around them. Suddenly, his words were finally starting to sink in—talk of demons and royalty filling in some of the blanks in her mind at last.

She too stared up at her new master as he spoke, feeling herself getting hot and bothered under his gaze as it swept across the crowd while he continued to address them. "He has completed the first two trials, and bears their marks on his chest," he added, pointing down at Lucas, who removed his shirt and showed what looked like two tattoos on his chest, both in the shape of the number six. The crowd roared and cheered, while Lucas smiled and fist-pumped the air happily. "Settle down, we still have one more trial, and this one is the toughest," Blake commanded, and the group were instantly quiet again. "I will now take him to the brink of death and back six times. If he survives, his trials are complete, and his soul will be considered by my mother for the ultimate prize: an eternal place at Lilith's side, as well as the gift of immortality and true demonic power. So, what are we waiting for? Let's begin!"

"Hail Satan, hail to the Dark Queen," the crowd roared following his motivational speech, including Brent. Tilly repeated the strange words quietly to herself, catching the green eyes that watched her from atop the altar as she did so, along with the slight curl of Blake's mouth as she continued to flounder in the black sea of followers around her.

They all watched in horror, or fascination for some, as Lucas was then beaten, poisoned and hung from his neck before them by the Dark Prince, who gave him no mercy and showed no remorse in any of it. Lucas would come back to life again each time, a little paler and less human with every gruesome near-death-experience, but back again all the same.

He then had his still beating heart ripped out of his chest by Lilith's bare hands, which she then proceeded to shove back in the cavity she had left behind, dark forces somehow healing Lucas' wounds inexplicably before them, and Tilly's stomach turned as she watched. Brent was then called upon by the powerful Prince and ordered to stab his father through the only just healed heart in his chest with a long dagger, all under the watchful eye of the malevolent adjudicator, and his eldest son carried out his order without question or hesitation. Blake brought Lucas back just in time again, healing the wounds, but it was obviously blackening his soul one little piece at a time, too. It was a realisation that scared the hell out of Tilly.

Before long, the sixth and final challenge of his death trial was due, and Blake roused the crowd, welcoming their suggestions on how best to torture Lucas one last time. He actually seemed to relish in the depraved and sadistic ideas that were called out to him.

"No, no," he shouted, silencing the crowd once again. "I'm thinking of a good one, let's see if any of you can guess it," he said, playing with the group and egging them on with a cunning smile. There were shouts from the followers as they made their suggestions: hot pokers, suffocation, drowning, beheading and mutilation—however none of them were correct, much to the disappointment of the Black Prince.

Tilly then let her mind wander, thinking of the many terrible ways to die. She suddenly thought of fire, flames licking the skin and burning off the flesh, and she shuddered, remembering the stories she had been told as a child of a poor boy who had played with matches and set his clothes alight. She'd seen him a few years' later, but he'd been barely recognisable thanks to his awful scars. "Got it!" Blake suddenly shouted, pointing his finger at Tilly and breaking her from her reverie as the crowd silenced and stared in her direction again.

More disturbing than the memory, was how in that exact moment she realised that this Black Prince had just read her mind. "Care to share it with the rest of the class?" Blake questioned her, stepping closer to Tilly as he spoke, an edge of appreciation and admiration in his tone.

"Fire," she said quietly as he neared her, not releasing her from his gaze for even a moment. She then cleared her throat and quickly added, "your majesty," as she bowed, and he moved back towards the altar with a satisfied smile.

"Good girl," he said, staring at Lucas again, and with a click of his fingers he set the poor man alight. He writhed in agony and screamed as the flames licked every inch of his skin. Tilly flinched and covered her nose as the smell of burned flesh filled her lungs, but thankfully it wasn't long until he stopped fighting the blaze. The crowd then watched eagerly as he lay there, seemingly dead, before coming to just a few minutes later, his body healing one last time before their wide eyes.

With the trial finally over, Lucas rose feebly to his feet and was greeted by cheers and applause from those who'd watched over his dreadful challenges. Blake then stepped forward, laying a hand on his chest for a moment before stepping back again, having left a new black mark on Lucas' skin. It was another six, and a shiver went down Tilly's spine as the realisation hit her.

"Six, six, six," she whispered to herself.

"Exactly," Brent said, moving his hand to take hers in his own, wanting to comfort her, but then he changed his mind and pulled it away again.

CHAPTER ELEVEN

The trial was finished, and, after cheering loudly along with the crowd in recognition of Lucas' achievements, Blake then shushed them again, and silence fell within less than a second.

"I shall take my news to the Dark Queen, and she will make her decision. In the meantime though—drink, fuck, sin aplenty, and relish in your dark delights my friends. So mote it be!"

"So mote it be!" the crowd all cried in response to his highly motivational closing speech, and every one of Lilith's loyal followers was grinning with pride at Lucas' achievements. Blake then stepped down from the altar, and they all kneeled before him one more time. Tilly was mindful to follow the lead of the group this time, and knelt quickly before him alongside her friends. She expected the crowd to stand again after a few moments and find the Black Prince gone again, but this time they didn't move. Everyone stayed exactly where they were, as though frozen in place, the silence around her pressing like a stifling force. She risked a peek to her side at Brent, but he was completely still, his eyes unblinking, and his breathing had slowed unexplainably.

A hand on her shoulder caused Tilly to jump and look up, bemused, and she found Blake looking down at her with a sly smile. He was every inch the dark and dangerous god, demon, or whatever he was. Either way, he both excited and terrified her.

"That's better. This is just how I like you—on your knees," Blake told her, his eyes speckling with black again as he peered down at her. "Rise," he commanded, and it was then that Tilly realised he'd either stopped time or frozen the rest of the dark congregation in place so he could speak with her a moment alone. She did as he ordered, craning her neck to keep looking up at him again even when she was stood tall. "I'm going now, but before I do, here are a few ground rules," he said, lifting a hand and cupping her cheek with it. Blake then pulled her towards him and leaned down so that he was just a few inches away from her face.

Tilly could hardly breathe. His touch sent powerful shockwaves throughout her entire body. He laughed, a deep, gruff sound, and then continued. "Firstly, educate yourself adequately. The next time I come you should be much better prepared to receive me. Get yourself a Satanist's Bible, and ask your friends here to help you, but either way I want you up to speed next time," he added, pulling back slightly to look at her expectantly.

"Yes," she replied, her voice faltering thanks to her excitement and fear.

"Secondly, you call me master, your highness, or your majesty at all times, Tilly. You are never to utter my name again, otherwise you will be punished, severely. Is that understood?"

"Yes," she answered, and then quickly added, "master."

"That's better. Thirdly, you belong to me now. Do you understand what that means?" Blake asked, commanding her eyes on his so that he could properly read her. Thanks to his mother, the Devil, he and his siblings had been given access to higher powers over the years. Like many sires of the hellish throne, he could heal himself in an instant, age himself if he chose to, and teleport anywhere he wanted. On top of those gifts, Blake could also read the mind of any being in his company, he had the physical strength of one hundred men, and he could control the body of any being he pleased, such as the crowd that were now frozen before him.

Tilly thought about what it meant to be owned by him, and shook her head in response to his question. She truly didn't understand it.

"Is it like what Lily—I mean Lilith—has here. A sort of, following?" she asked him cautiously.

"No," Blake answered, "because you're the only human who bears my mark, Tilly. There's no following for you to join. You are, quite simply, to obey my every command and order without hesitation, and do not ever keep me waiting. You may live your life how you see fit, but you're to always put me first and follow my rules and orders as I give them."

She gasped, both scared and excited by his explanation. Tilly understood him clearly now and couldn't disguise the little flush of pride she felt upon realising that she was the only human in his following, however she also couldn't help the twisting of her gut at the realisation that he now owned her, in more ways than one. "I'm sure that Lilith won't object to you staying as a guest in her circle. You already have friends here and they can help to teach you," he said, looking down at Brent. "But know this. You are mine, entirely. Mind, body, and soul. Whatever affections you once had for this boy are done. Do I make myself clear?" he asked sternly, and she began to tremble.

"Yes, master," she answered, stifling a sob at the realisation that her love for Brent had to be over with now thanks to her new allegiance to Blake.

"Good, because I do not like to share, Tilly. So if he, or any other man, woman, or beast touches you sexually, I will slit their throat as you watch and then make you bathe in their blood," he told her, staring into her eyes without even flinching as he delivered his sinister promise, both turning her stomach and sending a deep throb to her cleft as he did so. She didn't know how he did it, but Blake certainly knew how to both terrify and seduce her in an instant. "I don't even want you touching yourself. Your pleasure is mine to command now, and only I will deliver it when you've served me well and pleased me adequately. Let yourself succumb to me, and I will take you places you've never dreamed of before," he promised, a sexy smile curling at his lips.

Tilly was aroused by Blake's firmness, drawn to his dark pursuit of her, yet still truly afraid, and she vowed never to underestimate him. He wasn't joking, and this was all very real. She knew without a doubt that her life was no longer her own, and that thought scared the hell out of her.

Blake read her thoughts, and then reached down from her cheek, laying his hand over her chest as she quivered before him. "Stop thinking with this," he said, indicating her fast-beating heart, before trailing the same hand down to the hem of her dress and expertly splaying his fingers up her thigh and to her panties, rubbing her clit beneath his fingers gently. She felt weak at his touch, almost faint, but his other hand reached around to secure her back, and he pulled Tilly even closer, his body now pressing into hers. "And start thinking with this," he finished, planting a deep and delving kiss on her lips. Tilly swooned, the pleasure and the fear bubbling up inside of her as he continued to rub her and kiss her expertly in sync.

Blake then stopped suddenly before she could reach her climax and pulled back from their kiss. He kept her pinned to him, his hand still gripping her back and pushing her into his hard body, but the other hand stopped its rubbing of the now swollen and ready nub between her thighs. "Do you want me to make you come?" he asked her with a sly grin on his face as he spoke.

"Yes master, please," she begged, desperate for her release.

"Then you've learned your first lesson, my darling," he told her, bringing his hand away from her throbbing nerve endings, leaving her panting and weak in his arms.

"*My* pleasure comes first, then yours, but only if I have been fully satisfied. That's your top priority from now on—satisfying my every desire," he said, steadying her and then releasing Tilly from his strong hold before stepping back. "You need to earn your rewards," he added with an evil grin.

Blake then looked her up and down, licking his lips and smiling darkly as though he were contemplating many wicked things for her, but Tilly could not be sure what they might be as he gave nothing away. "One last thing, you are only ever to wear black clothes from now on. However, I do like you in red. You may occasionally wear red underwear, which will be for my eyes only, of course, Tilly," Blake said, giving the final commandment for now to his new slave, minion, or whatever it was that she would be referred to as from now on. She still didn't know for sure.

Tilly nodded her understanding and bowed slightly as he left, still feeling woozy and also horny as hell thanks to their intense encounter. The crowd then began to stir and rise once Blake had gone, his commandment lifting. Brent and David stood and joined her, which was lucky, as Tilly quickly felt too weak and light headed to stand, and then fainted, falling right into Brent's strong arms.

CHAPTER TWELVE

The brothers carried the still woozy Tilly out into the main hall and then up to the room, where they put her down onto the bed she'd been due to share with Brent before things had been changed dramatically for the two of them thanks to Blake's new claim over her. David quickly left them to it, guessing they needed to talk, and he was eager to get away from the tense atmosphere between them.

As she refocused, Tilly gratefully drank a large glass of water and then laid her head back on the pillow. She wondered for a minute if she'd imagined the entire thing, but one look at Brent's forlorn face told her it was all very real. She had to fight back the tears as she peered up at him; still not quite able to accept the fact they had to be over.

He looked back down at her, eager to know if she was okay, but he also kept his distance rather than hug her or hold her hand as he would have before. Tilly knew he had to be on his best behaviour around her now or else face Blake's wrath, and it simply didn't seem fair. After a few minutes, she started to feel better and sat up against the pillows, taking in the small room around her for a moment, still deep in thought.

She remembered her early morning back at the circus so clearly now, and replayed the once lost bloody rendezvous she'd witnessed between Lucas and Lily in her mind's eye. It almost made sense now, whereas at the time she hadn't been able to comprehend their creepy actions at all. Tilly lifted her arm, looking inside her wrist for the inverted cross that Lilith had drawn on her that same morning, but it was gone again.

"It's still there, but only *they* can see it. Demons and witches will know you belong to one of the royal family the moment they're near you, and because I bear Lilith's mark I can kinda sense it on you, too," Brent said quietly, sitting down on the opposite end of the bed and staring across at Tilly with a sad, defeated expression.

He knew she had many questions and decided to get right to it, needing her to understand so they could both move on. She needed to accept that there was no fighting her master's orders no matter their past or what she might still want. Resistance was foolish, and would only lead to more pain for them all. "Lilith's followers and others like us that have been marked by our demon masters' can sense another marked Satanist in their company. It's up to the follower whether they wish to declare who their master is, but it's an honour, and you must wear it with pride," he told her earnestly. "I thought something seemed different about you, but I guess Lilith blocked me from sensing her mark on you until she wanted me to know," he added, looking down at his hands. The door of the bedroom then opened, and in walked Lilith, without knocking or having been invited. She looked down at the two of them on the bed with a stern expression, but was quickly satisfied that they weren't up to anything they shouldn't be.

"Tonight didn't go as I'd planned for the pair of you, but plans change and we too must adjust in order to suit our almighty masters' wants and needs," she told them matter-of-factly, quickly dismissing their past love as though it were nothing. "You have been given a great honour, one that is not to be thought lightly of,

Tilly. Your master has never marked a human before, so you ought to be grateful," she added, staring at her fiercely.

Tilly went to respond, but Lilith raised her hand to command her against it, and she followed the demand. She knew that this would not be the last time she'd be ordered around, so she'd better start getting used to it. "Your master wants me to watch over you, and it is my absolute pleasure to do his bidding. You'll be taught our religion, our history, and our expectations of you as his devoted, loyal follower," Lilith continued, her tone softening as she spoke of the Black Prince so lovingly. "The two of you will remain up here for the rest of the evening. Brent will now be your teacher, a friend, and nothing more. Is that understood?" she asked sternly, her eyes dark and ominous.

"Yes, mistress," Brent answered, and Tilly copied his response, but was quickly silenced by Lilith's disgusted reaction.

"I am not *your* mistress. Your only mistress now is the Dark Queen. You may address me using my full name—Lilith," she corrected her and then left without another word.

"I've got a Hell of a lot to learn," Tilly said quietly as she slid off the bed and made her way to the bathroom to change into her nightwear, eager to get out of her tight dress.

"You've no idea," Brent told her with a scowl, staring out the window.

"Shit, I need some black clothes!" Tilly then shouted to him from the en-suite, tossing aside her blue pyjamas with a huff, and Brent threw her a black hoodie and some tracksuit trousers from his bag to wear instead.

"You're gonna need to go shopping tomorrow," he told her with a frown.

They were soon brought plates piled high with food by David

and Jackson, who disappeared again within seconds, both of them eager not to get involved in their depressive conversation. They rushed back downstairs in case they missed the festivities in the hall below them, and didn't envy their elder brother's responsibility to his now ex-lover.

Tilly and Brent thanked them and then sat crossed-legged at opposite ends of the king-size bed as Brent began telling her about the history of the Dark Queen.

"We need to start with the Devil's," he told her, chomping on a breadstick.

"Devil's, as in plural?" she asked, a puzzled look on her pale face as she pulled her plate towards her and started munching on a spicy chicken skewer.

"Yes, there was the old one and now the new one. Let's just start at the beginning, okay?" he asked her impatiently, and Tilly nodded, keeping quiet so Brent could begin telling her the strange tale. He reached over and grabbed a small notepad from the bedside table and a pen, and he then began writing a list while Tilly watched him quietly, making her way through some more food from her plate. "I suppose I should say, first and foremost, that we are not worthy of speaking their names, Tilly. The royal family are beings far above us and our lowly human status, and we will be punished severely for doing it, even accidentally. I've seen it, and trust me you don't even wanna know, or ever go through what they might do to you for the insubordination. He was incredibly lenient on you tonight, whether it was because of your lack of knowledge or because of his desire for you, I don't know. But either way you were lucky," he stressed, his blue eyes staring across at her intensely. Tilly thought back to how she'd said Blake's name, and paled at the thought of what her master might have put her through had he been in a less jovial mood.

CHAPTER THIRTEEN

Brent looked down and pushed the notepad towards Tilly on the bed. He then pointed to the first name he'd written on the pad—*Lucifer*.

"He used to be the Devil, and I'm sure you've heard the name before?" he asked her, and Tilly nodded. "He's your new master's father, but this entity is no longer known as the Devil. Most humans have no idea that everything changed in Hell, but according to Lilith, it happened around sixty years ago. Only our new bible makes it known, the opposite side remains the same. Also, as far as movies and literature go, he's still in charge and they're happy to let most humans believe so." He took a deep breath. "Anyway, over to your master. We're permitted to call him the Black Prince, and not his real name. He has a twin sister, whom we are allowed to call the Black Princess," he said, pointing to the name, *Luna,* on the paper.

"The twins are incredibly powerful. Your master is heir to the dark throne now and he is the most powerful of all the dark beings below the Queen. The twins do not come to Earth together if possible because their combined dark power brings about nothing but chaos, war, freak weather occurrences, and other such catastrophic events to mankind and our existence. They are bound by the moon and can only come to Earth during its full days, or on all Hallow's Eve—like tonight."

Tilly nodded, trying to take it all in. It seemed so simple, normal, and yet was so far from it her head ached trying to imagine the family of demonic creatures. "They have another sister, and she's younger. We may call her the Unholy Princess and I do not know her real name, no human does," he told her, pointing to the line below Luna's name where he had written their sister's chilling title. "But, it is rumoured that she is a child with no paternal father, only a mother, the Dark Queen. She's the fabled death bringer, Tilly. You want to hope you're never taken before her as she's famed to be merciless, cruel, and the epitome of all her family's dark powers combined. No human has ever seen her face or knows her true story, and we do not dare ask for it from our demonic masters. All we know is that she can never come to Earth. She would bring about the end to all humanity. The fabled, *end of days*. Does this make sense?" he asked her, stressing the point so hard that Tilly knew she would never forget it.

She nodded, looking pale again, and pushed what was left of her food away. The last mouthful was stuck in her suddenly dry throat, and she took a large gulp of cola instead. Tilly looked down at the next name he'd written on the page as Brent took a deep breath and continued, pointing down at the name, which read, *Hecate/Cate*.

"The new Devil. You may call her the Dark Queen, as well as Satan, or the Devil—she has adopted both of those titles, too. She's their mother, the all-powerful ruler of Hell, and our almighty mistress," he said, and with deep affection so clear in his voice at the very thought of the Dark Queen. It was a sense of devotion Tilly couldn't quite understand, not yet anyway, but she was sure she'd soon learn. "She was once married to the old Devil, gave him their children, and then went on to dethrone him. No one knows why, how, or where he is now. Only she knows the truth, and you can guarantee her lips are well and truly sealed. Not even your master knows what happened to his father, Tilly," Brent added, every ounce of seriousness in his tone, and she felt terribly for Blake. Losing a parent had to be tough, but losing someone as infamous as his father had to have left a void so deep it was no wonder he'd avoided letting any followers wear his mark.

Tilly wanted to ask him more, but Brent didn't seem ready. He leaned forward and wrote a few more notes on the page, but then closed the notebook and passed it over to her to keep rather than continue telling her the history. He knew that Tilly might be glad of the notes to jog her memory later on. "There are more of them. The Queen has brethren that live on Earth, but it can get complicated from here. I suggest you take one of the bibles home with you to read, and I urge you, read it thoroughly, for your master knows every word by heart and he will surely test you. I also suggest you think about performing a commitment ceremony, Tilly. Cleanse your soul of your old life and beliefs, and then embrace the new. Your master will no doubt be very pleased with you," he said, looking sad as he contemplated her future with Blake instead of him.

She nodded, thinking of her master and his intense stare. Those gorgeous green eyes had peered right into her soul, and not once had she wanted to stop him. She knew she'd do anything it took to please him, to feel his satisfied gaze fall on her again, and to reap the pleasurable rewards for her submission.

Tilly knew her once immense love for Brent was already waning. It was as if it'd dulled a little bit at a time over the past few hours thanks to her master's commandment that they were no more, and it shocked her how quickly she'd been swayed. She looked across the bed at her friend, who was until incredibly recently, her boyfriend and lover. He peered back at her, seemingly thinking the same as she was.

Brent had a dark look of regret on his face, and although he didn't dare say the words to express his loss or anger at losing the one woman he'd ever truly cared about, she felt it. Tilly jumped, realising that she was staring at him a little too longingly, and she busied herself with writing notes next to the names he'd written in the notebook, adding little annotations to explain who they were and a brief version of their story. When she was done, it was still early, and despite the strange events of the evening, she wasn't tired.

Her head was swimming with far too much information to rest yet, full of too many scary thoughts and dark memories to let her settle down to sleep. "Any questions?" Brent asked once she'd finally closed the book and looked up, careful not to stare into his blue eyes too deeply this time.

"Just a couple. How come we can say Lilith's name but not Bl...the Black Prince's? And why is it that she *is* allowed to say his name?" she asked, and was glad she'd managed to stop herself in time before saying his name again.

"She's a level one demon, just below the royal family in the hierarchy of Hell. Only level one's are allowed to speak the royal names, having earned their positions at the top of the ladder after years of evil service and unwavering loyalty. Many of them are the Queen's most trusted advisors that took centuries to rise to their powerful positions, and they're the only ones who know the royals closely," he explained.

Tilly couldn't deny she was shocked to realise that the so seemingly human Lily, was actually a very powerful demon. And level one—much higher than she'd previously imagined. "It's only the royal family that we are forbidden to say the names of, demon classification doesn't otherwise affect humans. If we know their name we can say it, that's kinda the rule. It seems old fashioned, but that's because it is. The rule goes back thousands of years. A human may consort with demons and pledge allegiance to one or more of them, but you have to be willing to ask them for their name in order to earn their respect. Some will give it willingly, especially if they want you as a follower, but others will make you work for it first, which can be fucking scary as they don't always want to tell us. The stories of demonic possession are largely exaggerated, but somewhat true, and by knowing their name you have a hold over them, so they don't give that up too easily. You should be fine though. You bear the Black Prince's mark so there's no reason for any demon not to want you to know their name. They're always on the lookout to progress higher up the classification levels and might use you to gain favour with your master." Brent took a breath and watched her for a moment, letting the information sink in. "You can tell a demon's level by the colour of their mark when called to the surface. Red means level one, green is level two, and then I think it's blue for level three. After that I can't remember them off of the top of my head, but it's in the books, and after level three they don't really get to have human followers anyway so you won't need to worry," he said, giving her a moment to jot all of that down.

Tilly knew she had a lot to think about. All this information about classifications of demons and dark royal families were so new and unnatural to her, and she knew it would take her a while to get used to all of the terminology and unusual rules. She had to admit; she could already do with a break from all of this studying.

"Okay, I could do with stretching my legs. Do you think we've finished our lesson for this evening?" Tilly asked him, hoping to get out of the small room and to break the awkward silence that'd descended after she'd finished taking her notes. Brent shrugged, checking the clock.

"Yeah, I suppose so. We can get you your books and some new black clothes tomorrow. I'm guessing that was one of his orders while we were frozen?" he asked her, seemingly understanding Blake's control over the crowd without question. Tilly nodded, realising then that she'd always seen him wearing black too, but had never thought about it before.

"Yep, and nothing but black. I might as well throw out half of my clothes now," she replied with a pout and Brent smiled. Despite the changes in her she could still feel that spark lingering between them, and decided that they really didn't need to be alone in a room talking and smiling at each other like old times right now. "Do you think Lilith will let us join the party?" she eventually asked, hopeful that they could head back down to the crowd and join in on Lucas' celebrations, eager to clear her mind and have some fun.

CHAPTER FOURTEEN

Brent grinned over at Tilly and then grabbed his jacket from the hook behind the door, reaching in the pocket for his mobile phone. She watched eagerly as he gave David a quick call, asking him to speak to Lilith and seek permission for the two of them to leave the upstairs room. He seemed hopeful that his younger brother might have the chance to use Lilith's good mood to their advantage.

"Yeah, let me go and ask if..." David began, but was quickly silenced and then ordered to immediately pass the phone to his mistress, while Brent winced. Deep down, he knew he and Tilly were pushing their luck after just a couple of hours' on their own.

"Do you mean to tell me that you feel as though she's learned everything already, son?" Lilith asked him, in a stern but slightly softer tone as she addressed the boy she was so closely linked with. She'd always called Brent her son, and considered him and the other two boys as such. Lilith had even offered him her backing if he wanted to attempt the demonic trials someday too, which he knew was a rare gift that countless other followers would give anything to receive. And yet, he'd never flaunted her care for him, or had used it to his advantage—until now.

"Yes, well, what I mean is," he mumbled. "She's learned enough for now, mistress. I've taught Tilly the basics, and while there's still more for her to learn, I feel she may benefit further from the group experience. Enjoying the party and speaking openly with my father about his experiences will surely help her understand, rather than us hiding away up here all night?" he replied, hoping she would be lenient on them.

"Very well. Has she changed her clothes?" Lilith asked curtly, and Brent smiled.

"Yes, mistress," he replied, crossing his fingers hopefully.

"Then you may come," she told him and hung up the phone without another word. Brent turned and smiled at Tilly, letting her know they had been given permission to go. She jumped off the bed and checked her suitcase again, remembering she'd packed some black items after all, and she soon found a black skirt and tights that she paired with Brent's black hoodie, feeling much more comfortable than she'd done in his tracksuit trousers.

Within minutes, the pair then headed down the stairs and into the great hall. The darkness inside enveloped them as they made their way through the crowd, but she wasn't as apprehensive this time.

The altar ahead had been transformed into a kind of bar area, and a variety of drinks had been lined up for people to help themselves to. Lucas was there, chatting away animatedly to some other men, all of whom Tilly had seen in the dark crowd earlier that night, and he downed shots as he relished in their congratulatory toasts. He smiled happily to his friends, seeming just like the same man Tilly had met so many times before, and he continually planted kisses on his wife's dark-red lips, who also still appeared just like the same woman Tilly had seen all those times at the circus, too. They seemed so happy together, and she couldn't help but watch the pair as they interacted so comfortably, feeling surprised that a demon and human could possibly be so in love with one another.

"It is possible, strange as it might seem at first," Brent's voice said quietly from behind her. He'd seen her watching them and somehow knew exactly what she was thinking. "But, they've had many years together now, and in that time their goal has always remained the same—each other," he told her, looking over at them fondly. Tilly smiled, hoping she may truly understand or possess a bond that strong with her master in the future, but it seemed very hard to even attempt to predict what that future might be like. She hated the idea that it was scarily out of her control right now, but knew she was nothing more than a puppet in whatever game Blake wanted to play. Love might never even come into the equation.

"What's with the blood-sharing?" she then asked him, looking up into his dark blue eyes in the dim light and remembering back to that morning in the tent.

"Demons can use their blood to control humans, like she did with you that day so you'd forget both what you saw and the fact that she'd marked you. But, that's not what *they* do it for. Their true love allows for the sharing of blood between them without control or power being the reason behind it. It's a sharing of one another's essence, a declaration of mutual understanding, and a sign of both their individual strengths and their strong bond as a couple," he replied and she could hear the admiration and respect in his tone as he watched them for a moment beside her.

"So, they make each other stronger? Like equals…" she asked, and Brent nodded before taking her elbow and gently leading her on through the crowd once again. They reached his family, and Brent received a tight hug from his father and brothers before he bowed to Lilith and kissed her hand in respect. Tilly watched them all interacting as though this old-fashioned approach was so normal to them and she couldn't help feeling awkward, like an outsider. After a few minutes, she made her way towards Lucas, and Brent stayed behind to talk quietly with Lilith. In all honesty though, she was glad to have some time away from the scary demon. "Congratulations," she told Lucas after he gave her a hug, and made sure to look especially impressed at his new tattoo-like mark that completed the three sixes on his bare chest. He smiled and thanked her, looking Tilly up and down as though seeing her for the first time, and she realised he was sensing something different in her, too. She wondered if perhaps it was the change in her thanks to her new black mark and smiled back at him coyly.

"And congratulations are in order for you as well, Tilly," he replied, excited for her, but seeming to understand her reservations and fear at her new gift. Lucas watched her for a moment longer, his expression softening, and then he looked at her like he would do his own daughter—with a warm and gentle smile, and understanding eyes. "You have a lot to learn and I understand you have your fears, but if you take advice from no one else, please listen to me for I have been where you are now," he said, and she looked up into his deep blue eyes. There was darkness in them now that she was sure wasn't there before he'd completed his death trial. But, she still wasn't scared of him in spite of it.

She could sense that he was still the same man, a good man, and she thought that perhaps the darkness that was now inside of him was not just to be feared, but it was to be respected as well. "I was once just a man, with a wife and three young boys. I wasn't a Satanist back then, in fact I wasn't religious at all, and then when Jackson was five years old my wife left us, saying she had found another. It turned out she'd fallen in love with my only brother, and that they'd been having an affair since Jackson was only a baby. I was furious, enraged and betrayed, so I prayed to the gods above for vengeance. They did nothing. And then, as though by some unholy intervention, I crossed paths with the mesmerising and beautiful demon that I am now truly honoured to call my wife," Lucas told Tilly, looking over admirably at his demonic lover.

Tilly gasped, but he simply smiled. "Lilith and I helped each other. She was lost too, but she showed me a world I'd had no idea about before, a life I never knew I could have, and she also taught me how I could punish those who'd crossed me. With her help, I destroyed them both. I relished in their misery, and never once felt an ounce of guilt for my evil actions. I finally got my vengeance, and I loved her for showing me how. My brother eventually went crazy and killed my ex-wife. He then tried to take his own life but failed. He's in prison now, rotting away like the coward he is and when he eventually does die, Lilith will make sure his soul is tortured for all eternity," Lucas finished.

His eyes seemed sad for just a moment but he quickly shook it off, regaining his composure, and then he offered her a shot of whisky from atop the bar with a sly grin. Tilly smiled back at Lucas and accepted the small glass, nodding in understanding and gratitude for him having shared such an intimate story with her.

Although he was now very dark, damaged, and obviously still burdened by the memory of his ex, Lucas could still show her a warmth and kindness she wouldn't have thought could exist in this strange world she'd just joined. He brought her comfort, and Tilly happily clinked his glass with her own and then drank down the strong alcoholic shot to celebrate with him, reaching for another at the same time as Lucas, which made him smile even wider.

Later, as Brent escorted her back up to their room and grabbed his things, intending to share a room with Jackson instead, he hovered at the doorway for just a minute. He stayed to look at

Tilly, leaning against the frame thoughtfully.

"I'm truly sorry about all of this. I never intended for you to get involved in this part of my life. But, I guess it was never going to be my choice was it? I should've known Lilith would find a way to mark you, whether I was ready for her to or not," he told her, looking forlorn, but as though he needed to get it off his chest once and for all. Tilly stepped closer, and then slapped him across the face as hard as she could manage. Brent took the hot, stinging pain as if he felt he deserved it, and without any anger in his eyes towards his ex or even a hint of a flinch.

"You should've always known she would do it, of course she would. Don't make pointless excuses, Brent. I love you, or should I say *loved* you," she said, tailing off and having to stifle a sob at the finite words. But, she'd already begun to accept the fact that they were over. It was one of Blake's first orders to her and there was no way she wouldn't follow it. "There would have always come a day that you would've had to tell me about all of this, but in the end you were just too busy being a fucking coward to do it yourself," she snapped.

His sad eyes angered Tilly and she refused to let him play the martyr. After all, it wasn't his life that had just been changed forever. Brent had chosen this life years ago when he willingly became another of Lilith's followers, and had clearly always planned to live the rest of his life under her rule. Tilly had been forced into their world without ever having been asked if she even wanted it.

Something told her she did want it, though, and she turned away and closed the door in Brent's face. One thing was for sure, she was already undeniably excited and attracted to her new master, despite only having been with him for a few minutes, and she felt the flutter of butterflies in her stomach at the sheer thought of what dark delights might be in store for her under his rule. At the same time, she was also truly terrified by Blake and all the wicked things he might also decide to do to her, so vowed never to make it easy on Brent for having forced her to become his plaything, regardless of where this path took her.

CHAPTER FIFTEEN

The next morning, Brent and his brothers took Tilly to the city centre to do some shopping. She picked out some black dresses, skirts and jeans, before also treating herself to a biker jacket and boots to complete her dark new look. She felt amazing in all of it— gothic, sexy, and confident. Tilly didn't take too long either, much to the boys' delight, and they then stopped by an old church on the way to the train station afterwards. It was a hidden building that no one would even know existed without being shown to it, but she wondered if perhaps that was precisely the point. Brent grabbed her some books from the back room and gave the church a large donation in return for them. He then introduced her to some of the dark ministers, whom she could sense were marked. She somehow knew that their marks were black and they were under royal ownership, just like her. But unlike her, they weren't free to carry on living their lives. They lived and breathed their mistress' cause, and she was awestruck by their reverence.

The human ministers wore long robes embroidered with black roses, and they had hoods that covered half their faces, concealing their eyes. Despite the sinister look, the few she met were kind and warm. They told her how they'd started out as devout followers to the Satanist religion, and that the Dark Queen herself had handpicked each to climb the human ranks to become her clergymen. Each one wore his mark with so much pride that Tilly couldn't help but smile. She rubbed the inside of her right wrist with a strange sense of anxious pride, feeling special and blessed, or perhaps it was cursed—she couldn't be sure yet.

An hour later, and after saying goodbye to her friends, she boarded the train. Tilly was glad to be able to slump down into the comfortable first-class seat once again, and for the time alone at last. She was tired but couldn't seem to rest, so after polishing off a tall coffee and a bagel, she picked up her new reading assignments. First, she flicked through the pages of the Satanist's bible before settling down to read it more thoroughly with her second cup of coffee in hand. By the time she got home, Tilly was pretty well versed in the dark texts and rules surrounding her new world, though hardly any clearer on it all.

She popped into the main house to quickly greet her parents, informing her mother that she and Brent had decided to split up. She blamed their long distance relationship, but didn't say any more. Tilly already knew that she'd have to get used to concealing her dark life from her parents from now on, so figured she'd start there. Robert stayed quiet, but after a little quizzing, her mother, Bianca seemed convinced enough. Tilly gave her a hug and excused herself, and then went out to her little nook to be alone, and she was exhausted so fell immediately into bed and into a deep, dreamless sleep.

The next morning, Tilly awoke and quickly proceeded to throw out all of her colourful clothes, slipping them into bags ready to give away via the charity shops in town. She then continued to study the books Brent had given her, absorbing everything she could about the Satanic world, while making notes and researching online for more information and rituals, poring over every piece of information she could find.

Tilly soon found out that Brent had been right about Blake's extended family. His aunt, uncle, and cousins were powerful extensions of the Dark Queen's brood, but they lived on Earth rather than in Hell, and ran a secretive order by the name of the Crimson Brotherhood. She couldn't find anything else on them so guessed she'd have to wait until she'd be allowed to know more, presumably by Blake himself. The secret, she imagined, was something told only to those deemed worthy of the knowledge, and she was sure delicate information like that wouldn't be given out to just anyone. Tilly simply made a note about it in her book and then carried on researching the many other aspects she needed to educate herself on in order to feel more comfortable in Blake's following, adhering to yet another of his orders without hesitation.

She searched the Internet some more, and eventually came across a commitment ceremony the next evening. She remembered Brent's advice, and decided that she might as well do it sooner rather than later. Tilly knew Blake could only come Earth during the full moon, but couldn't be sure when the next visit from her master would happen. Perhaps he might not want to. Either way, she wanted him to be pleased with her progress when he eventually did come to her. Tilly knew that the next step was to fully commit herself—mind, body, and soul.

She set up a small altar on her desk—as per the website's instructions—complete with a black candle and small knife she'd had to sneak out of the main house. Tilly then drew a pentagram on some paper and lit the candle, before pricking her finger and dripping the blood onto the page as she prepared to recite the strange text. She then took a deep breath and spoke the binding incantation, meaning every word of the powerful spell as she spoke.

"I call upon the darkness to hear my call. I hereby renounce all others and pledge both my allegiance and my soul to the Dark Queen," she said, before setting fire to the bloody page with the candle. "So mote it be, hail Satan," she finished, then blew out the candle and cleared up the mess before heading off to get changed for bed. Tilly didn't feel any different following the ritual, but hoped it'd worked, or that it was least appreciated that she'd made the effort. She then climbed into bed and fell straight into a deep sleep again.

Tilly was stood before the huge mirror in her small bedroom, dressed in a beautiful long black gown that was made up of a boned corset on the top and a layered skirt underneath, and it covered her all the way down to her feet. Her dark-blonde hair was pinned back in a side-bun that was wound with black ribbon, and she had charcoal, smoky shadowed eyelids and long, black lashes. Her inverted cross was now clearly visible on the inside of her right wrist for some reason, and she couldn't help but think that it looked almost like a tattoo. The mark looked amazing at her side beside the black dress that clung to her hips alluringly, and Tilly felt wonderful, as though she were a princess ready to go to a ball. She gazed at herself for a few moments, taking in the gothic look she'd so easily taken to with a satisfied smile.

Two hands then reached up her bare arms from behind and held her shoulders for a second, one of them then moving around inside her left arm to her torso and gathering Tilly around her stomach as the other reached over her right shoulder and grasped her neck softly, yet powerfully. A set of bright green eyes then appeared over her shoulder and Blake's face materialised from within the shadows, looking sultry and incredibly sexy. She smiled, leaning into his strong hold and succumbing to him, staring back at her master through the reflection in the mirror.

"You're here," she said, her voice almost a whisper, and she was surprised to find herself genuinely pleased to see him.

"Yes, Tilly," he answered, kissing her neck softly. She groaned, having felt it for real, along with an excited tingle that coursed through her at his touch. "I figured it was high time I checked in on my new prize." His teeth grazed her skin when his lips curled in a smile, and she swooned.

"Is this real?" she asked him quietly as he trailed his lips up and down her exposed collarbone, his gentle touch making her tremble before him with both anticipation and nervousness.

"No," he answered with a gruff laugh. "You're dreaming. But, your body will respond to any stimulation I give you in your dreams as though it were really happening. You'll feel everything I do to you as if I am really there," he told her with a wicked grin, before lifting his head up and looking into her eyes through the mirrored reflection. "Tell me what you desire from your life, Tilly—what you crave. Show me," he said, and then the mirror before them seemed to blur and darken. Their reflected image was soon gone from it completely, and moments later, it was as if a video was showing through the large framed screen. It was a clip of her, and she was just a few years older than she was now. In the vision, Tilly was a famous chef. She'd made it at last and was running an award-winning restaurant, signing her recipe books, and making television appearances as her adoring public watched on. Fame and fortune, being desired and respected by all that watched from the audience—that was what she yearned for.

"Yes, this is what I want, master. I want to be successful, rich, renowned, and adored," she told him, ashamed somewhat by her shallow aspirations, but Blake was completely unsurprised by it.

LAURA MORGAN

Power, wealth and fame were what everyone wanted, and what almost all the humans he and his demons encountered along the way sold their souls for.

He smiled down at her as the image before them changed again. Tilly couldn't control them. It was as though he was showing her what was inside her own head, and she had no idea what nuggets of truth and desire he might pluck out of her next. The following scene was that of her and Blake, naked and lying in bed together. They were making love and he was staring into her eyes, telling her that he loved her. Tilly blushed at the image and gasped as he tightened his hold on her, silently commanding her to keep her eyes on the screen.

"And this?" he asked, his voice a rough groan in her ear, and she nodded. She blushed harder but ignored her embarrassment and lifted her hands, covering his as they held her in his still strong grip. "Are you sure it's not this that you want?" he asked, altering the image to replace himself with the image of Brent's naked body. His blue eyes were peering into Tilly's as he too spoke the same words of love that Blake had just done in the previous, matching movie. She stiffened at the sight before her, but knew it wasn't true. She wanted the first variation of that image now, more than ever. The look on his face as Blake had proclaimed his love for her was all she wanted, and Tilly knew she'd do anything to have it.

"No, master," she said, and she turned to face him, wanting to get away from the image of her and Brent so intimately together. She dropped to her knees and looked up at her Black Prince as he stood towering over her. He looked gorgeous, like a beautiful statue of her dark god that belonged in a museum somewhere, rather than here in her tiny bedroom. He was wearing a perfectly tailored and entirely black suit, with a matching waistcoat, shirt

and tie, every inch of him exuding the powerful force she was now so drawn to. Blake looked down at Tilly, a smile curling the edges of his lips, and she could tell that she'd satisfied his curiosity on the subject at last.

"Good. Now, as much as I adore seeing you on your knees, you may rise," he ordered her, and then pulled Tilly close and planted a deep, fierce kiss on her lips when she did as he commanded. She could feel his grip on her as though he were really there, feel the pressing of his lips against hers as he took possession of her mouth, and she kissed him back fervently. His hands slid behind her as they kissed and he then unzipped the black dress she was wearing, causing it to immediately fall at her feet. She realised then that her imaginary form had been completely naked underneath the gown, but didn't care.

Blake eyed her for a moment and then lifted Tilly up into his arms and took her over to the bed, laying her down on the duvet before lifting himself over her trembling body. She was utterly naked before him while he remained in his perfect suit, and Tilly was pretty positive that he had absolutely no intention of removing it this time. His mouth found hers again and they kissed lasciviously, his touch and the taste of him sending her body into overdrive, and she found herself desperate to run her hands through his dark curls, but she didn't dare reach up to grab them. Instead, she gripped the duvet beneath her tightly. "I know...what you did," he whispered in her ear between their kisses, and Tilly couldn't help but tense up, wondering if she'd done something wrong.

Blake immediately laughed though, letting her know that she wasn't in trouble with him, and he lifted himself up on his hands to look down into her eyes. "You committed your soul to my mother, and to me," he told her, smiling down at Tilly as he cupped her *cheek with one hand. She was instantly mesmerised by his deep green eyes again as he spoke to her quietly, his tone much softer than when he delivered his stern orders at the castle. "You're to be rewarded, Tilly," he then added with a wry curl of his lip.*

Without another word, he laid his mouth on her now so sensitive skin again, trailing kisses across her chest and to her breasts before sinking lower on the bed and opening her thighs before him. Tilly let all her inhibitions go as he possessed her, and gripped the duvet beneath her even tighter in her hands. She gasped as he kissed her other lips and began caressing her tender nub with his mouth. Blake then delved his tongue expertly inside her cleft and then slid it out and upwards to flick over her already swollen clit. His fingers filled the wet void, rubbing her skilfully inside as his tongue pursued her climax from above. She cried out, being careful not to say his name as a wonderful orgasm rippled through her, but she could barely form words at all thanks to the so strong and mind blowing waves as they reverberated throughout every inch of her being. Her body continued to pulsate even as he pulled away and stood over her, smiling down before disappearing into the darkness again...

Tilly woke up from her wonderful dream with a start, gripping the bed covers tightly while drenched with sweat, and with her core still tensing wonderfully from her climactic release. She lay back and revelled in the afterglow, panting and feeling so delighted after Blake's wondrous gift.

"Whoa," she whispered to herself before falling back asleep, and she was disappointed that he wasn't there to greet her this time, having already delivered Tilly with her sublime reward.

CHAPTER SIXTEEN

Blake's eyes flew open, as though he too had just awoken from a deep sleep. Being inside Tilly's consciousness was strange, but fun, and he looked forward to spending more nights in her dreams in the future. The powerful Prince quickly found himself eager to strengthen their already amazing connection further, but he was willing to wait until he saw her in the flesh before joining Tilly in bed properly, wanting nothing but the real thing from his new endeavour. The link between them was stronger than ever now, thanks to her having performed the commitment ceremony, and he'd been pleasantly surprised that she'd decided to do it without him having to order her to. Blake had high hopes for this intriguing human and he expected nothing less than complete submission, obedience, and loyalty from her from now on. He lay back on his bed, thinking of her and her delicious body for a moment with a satisfied smile.

His twin sister, Luna, then came bursting into his room, disrupting his wonderful daydream without a care, and he glowered across at her.

"Hey, brother," she said, ignoring his scowl as she flopped down on the bed next to him and eyed him curiously. The two of them had always stayed close friends as well as siblings despite their many years in Hell together, and they still shared a strong bond regardless of their age, power, and the individual strengths and responsibilities they'd developed along the way. She'd sensed it instantly when he'd marked Tilly, having felt the connection appear somewhere deep inside of her, and she'd been excited for him to finally share that part of himself with someone. He'd insisted that it meant nothing, but Luna knew him better than that. While she'd chosen not to tease him about it, knowing better than to push him, she'd still given him a knowing smile in return. Marking a human never meant nothing, and they all knew it.

Luna had only marked a handful of humans in her lifetime, but she'd shared strong bonds with each of them and had taken them all as her lovers at some point, whether male or female. She used to visit each of their dreams frequently while stuck in Hell, as well as going to Earth during the full moons to be with them properly, and it'd been wonderful having her own small following to both command and love in one way or another. She'd eventually granted one of them a place in her coven. A once tortured soul, she'd grown to truly love Ash, and knew he was her soulmate. He hadn't been deemed strong enough to complete the demonic trials, so had instead settled for spending eternity by her side as her servant. He'd been granted magical powers and immortality by her mother, and had then gone on to quickly become her chief warlock. The two of them were now inseparable, and Ash would beg Luna to marry him on a daily basis. He was careful only to proclaim his love to her in private due to his lowly status when they were in the company of others, but the sentiment was true. She wanted to say yes, to allow him a more respected position in their dark hierarchy, but it was too soon. They'd only been together twenty years, and had many more to come yet. She never understood why he wanted to rush it all when they had hundreds of lifetimes together, and years to finally do all of those things. Ash would just smile knowingly and bow to his mistress, but then fall to his knees before Luna and ask her again the next day.

Her mother, the Dark Queen, always smiled when she moaned to her about his proposals with a pout. She told her daughter that it was simply because Ash loved her so very much and couldn't bear the thought of not calling her his wife. Luna knew that Harry had felt the same way towards Cate half a century before, and had asked her to marry him the moment he'd made it to the highest level of the demonic hierarchy following his transition from man to demon at her request. Cate had said yes to him immediately, of course, and they'd been married before the day was over. The couple had been together in secret for years before that, ever since her mother had returned home with Lottie, their surprise little sister, as well as having created the first new demon in centuries. It was very much to everyone's surprise, but they'd soon figured out why she'd done it, and how the young demon was the missing half of their Dark Queen's heart. After years of her trying to ignore the loss, Cate had finally found him again, and admitted all to her eldest children. Blake and Luna had taken to Harry instantly, and their newly discovered sister, Lottie, spoke so highly of him that the five dark beings had soon became a formidable and extremely close family.

Cate had then lifted the ban on making new demons, but all willing candidates had to complete the almost impossible demonic trials first, and then she could still turn them down if she didn't deem them worthy for the highly coveted powers. The final ritual could only be carried out in the Queen's presence as well, and while her time was considered too precious by some to spend on human matters, she didn't need to attend hardly any, as almost all who tried didn't even make it to the council table for her consideration. Harry had been the only new demon for many years, followed eventually by a second, Eliza, but she'd only made it to a level four position in the demonic hierarchy. In then end, her innocence had halted her progress, much to her new sire, the level one demon Asmodeus' despair. He'd fallen in love with the human while she was in his following on Earth and wanted her to be his demonic bride, which she'd still become after her initiations were over, but the pair were not welcome in the company of high ranking demons thanks to her two failed attempts to climb higher in the initiation arena. They would have to wait centuries for her to try again, and in the meantime, Asmodeus would have to attend the higher-level gatherings alone. Listening in on his sister's thoughts, Blake simply couldn't understand how a powerful demon such as Asmodeus would settle for a lower level existence. And for what reason? So that he could be with the woman he loved? There was no way he would ever give up his high status for something as foolish as love.

"One day you'll see why he did it. Perhaps you might even risk it all yourself. Why are you so unsatisfied? I thought you just went into her dreams?" Luna asked Blake, pulling him out of his reverie. She could sense his frustrations at only having given Tilly her pleasure in the dream rather than having had his own release. In truth, he'd wanted more, wanted to gratify his own needs as well, but had decided against it. He'd never tell Luna, but there was a strong part of him that wanted to wait until he could be with Tilly properly, in full physical form for their first time together. Then, they could make love for hours, gratifying both their needs over and over, and he wouldn't settle for anything less than perfect.

"She woke up," he told her dismissively with a nonchalant wave of his hand. "And, I owed her one after leaving her hanging on Halloween."

"You need to work on that then, she's not meant to wake until you release her," she replied with a smirk.

"Did you actually want something?" he asked Luna impatiently, feeling sick of her leading questions.

"No, I just wanted to figure out if you had finally fallen in *love*," she teased, nudging him with her elbow and fluttering her eyelashes, but she teleported away before he could even answer her. Luna knew that Blake thought himself incapable of love, he'd told her many times that he'd never let himself fall, and yet she still hoped that this human girl might just break down those incredibly high walls of his. That, or at least make a decent dent in them before he discarded her and moved on to his next distraction.

He sneered and lay back down on his dark pillows, then closed his eyes and focussed. Blake mentally closed himself off to everything and everyone around him, which was his usual mind-set. This was how he'd always managed to keep his walls so highly built and his darkness so strong. He kept his emotions at arm's length, which was easy; you just had to become numb inside—a cold, closed-off shell of a man fuelled by power, strength and purpose, rather than by love or emotion. He'd learned how many years before thanks to his father's teachings, and those terrible lessons simply could not be forgotten no matter what the female romantics in his family wanted for him. By never letting anyone else invade his little bubble, Blake had maintained his ominous strength and incredible power perfectly, never allowing nonsense such as love affect his decision making abilities or cloud his renowned judgement. If he was horny, he would fuck, and he had plenty with whom he could do it. But, right now he just wanted to sit and be melancholy for no reason other than that he wanted to, and he didn't have to explain himself to his twin sister.

CHAPTER SEVENTEEN

Home and work life continued on as normal all around Tilly, as though everything was still exactly the same as it'd always been. She supposed that to everyone else, life still was the same, but nothing was as it'd once seemed for her. The world had become a new and scary place ever since her life-changing night at the castle, and Tilly knew that it would only get crazier as her time as Blake's follower went on.

The following week, she returned to college, and her new wardrobe colour immediately attracted negative comments from Renee, who called her a Goth and then rolled her eyes when Tilly told her just where she could stick her opinion.

She simply got on with things, but in the food hall later that week, Tilly felt a strange little beacon from somewhere deep in her gut, and couldn't understand what it must be. She looked around the large room to try and figure it out, and that was when she saw a girl dressed entirely in black watching her from a small table in the corner. She sat alone, and beckoned Tilly over with a wave, smiling and seemingly eager for her to join her once they'd made eye contact.

"Hi there, fellow follower," the girl said as Tilly sat down opposite her, and she was gobsmacked. She realised that must've been what the strange little feeling was, and guessed she could sense the other girl's mark even from across the room.

"Hi," she said back, instinctively rubbing her wrist where her hidden mark was. The girl saw, and realised that she must be new to all of this, so helped her out.

"Are you new?" she asked excitedly, her dark-brown eyes wide and her black hair bobbing up and down on her shoulders as she talked enthusiastically. Tilly nodded and smiled, looking all around her at the other people milling around in the hall to check they weren't going to be overheard. "Well, don't worry, okay. I am not gonna start shouting about it in the dining hall," she added, and laughed, making Tilly smile and instantly drop her guard.

"My name's Sapphire, and my master is the demon Belias," she informed her formally, and then waited for Tilly to do the same in return.

"Well, my name's Tilly," she said, but hesitated as to what she should say next. "And, urm."

"It's nice to meet you, Tilly. You don't have to tell me who your master is if you don't want to. It's our choice whether to divulge the details or not, and it's okay if you don't want to say it yet," she said with a warm smile as she rose from her chair and offered her a cigarette.

Tilly shook her head no, but joined Sapphire outside to chat to her some more as she smoked, grateful to have a new college comrade who knew all about her secret world. They became friends right away, and Sapphire never pushed Tilly to find out who her master was, seeming to understand and respect her privacy much more than her other friends would ever have done if she kept anything so important from them.

A couple of weeks later, Tilly and Gwen were informed that they were all going out to celebrate Renee's birthday in Coventry.

The plan was to hit the bars and end up at one of the huge nightclubs there to dance the night away and get insanely drunk. She said yes, eager to let her hair down, and thinking that, after all, Blake had told her she could live her life however she wanted while she wasn't given any orders to follow. She was absolutely certain that they'd behave themselves while out in town, and maintained that she would just have a few drinks with her friends, not intending to get too drunk and potentially disappoint her master quite so soon after being marked by him.

Tilly also had no idea when she would see her Black Prince again, and hadn't heard from him since that wonderful dream. She was desperate for some contact though, so figured she could do with the distraction that a night out with her friends would give her. Gwen agreed to come along, and the three of them happily barhopped their way up the high street before drunkenly making their way into one of the busy nightclubs. Tilly had decided to wear her dark-blonde hair in a high ponytail with smoky eye makeup, and she'd gone for a black skater style dress with fishnet tights and very high-heeled black boots. She topped it all off with a thick silver necklace and cuff bracelet, and teemed with her biker jacket—she knew she looked amazing.

Not a single one of them noticed the bright and very full moon that had risen in the sky above them as they went along the busy high street and then hurried excitedly into the bars for their next round, the energy of the night calling to them. Tilly was having a great time, laughing and joking with her friends as they made their way through far too many cocktails and shots while Renee flirted wildly with many a handsome barman or fellow drunken comrade on a night out. By the time they had gotten to the club, Tilly had to admit she'd had more than enough to drink, thanks to the two-for-one deals in the bars that'd lined their path there. So, she headed straight towards the bustling dance floor once she was inside rather than to the bar with Renee. Gwen joined her and they happily throbbed with the heavy crowd, keeping hold of each other as they were thrown around a little when the music picked up speed. The loud bass hurt Tilly's ears, but she didn't care. She hadn't been out dancing in such a long time and was enjoying herself far too much to worry about having ringing ears for the next day or so. Renee appeared at their side after a few minutes with drinks in her hands, which she passed to them.

"Thanks," Tilly shouted as she took the cool drink and greedily downed a large gulp—whisky and cola, her favourite.

"I didn't buy them," Renee told her with a sly grin, and had to lean in closer and shout over the music for Tilly to hear her better. "I met three totally gorgeous guys at the bar, and they bought them for us," she said with a pleading look. "I promised we'd go over after this song has finished to say thank you. They are so hot, trust me!" she shouted with excitement and Tilly shook her head.

"Nope not interested, Renee," she said, looking at Gwen, but her other friend's big brown eyes were looking at Tilly pleadingly too, and she groaned in defeat.

"Just because you're not interested, doesn't mean we can't pull some hotties. Come on, for me?" Renee asked with a smile and a flutter of her long eyelashes. Tilly conceded, and nodded in agreement, finishing off her drink with a large gulp. She then followed Renee over to the bar in search of these so-called, 'hot guys,' that her friend had promised would be waiting for them there, and caught Blake's green eyes watching her from across the room before seeing him properly in the crowd by the bar. She nearly squealed with excitement as she neared him, catching the sly grin curling at the corners of his mouth as he watched her approach.

CHAPTER EIGHTEEN

"There they are," Renee said, pointing in the direction of Blake and his two friends, but Tilly already knew they must be the guys she was talking about, and she could somehow sense that his two companions were demons. Renee led the way, and a few seconds later, the trio were stood beneath the terrifyingly seductive gaze of the three dark and powerful beings.

"Tilly, Gwen—this is Luke, Bob, and Levi," she introduced them with a satisfied smirk, eyeing her as if to say, *I told you so.*

Blake didn't take his eyes off Tilly, and she felt her knees go weak under his intense gaze. She smiled, reaching out to shake his hand, while the other two men focussed on obtaining her friends' attentions. She then began to wonder if they'd been ordered to keep the other two girls busy so that Blake could have Tilly to himself, and hoped she was right.

"Pleased to meet you," she said, performing a small and unsuspecting bow to her master, before then graciously accepting another whisky and cola that he offered her. He hadn't even needed to ask what she might like to drink, and even though Tilly knew that he could read her like a book, so wasn't surprised he knew what to get her, she loved the gesture anyway.

"Well if it isn't the girl of my dreams," he said quietly, smiling as he watched her sip the drink, tipping the glass higher to try and hide her blushing cheeks.

"I suppose I can't say you're the *man* of my dreams, but perhaps the master of them," she eventually managed to reply quietly, smiling up at him sheepishly. He laughed gruffly and grinned back before he then took her hand in his and pulled Tilly away without another word. Blake only stopped when they reached a dark corner where he then pinned her up against the wall and kissed her deeply. She swooned in his grasp and kissed him back with a passion and need for him she hadn't even realised she'd built up during his absence. He finally broke their intense kiss and pulled his head back to stare into her eyes, and she didn't miss the flicker of surprise in his gaze, too.

"Ready to get out of here?" he asked, looking around to make sure no one was watching the two of them.

"Of course, your majesty," she replied in a whisper, panting and trembling before him, having completely forgotten all about her friends and the busy club around them.

In less than a second, they'd teleported away and arrived in a dark foyer, and Tilly had to give herself a moment to find her feet. The whisky and cocktails coursing through her system weren't helping matters either. "Did we just..." she started to ask him.

"Teleport? Yes," he answered, laughing as she shook her head in bemusement and gripped the nearby wall to help steady herself.

"Cool," she muttered as Blake wandered over to one of the walls. He turned on the lights and then unlocked a huge set of wooden doors that were before them. The lights inside had flicked on too, and Tilly could see into a huge penthouse flat that stretched out before her. It was darkly decorated in blacks and reds, but was lavishly furnished and the walls each held dark, erotic and ominous art. She'd never seen anything like it before and stood for a few moments, taking it all in. Tilly couldn't help feeling common and unrefined in this luxurious home fit for nothing but millionaires and socialites, and she shrunk back.

Blake didn't address her angst. He simply shook his head, took her hand, and then led her inside, locking the doors behind them so as not to be disturbed. Tilly felt her heart flutter with excitement at being there alone with him, and hoped he was intending on showing her exactly what it meant to be his one and only devoted follower.

Her master then led her over to a small bar area near the lounge, where she sat down on a stool and watched him intently as he poured them both some whisky over perfectly square cubes of ice.

"Any chance I could have some cola with that please, master?" she asked timidly, hoping not to annoy her powerful companion. He smiled, but sighed and shook his head again as he pushed the glass towards her.

"This is a ten-thousand pound bottle of whisky, Tilly, you absolutely do not mix it with cola," he told her authoritatively, but with an edge of playfulness about him.

She hadn't seen him be so relaxed before, but liked it. His cold, business-like manner from the night of Lucas' trial was gone now, giving way for his more playful and fun side to shine through. She enjoyed this side of him, and smiled in gracious defeat as she picked up the crystal tumbler. Tilly swirled the ice around in the thick, dark spirit for a moment, coating it with the strong drink, which helped to water it down slightly. She then raised it to her lips and took a small sip while he watched her intently. The whisky really was lovely, and far better than the cheap stuff she was used to. She couldn't help but concede to his triumph in this matter, shrugging and nodding with a coy smile before she took another sip. "Good, you'll soon learn to trust my judgement without question. But first, let me give you the tour," he said, taking her hand and pulling her close.

"It must be nice always being right," she murmured, smiling up at him. He couldn't seem to help but grin back down at her, taking her in silently as though surprised by something, before leading the way around the huge penthouse flat. There must've been six bedrooms, and each of them was stunning and lavishly decorated, just as the lounge had been. Along the corridors revealed more rooms. Blake showed her a library, office, huge television room, home gym, and then finally—the master bedroom. That one room was almost as big as the lounge, with patio doors that led out onto a shared terrace with the living room, and it had massive windows on the other side that had huge black curtains over them. In the centre was a gigantic bed, with four black-curtained posts on each corner and black satin sheets covering it.

Blake led her inside and placed the whisky glasses on a chest of drawers beside the patio doors, and he then turned on a music system that also sat atop the wooden unit. Acoustic rock music immediately filled the room, seductive guitar riffs along with the deep, yet gentle voice of a man singing. It was beautiful, and Tilly couldn't help but close her eyes and let the sound wash over her. This was much better than the thumping club music they'd been listening to less than half an hour earlier. It was soulful. Stirring. Tilly listened intently, the lyrics suddenly speaking volumes to her.

"I'll follow you forever, through the darkest nights and darker days.
No need to compromise, join me in the shadows.
Your darkness is no burden. I'll carry its weight in my soul.
Never apologise, just make sure your soul obeys.
I'll follow you forever, just say yes."

"I'm glad you like it," Blake said, breaking her dreamlike reverie, and Tilly opened her eyes to find him standing just in front of her, his face only a few inches away. He reached up to cup her face gently in his hands, staring down into her eyes as he read her thoughts.

"You didn't mind me going out to the club tonight did you, master?" she asked him; suddenly worried she might have needed to ask his permission or something.

"No. I told you before. You may live your life as you wish. All I ask is that you follow my rules and orders, and you come to me when I summon you," he said, still staring into her blue eyes alluringly.

She couldn't help but laugh, thinking that even if that was all he wanted from her, it was still an incredible amount to have to take into consideration, but she knew she'd do so willingly if it meant more nights like this.

"Did you summon me tonight?" she wondered aloud, hoping she hadn't accidentally ignored his commandment in her slightly drunken haze.

"Trust me, you'll know it when I do," Blake answered, and laughed deeply, but didn't mock her. "I read your thoughts while I was in Hell, Tilly, and I knew that you and your friends were planning this night out. Why did you think I bought along some 'hot guys' to help distract your friends for me so that I could get you alone?" he asked with a fiendish grin, confirming her earlier suspicions on the subject.

"Ah, I thought that was a happy coincidence," she replied with a smile, her eyes lighting up as she peered up at him.

"There are no coincidences, you should know that by now?" he teased, however he didn't wait for an answer. Blake pulled her towards him, capturing her mouth again with his, and they kissed deeply. Tilly had to grip his shoulders to stop herself from falling. She was so woozy from his wonderful kisses, weak from his powerful prowess, and commanded by his almighty power, that she nearly forgot to breathe. His hands reached down to support her, pulling Tilly even closer into his embrace. "Strip," he then commanded, just a whisper but so incredibly clear and powerful that it was as though she heard him in her mind as well as in her ears.

"Yes, master," she said, understanding now that there really was a big difference between him asking and him telling her. Tilly reached down and began pulling off her dress, slipping it down and then throwing it onto a nearby chair. Her tights soon followed and then her underwear. She stood before him, naked and trembling with anticipation, and looked up into his satisfied green eyes. Tilly smiled, relishing in his pleasure with her. "Déjà vu," she whispered, looking him up and down, taking in his complete outfit while remembering her dream where she was naked before him then, too. He laughed and reached down, scooping Tilly up into his arms and then pulling her legs up to wrap them around his waist as he carried her over to the bed.

"This isn't going to be like anything you've had before, Tilly. I absolutely guarantee it," he informed her as he placed her gently on top of the sheets and stood back, pulling off his black shirt before unbuttoning his jeans. She sat back and crossed her legs, gazing up at him—her dark, sexy, godlike master, and she almost drooled as she finally got to take in his perfect, half naked body when he stood before her. His arms and torso were so muscular, so defined and sexy, and his open fly showed off those sexy hip muscles that made Tilly excited to think what was coming next. Blake laughed, almost coyly as he read her wicked thoughts about him and his glorious body. She just grinned and climbed up onto her knees and sat before him on the bed, licking her lips while silently pleading with him to continue undressing for her.

He obliged, pulling off his jeans and boxers, and releasing his hard cock at last. "Come here," he commanded, and Tilly shuffled forward, eager to touch him, to feel his flawless skin against hers. Blake leaned in and kissed her, grabbing her lower back and pulling her closer, pressing his hard body into hers. He then lifted one thigh up and wrapped it around his waist, opening her up for him as they continued to kiss passionately. He finally pulled his mouth away, needing to ask her just one last question before they could proceed. "Are you ready to fuck me, Tilly?" he whispered, his gorgeous green eyes staring at her intently. He didn't want to go slowly, not yet. Blake was a creature of desire, bound by its allure, and fuelled by the spoils. He wanted to fuck Tilly, to take her in every way he imagined, and own her body in ways the inexperienced young thing had no idea of.

"Yes," she whispered back, her voice trembling with anticipation.

In less than a second of her response, Blake pulled her closer with one strong thrust, and he was inside her before she could take her next breath. Tilly gasped as she enveloped him, her muscles tightening wonderfully, and her body moistening for him in an instant. He pulled her back and forth, commanding her body with his. The wonderful strokes he delivered to the tender spot inside of her made her succumb to him subconsciously, and without hesitation or fear.

His kisses grew deeper, more intense and eager as he moved harder and faster inside her hot and welcoming cleft. She came quickly, unable to contain the pleasurable release no matter how much she tried to slow it. He didn't care that she was alight, the climax bursting from her like a wave of all-consuming pleasure, and carried on. Her body clenched and tensed, and Blake let himself enjoy her climax while continuing in his pursuit of his own release.

After her body calmed down, he laid Tilly back onto the bed, but she continued to tremble in his strong grasp thanks to having had the most satisfying and intense orgasm of her life. Blake turned her over onto her stomach before him with a satisfied smile. After finally joining her on the bed, he then climbed over Tilly and slipped inside her from behind, his strong body pressing her fragile frame into the huge bed as he thrust hard inside of her again. She groaned with pleasure as he continued his strong and heavy thrusts, grabbing at the sheets with her hands and pushing back to welcome him even deeper, eager to give him every inch of room she was able to open up for him. She came again, deep and breathtakingly intense, as he pushed even harder inside her, and cried out for him.

Blake flipped her over again, this time to face him before he sat up, pulling Tilly onto his lap so that she could ride his long length while he watched. She happily obliged, climbing atop her Adonis, and she slid him back inside her still wet, ready, and willing opening. Blake watched her with a smile as she rode up and down, and then grabbed her hips and deepened the thrusts, unable to help himself.

He sat up further, cradling Tilly in his arms and taking her mouth in his again as she continued to pleasure him, eager as he was for him to reach his climax. She was desperate to give him his gratification and pushed her body way beyond its normal limits in order to satisfy her dark master. She cried out uncontrollably again as a third orgasm rippled through her, the aftershocks making her weak, and her human body finally started to struggle to keep up with his relentless lovemaking.

Blake pulled her closer to him, stopping his thrusts for a few moments, and kept still so he could enjoy the sensation of her inner muscles as they clenched around him from deep within. He looked up at Tilly, and kissed her gently, staring into her blue eyes as he revelled in her pleasure, basking in her satisfied glow. She was dusted with sweat, red-faced and truly beautiful. There was no way he could stop now. No way on Earth he wanted anything but more of what she was giving him.

Blake then laid Tilly back onto the bed; his strong body lifting her easily before he then wrapped himself inside her trembling thighs. She peered up into his gorgeous green eyes again as he continued to slide in and out of her soaked core, slower now and less urgent, but still hot and hard for her as he leaned over her. Blake gripped her thighs with his strong hands, lifting her hips to meet his. She ran her hands up to his shoulders and then through his dark-brown hair, smiling up at him through her woozy haze of emotion, lust and even love. She was falling for him, she could already feel it, and knew she couldn't control it.

They continued for hours, and eventually Tilly was left panting and exhausted after her sixth orgasm while Blake grabbed her tight and pulled her closer one last time. The bed beneath them then shook as he came, his hot bursts throbbing inside of her as he reached his powerful climax and cried out, kissing her feverishly as he revelled in his glorious release at last.

Tilly lay in his arms afterwards, feeling both relaxed and wonderfully exhausted. She watched the sun as it streamed into the bedroom through the open curtain as she rested, her head on Blake's chest. She was too exhausted to talk, yet still too buzzing to sleep, and so she just let her mind wander, knowing he would be listening in. Blake lay there in comfortable silence as well, smiling and caressing Tilly's bare back with his hand while she draped herself over him. He wrapped her protectively in his arms, working hard to push away the feelings that were threatening to creep into his heart for her, too.

"I can't give you what you want, Tilly," he told her later that morning after she'd managed to drift off for a couple of hours' sleep. He'd stayed with her, but hadn't let himself fall off to sleep beside her. Instead, his mind had been running through every possible scenario for the pair of them and their future together.

"What do you mean, master?" she asked, confused by this sudden, bleak statement.

"The image of us you showed me in your dream," Blake told her, and her face fell. "I can never love you. Don't live in hope that I'll ever say those words to you, Tilly. I'm not capable of love," he added, his tone quiet and sombre, but he wanted to be honest with her. Blake knew that she was falling for him, and he wanted her to be his, he wanted to control and possess her entirely, and have her at his every command, but that was all he could ever offer the innocent, young girl. Possession was all he knew. Love was something long forgotten, and he knew that he could never love Tilly back, never give her the love she deserved and wanted so desperately.

"Will you hurt me?" she asked him, leaning up on one elbow so that she could look into his hooded green eyes properly. Her response surprised Blake, having expected her to cry out or try to reason with him, or even beg him to reconsider—like all the other lovers before her. This was an unanticipated reaction. For some reason, she accepted his harsh explanation. He could sense it in her calm, decisive thoughts. Tilly took his dark words like a strangely profound promise, and was willing to live with them, even if it meant loving him for the rest of her life and never having him love her in return.

"Yes," Blake answered, knowing that in all honesty he most likely would hurt Tilly eventually, both mentally and physically. He was bad news, no matter how either of them looked at it, and he knew he'd probably just end up using her to satisfy his needs and then leave her once he'd had enough. That was simply his way. He'd always blamed his black heart for it, despite knowing how his siblings and mother didn't suffer from the same aversion to emotions that he did, but didn't know how to change. Blake had never had a relationship with a woman in the past that didn't involve fucking them and then leaving, calling on them again only when he was horny. His witches and lower level demons had seen to those needs perfectly well in his almost eighty-year existence, so hadn't bothered to look elsewhere. He certainly didn't stick around for the declarations of love, cuddling, or date-nights, and knew he never would.

Tilly stared into his eyes thoughtfully, trying to read him, but was unable to understand the true motives behind his words, or properly sense the emotion he was fighting so hard to keep hidden behind his stoic features. She decided to trust her gut, and smiled down at him before kissing Blake's lips gently. She knew there was no getting out of his ownership, and that she was already far too close to being in love with her master to want to. Tilly also couldn't bring herself to care that he might never love her in return. After all, she was his possession now and if he never saw her as anything more, she would just have to get used to it.

"Well, I'm sure you know just how much I can take—whether physically or emotionally—and still be able to come back from in one piece, so do it. I'll take it. I made a vow to dedicate myself to you and I will honour it, regardless of what I have to go through in order to do so," Tilly told him, and Blake knew she meant it. Her body was weak from their lovemaking, sore and tired, but she was strong in other ways and knew her mind, so spoke it confidently without being scared of him now, not in this moment.

It was the most truly honest anyone had ever been with him, and Blake couldn't find the words to respond, honestly taken aback by this beautiful girl and her incredibly strong nature.

CHAPTER NINETEEN

They rested together for a while longer, and then Blake climbed up out of the huge bed and pulled on his black jeans. Tilly had been dozing in his arms again and groaned as he moved away. He laughed and kissed her cheek, heading off through the penthouse in search of some coffee.

She forced herself to wake up too and, after a quick shower, joined him in the large kitchen. She'd found his shirt folded neatly in the bedroom and pulled it on, but wore nothing underneath, and plodded into the heavily coffee-scented kitchen with a smile while she pulled her still damp hair into a ponytail.

Tilly caught sight of Blake's perfectly toned back as he stood at the kitchen counter, his flawless body already making the butterflies return to her belly. She figured it was impossible to want him as much as she did, and so soon after their last round of epic sexual discovery, but her body was saying something vastly different to her mind.

"Oh really?" he asked her with a grin as she joined him and grabbed a mug. Tilly smiled and shrugged as he filled it for her, and she sipped it after inhaling the delicious scent dreamily. "And what a daring choice of outfit," he added, watching her from the corner of his eye.

"My clothes were all crumpled and dirty, balled up on the

floor of the bedroom. I didn't think you'd mind, your majesty?" she asked with a cheeky smile. "But, I think I might be in trouble wearing this shirt in particular," she added playfully, taking another sip of the dark drink.

"And why is that?" Blake asked, taking the bait. He turned to look her up and down as she stood before him, her bum only just about being covered by the dark cotton.

"Because, my master is a naughty boy, and I'm pretty sure this is dark grey, not black," she said, looking up to him as she spoke, hoping that she wasn't pushing her luck by teasing him.

"You're right, good girl. You'd better take it off this very instant," Blake commanded her, smiling down at Tilly, and she unbuttoned the shirt and then draped it over the back of the stool next to her. He took in her stunning, naked body as she stood before him, while he sipped on his hot, black drink. Without a word, he reached into the drawer beside him and pulled out a small knife. Tilly looked on in shock for a moment, unsure what he was planning to do with it, and watched as he poked his finger with the tip of the blade, drawing a small drop of blood to the surface, which he then offered to her.

"You'd best have this then, Tilly, because I need to fuck you again right now and you're gonna need the strength," he told her with a wicked grin, relishing in her brazenness and groaning with pleasure as she stepped forward without even a moments hesitation, and willingly sucked the blood from his fingertip.

Within seconds, she felt its effect on her, immediately soothing her soreness and delivering her with the energy and strength she needed to start again. After just a few seconds, Blake pinned Tilly to the kitchen side and he kissed her deeply, pulling her legs around his waist. He then ripped open his fly and forced himself inside her, while she clawed at his shoulders and groaned loudly, eager and ready to satisfy him again and again.

A couple hours' later, Tilly stood at the large living room window that overlooked the city. She was still naked following their second round of fantastic lovemaking and her core still trembling thanks to the wonderful memory her muscles simply could not let go of. Blake came up behind her and pressed his rippled torso into her back as he grabbed and embraced her in his strong arms, before pulling her chin up and back so that her lips could meet his. He was surprised, but felt as though he needed to taste her again more than he needed anything else in the world.

She then began to wonder about the blood she'd taken from him, thinking back to her conversation with Brent about how demon's used their blood to control humans. The lore was quite similar to the popular tales of vampirism—monsters feeding from humans, or else turning them using their blood and then ordering their sired progeny to do their bidding, but she didn't feel like he'd used it that way. In fact, other than her healed body, she couldn't figure out what'd actually passed between them in that little drop.

"Demon's do use their blood for control, you're right. A taste of either parties' blood gives one demon power over the other, unless their bond is strong, which you already know from your experiences with Lilith and Lucas," he said, replying to her thoughts. "It's my choice what I use mine for, Tilly. And, my blood is incredibly powerful, so just a drop at a time will do. I used it today in order to heal you, to rid your body of its tenderness and fatigue. That's all," he told her, and she smiled up at him, grateful for the explanation.

"Thank you," she replied, and kissed his cheek tenderly. "Are we in London?" Tilly then asked him, looking back out at the skyline.

"Yes," he answered, keeping his arms around her. "We keep this penthouse as a base for when we come to Earth. Luna and I often come during the full moons. Our mother rarely comes up anymore, but she's been known to throw a party or two here over the years. My other family are not bound by the moon so can come whenever they please. They live on Earth permanently at the moment, so don't need to use this apartment as a base," he told her, opening up a little bit about his family. Tilly looked back at him, and then turned herself around to face him and looked up into her master's eyes.

"Do you mind me asking, why is it that you cannot come here whenever you want?" she asked him hesitantly, but hoped he was happy to be more forthcoming with the details that still had her confused.

Blake looked at her thoughtfully for a moment, but wasn't angry. It wasn't the sort of information his family would readily give out to the masses, and it most certainly wouldn't have been in the books she'd used to help her learn about him and his unusual brood.

"My uncle and aunt are half human, and so are their children, my cousins Braeden, Leyla and Corey. This allows for them to travel freely between the two worlds and stay as long as they wish in either one. My mother was once half human too, but since she took the throne she has been transformed and is now one hundred per-cent pure darkness," he said, pausing to check that she was following. "Luna and I were born while she was still the same, but our father's full darkness made us only one-quarter human, so we are bound by the moon just as he was," he added, and his face fell. Blake hadn't spoken of his father in a very long time and it felt odd. Tilly reached up and touched his cheek gently before placing a light kiss on his lips.

"I'm sorry. Thank you for explaining it to me," she replied, quickly breaking his sad mood. She thought about the family he'd just told her about and the children that were born into their powerful line, and then panicked about whether she needed to worry about contraception with him. Blake laughed to himself, shaking his head as he read her thoughts.

"There's no need to worry. It's not as simple as you might believe. I'd have to ask you to bear my offspring, and you would have to say yes first—free will and all that. Plus, we'd most likely need my mother's permission first. Accidents don't just happen like with humans, it all takes a bit of, *planning*," he told Tilly, putting her instantly at ease.

He then smiled down at her and kissed her deeply before finally releasing his hold on her and heading back to the kitchen. Tilly followed him, and found Blake pulling on his black jeans again. He picked up the shirt from the stool where she'd put it earlier and handed it to her. "You'd better put this back on," he said with a wide, knowing smile.

"Why?" she asked, just as a knock at the door made her jump. The two demons she'd briefly met the night before, Bob and Levi, entered a moment later, only just as Tilly had finished buttoning up the dark shirt. She still felt exposed though, knowing she had nothing on underneath it, and that the hem of the shirt was so very high. In an attempt to cover her backside, she leaned back against the side of the kitchen counter, and smiled warmly at the two demons as they entered.

"Good evening, your majesty, you're looking buff tonight," Levi said with a cheeky smile as he took in the sight of his half naked Black Prince, but he still bowed to his master respectfully, and Bob did the same.

"Hey guys," Blake replied with a grin, flexing his biceps

jokingly to break the formality, and he then slid them both a mug filled with steaming black coffee. He handed one to Tilly too, and she smiled, thanking him quietly. It was strange for her to see him with his friends, joking around and having fun, and she liked it. "Did you have a good time after we left last night?" he then asked with a wink.

Both demons sniggered and Levi spoke first.

"Yeah, that Renee girl was certainly a fair bit of fun. She couldn't handle me all the way till the end though, so I had to finish in her arse. But you know I'm never against a harmless bit of anal," he said, laughing. Tilly gasped and blushed, which only made the others laugh even harder.

"Gwen was a real nice surprise, too," Bob told Blake. "Rode me for hours," he told him with a wink and Tilly buried her face in her mug, not wanting to hear any more intimate details about her friends. "Seriously though, I was pleasantly surprised with her. I'm thinking of marking her now that I'm due to stay here on Earth for a while. What do you think, boss?"

Blake looked at Tilly, reading her reaction for a second before answering him. She was shocked, but actually liked the idea of having a close friend who knew the truth, and with whom she could talk to about all this demonic business. She figured perhaps they could help each other get through the transition.

"Good idea, but mark Renee as well. It'd be good for Tilly having her friends in the upper circle of followers," he told him, a commanding order to his friend and servant, who nodded in agreement. "Speaking of. Tilly, don't you have something you need to ask these two?" he said, reminding her of the rules when it came to associating with demons.

"Yeah. I guess I'm supposed to ask you both for your names, right?" she asked, ashamed that she was still so new to all of this.

They both smiled patiently over at her, and Levi spoke first.

"Well, my name's Leviathan, but you can call me Levi if you'd prefer," he told her, reaching out to shake her hand, eyeing her bare legs when she stepped forward to take it. A dark scowl from Blake stopped them both in their tracks, and Tilly jumped back just as Levi stopped his flirtatious, wandering eyes and held up his hands, a silent apology passing between him and his Black Prince.

"Keep your hands to yourself, your eyes up on her face, and your thoughts out of the gutter, Leviathan," he warned him, and the demon bowed in apology. Tilly remained still while the air around them seemed to buzz, Blake's ominous power emanating from him for a few seconds, before he noticeably calmed himself down and took another sip of his coffee. He nodded to the other demon, who stepped forward with an anxious smile.

"I'm Beelzebub, or Bob if you prefer," he told her with a grin, and Tilly smiled back at him, glad that he'd broken the tense silence.

"So why do you go by the name Luke?" she asked Blake, forgetting her place for a moment, but being reminded instantly as he turned cold, almost black eyes on her and the two demons slunk back noticeably.

He stared across at her, his eyes growing darker. Tilly sent him silent pleas and apologies through her thoughts, and she tensed up, ready to take his punishment while mentally kicking herself for being so foolish.

CHAPTER TWENTY

"Luke's an alias my father always used to use. There's no real way to alter my name and I thought I'd use it last night so you had something to call me in front of your friends," Blake told Tilly coldly, but then suddenly switched back to his playful self as he locked away the feelings that threatened to bubble over, and forced away the darkness that'd crept into his eyes. She stood still as she watched him, desperate to take back her foolish words, but he thankfully moved the conversation on rather than dwell on her mistake. "I think we should have a party tonight, what do you think?" Blake then asked them all, and the two clearly relieved demons turned to their master with cunning grins.

"Absolutely," Leviathan answered excitedly.

Blake then nodded and grabbed Tilly before turning her and leading her away from the kitchen. Her body was still tense after seeing his small amount of fury at her foolishness, and he almost had to move her arms and legs for her as he led her away. He didn't bring attention to her fear; in fact he ignored it completely.

"Get the word out boys, upper level demons and their hand-picked followers only, oh and get those two girls down here as well," he called, another order to the two demons as he and Tilly made their way out into the living room. She looked up at him, trying to read her master but he was giving her nothing, so she pushed her fears aside and followed his lead.

She then heard the main doors to the penthouse open behind them just a few seconds later and turned to see a group of women enter through them. She assumed Blake must've sent out a silent order for them to come to him, and was awed by his power once again.

He left Tilly's side for a moment and went over to welcome them, talking first to a tall and beautiful, dark-red haired woman while the others began fussing about with the décor and moving the furniture around in the main living room.

The young woman gazed up at him with lust and carnal desire in her eyes, but Tilly could tell that Blake wasn't even bothered by it, perhaps far too used to being looked at that way by his devoted minions. He gave her his orders and then led her over to meet the still scantily clad human.

"Tilly, this is Lena. She's the high priestess of my coven," he told her, and waved his hand around to indicate the other women that had arrived with her. Lena smiled at Tilly and bowed her head to her master respectfully.

"Hi," was all Tilly could think to say to her, unsure of how to address the witch just yet, but he could sense the woman's incredible dark prowess, and suspected that she must be very powerful if she was his high priestess.

"Lena will help get you ready. There's a selection of clothes and shoes for you in the main bedroom, as well as products and makeup for you to use. I want you ready in half an hour," he ordered, and the two women bowed—Tilly carefully—and left him, rushing off to go and get her ready in time. Lena barely said a word as she led Tilly away, but then tersely told her what to do once they reached the bedroom.

"Get in there and take a shower, shave every inch of your legs, armpits, and pussy, and then apply a generous layer of moisturiser to every bit of your skin as quickly as possible," she barked, making Tilly feel uncomfortable, but she quickly did as she was told.

***

In his office, Blake chatted quietly with his old friend, and loyal demon, Leviathan. They discussed his current orders, and Levi's plans for the future. The powerful demon hoped, as always, for a coveted place on Blake's dark council, but the Black Prince refused him yet again.

"You're not right for it, too mischievous. I need dark and brooding," he told him.

"Fair one, I never was any good at that. I prefer the lure, the seduction, and then the attack," Leviathan admitted, grinning broadly at his master.

"Don't get me wrong, I like that too," Blake admitted.

"Like with that girl?" his friend asked, one eyebrow raised.

"I suppose. She's a good girl, Levi. So sweet and pure, and you know what that means?"

"Oh yes," the demon replied, a satisfied smile curling at his lips. "Good girls turned bad are always the most tantalising of trophies."

"Exactly, and I have this girl exactly where I want her," Blake said, an evil glint in his eye as he smiled at his friend before heading back out to the lounge.

***

When Tilly emerged from the bathroom, having done as Lena

had asked, she wore just a black robe with a towel that she'd wrapped around her head, and the witch was at the ready with a hairdryer and brush.

"He prefers curls, and likes hair to be left down, not up in a ponytail," she informed Tilly matter-of-factly once her hair was dry and she then began twisting hot irons around her long, dark-blonde locks.

"No," a voice boomed from the doorway and Blake joined them, making Lena jump. "Put it up, in a side-bun, and she's to wear this," he said, taking a black corseted dress from the wardrobe that flowed beautifully down to the floor from under the boned top. He smiled at Tilly in the mirrored reflection, and she blushed and smiled back at him, knowing he was thinking of her dream, and that he wanted her dressed in exactly the same way she'd been then.

Lena nodded and immediately began working Tilly's hair up into a neat bun instead, letting just a couple of curls fall down by her face before applying some dark makeup. Blake stripped and Tilly couldn't help but look at his gorgeous form as it too was reflected in the mirror, but she also noticed Lena's eyes dart up to look at his reflection as he wandered naked into the walk-in wardrobe. The witch then caught Tilly looking at her, and quickly composed herself again, working on the finishing touches silently.

Blake emerged from the wardrobe a few minutes later, fully dressed in a perfectly tailored black suit, with matching waistcoat and with a crisp black shirt and tie. It was the perfect match to the outfit he'd worn the night she'd dreamt of him. She blushed again, the two of them sharing their little secret while the witch finished off the last of Tilly's makeup.

"Good, you may leave us now, Lena," Blake ordered, barely even looking at her.

"Yes, master," she said quietly, leaving the two of them alone in the bedroom. Tilly stood and took in the sight of him before her. Seeing Blake in that suit sent all kinds of wonderful messages around her body, and she bloomed with heat simply remembering how he'd touched her that first time. He smiled and grabbed the belt of her robe, pulling her towards him for a deep and passionate kiss, and he untied the knot and pulled the robe off, leaving Tilly standing naked before him again.

"Déjà vu," he said with a sly grin, and Tilly heard a faint *click* from behind him that told her that the bedroom door had just been magically locked shut. "Lay on the bed," he ordered her, and she followed his command immediately, eager to please her master in the hope of the reward she prayed might come next. Blake kept his gaze on her as he lowered himself down, kissing her breasts and stomach before slowly making his way lower. Tilly gasped and gripped the covers tightly when his mouth took hold of her ready nub and began caressing it, delicately at first, then harder and stronger. His hands wrenched her thighs apart further, opening her cleft to him as he began stroking his strong tongue up and down her tender lips. Two fingers slid easily inside and he pushed down on her g-spot, making Tilly gush and come for him almost instantly. She groaned loudly, gripping the covers beneath her tighter as she rode the wonderful waves of ecstasy that her wondrous master had given her.

Blake then pulled her legs closed and stood, watching as she came down from her high with a satisfied grin. He then grabbed some red panties and a matching strapless bra from one of the drawers and passed them to her. "Put these on," he commanded with a wink. "No one will know but me," he then added before he ducked into the bathroom to freshen up. Tilly slid on the underwear with trembling hands, her body still reeling from her climax.

He returned to the bedroom a couple of minutes later and helped her into the beautiful dress. Blake then stepped back to take her in. She was still flushed from her orgasm and looked amazing, just like in the dream with her smoky eyed makeup and side-bun. He came around behind her in front of the huge mirror and gripped her the same way that he had in the dream, trailing kisses along her collar while she stared into his eyes through the reflected image.

"Wow, don't you two just make the most gorgeous couple?" asked a woman's voice from behind them, and Tilly jumped before turning to look at who'd broken the silence.

A young woman stood before her, with long, dark curls that fell by her beautiful face and she had deep green eyes that bore into Tilly's skull. Suddenly terrified, she then dropped to her knees, realising at once that the new arrival had to be his twin sister, Luna.

CHAPTER TWENTY-ONE

"What're you doing here?" Blake asked, stepping forward to embrace his twin and kiss her cheek in greeting.

"I just thought I'd pop up and see what this party's all about, but don't worry, I won't stay long," she joked, eyeing him thoughtfully. She then looked down and took in the sight of the young woman that was still kneeling before her. "You can stand up, Tilly. I don't want to get you in trouble for ruining that beautiful dress of yours," she added, reaching down to help her up. Tilly took her hand gratefully and bowed to her once she'd climbed to her feet, not sure how to act or what to say to the powerful, beautiful woman.

"Thank you, your majesty," she then said, feeling uneasy under the Black Princess' intense scrutiny.

"You may wait for me in the hall, Tilly," Blake then commanded, and she left the siblings to talk, bowing to them before she ducked out into the hallway and closed the door behind her, grateful for a moment to herself.

"She seems nice," Luna said to her brother once they were alone, and Blake raised an eyebrow at her.

"What are you *really* doing here, Luna?" he asked impatiently.

"I felt a change in the air—in you—so I thought I'd pop up

and see what was going on. You two seem really happy, closer than I've known you get before. However, I sense some hesitation from you, and you know I cannot keep my nose out," she told him, and he tensed, prickling angrily in an instant.

"You'd be wise to keep your curiosity to yourself, Luna. I'm sick of you trying to interfere in my life. We're having fun, that's all. Don't try to push me," he said, his features mashing into an angry stare.

"I'm only here because I love you, hard as it might be for you to hear, Blake, but I do love you—we all do. And yet, I know that you're thinking of him, remembering him fondly and using his alias. Why? Why would you choose to think of him over our mother?" she asked, getting angry herself now. "Did you know that he was a tyrant, and that he forced his will on everyone and tortured those he was supposed to love and protect?"

"You know as well as I, just how well I know all of those things, Luna. Who told you to say that to me? Mother?" he snapped.

"You know she'd never speak of such things. I've listened in on other's thoughts, Blake. Alma, Dylan, and even Devin opened up to me. She knows I've quizzed them, and hasn't tried to stop me. She wants me to know the truth and for you to learn it, too." Luna knew this was getting too heated, but she couldn't stop herself. Her brother had to hear it, even if he didn't want to. "Stop trying to pretend you don't care what happened to her, what happened to them both after she was taken that night in the park. And stop blaming yourself for his dethroning. He deserved it, Blake, and you will never be King if you continue to be like him: cold, manipulative, black-hearted, and cruel," she bellowed, her eyes turning dark as she too grew more and more angry.

Blake looked down at her, his eyes becoming completely

black now too as he absorbed his sister's harsh words. The floor beneath them both started to shake, an earthquake seemingly beginning from Blake while he stood stone-like and scarily cold before her.

"Who the fuck do you think you are, Luna?" he shouted in her face, the anger pouring out of him uncontrollably. "Get out of here right now before I do something I might regret!" he bellowed, and Luna teleported away, not wanting to have this out with him on Earth. Her beautiful face was forlorn and she wanted to kick herself. This certainly wasn't how she'd expected their conversation to go.

Out in the hall, Tilly grabbed the doorframe while the shaking building jostled her around uncontrollably in her high-heeled shoes. Lena came running down the hallway towards her, going to the door with the aim of going inside and finding out what was going on, but Tilly blocked her path.

"Stop," she shouted to her. "He's in there with his sister, you mustn't disturb them."

"Well that explains it then, get out of my way," Lena shouted, shoving Tilly aside as she burst into the bedroom.

"Master, there's an earthquake. Send your sister away..." Lena began, but was cut short as Blake turned to look at her, his eyes still black and his anger further fuelled by the unwelcome presence of his witch. Invisible hands gripped her throat and pulled Lena off her feet. He stared at her coldly as she writhed in panic and fear, and then with a flick of his head she was tossed across the room, where she slammed into the wall and fell to the floor, limp and seemingly dead. Blake stared at her for a moment and then looked up and out the open doorway where Tilly stood staring back at him from the hallway. She was rooted to the spot in fear, her mouth open, and he stormed towards her, covering the ground in three easy, long strides. Her breathing was fast and shallow, terror pouring out of her after seeing his dark features and what he had just done to his high priestess, but there was nowhere for her to run. Tilly couldn't help but let out a small scream as Blake reached her and grabbed her by the throat, lifting her off her feet and then pinning her against the wall behind. He then pressed himself into her with such force that her back ached and she winced as he pushed her harder into the cold brick.

Tears flowed uncontrollably down Tilly's cheeks as he pinned her there, but for some reason, he didn't say a word to her, nor did he squeeze her throat any tighter. Blake just held her there, his forehead against hers and his eyes closed. He too breathed fast and hard against her skin, and Tilly could somehow sense that he was trying to calm himself down. She slowed her own breaths, holding back her tears with all her might, and she reached up and touched his face, gently cupping his cheeks with her palms.

"Please…please," she begged, imploring him to calm down, to regain his usual composure again. Blake opened his eyes slowly, the green returning to them a little at a time, and he eventually loosened his grip on her neck. He then took his hand down and placed it over her heart, distinguishing as the beat slowed beneath his touch when she took control of her panic. It calmed him, as did just having her close, and breathing in her scent somehow helped to lull his rage. He kissed her, deep and passionately, eager to release some of his emotion. When he finally broke away and placed her back on the floor, instead of shrinking back in fear, she slipped her arms under his. Tilly wrapped them around his ribs to his back, pulling Blake into a tight hug and resting her head against his chest. "Please," she begged again, feeling him slowly coming back to her. Blake wrapped his arms around Tilly and held her close for several minutes before breaking the embrace. He then looked down at her and smiled at last.

"Thank you," he whispered to her, kissing her on the lips softly and wiping the tears from her cheeks with his thumbs. Her heart was no longer pounding in her ears and she suddenly realised that the earthquake had long since stopped, and that there was now music playing from the main lounge of the penthouse.

"Let me just sort myself out and then we can go in, okay?" she asked Blake, smiling up at him before heading into the bedroom once again. She couldn't help but look down at the floor where Lena had dropped, but she was gone.

"I sent her back to Hell, where I'll deal with her later. She isn't dead, don't worry," he told her, having read her thoughts, and the news was a welcome relief to Tilly. "I know you tried to stop her, well done," he added, watching as she re-applied her makeup and checked herself in the mirror. Her eyes were a little red, as was her neck, but other than that she looked fine, so shook it off, took a deep breath, and then headed back over to her master.

She checked his suit, smoothing the front where she'd leaned into him and accidentally left a tearstain. A click of his fingers and the suit was perfect again, as was her dishevelled dress, giving nothing away of the anger and pain that'd just been pouring out of him minutes before and its destructive power over him and everything in his vicinity.

Part of her wondered if he was prone to such outpourings of rage, but she didn't dare ask, nor did she want to know what his sister had said or done to incur such a devastating outburst. She just hoped it was all over with, for now at least. "Let's forget about all of this and go have fun, okay?" Blake asked, taking Tilly's hand in his. She nodded, and followed as he led her towards the doors that took them back into the living room.

CHAPTER TWENTY-TWO

"Ground rules first," Blake said as he stopped in front of the huge doors for a moment before he and Tilly went inside. "You're to stay by my side, unless I release you. You do not speak unless spoken to—just smile and nod, okay?" he asked, and Tilly smiled and nodded, eager to bring the playful Blake back, and he couldn't help but smile down at her. She knew he was testing her, but was more than willing to play along if it kept her in Blake's favour. "Good. And, I'm gonna need a lot of alcohol tonight thanks to my dear sister's visit. You're in charge of making sure that I have a glass of whisky in my hand at all times, Tilly. Fill it just two fingers deep, with one ice cube. When I start to get low again, tell me with your thoughts that you need to get me another glass and I will let you go to the bar, got it?" he asked, gazing down at her with a cheeky grin and she nodded, reaching up on her tiptoes to plant a kiss on his cheek.

"Anything you need, master," she whispered. She meant it. Being his arm candy was worth it if she got to have his company a while longer, and it surprised her that she was so ready to become his doting servant. She then took his arm and let Blake lead her into the now busy living room of the huge penthouse.

All eyes turned their way as he and Tilly made their entrance. Smiles and gasps greeted the gorgeous couple, along with the numerous demons and other dark beings that moved towards them, eager for a moment with their Black Prince.

She slipped away once inside, instantly grabbing Blake a drink, and then returning to his side as quickly as she could. He talked animatedly to many of the guests, introducing some of them to Tilly. She smiled and shook their hands or nodded along to their stories and anecdotes just as her master had ordered, but still felt out of sorts in their company. It was a relief when she had the chance to disappear again to grab her master another drink, and she soon realised that she wasn't missed when she did. The dark beings only really wanted Blake's attention. When they eventually had a quiet minute to themselves, he leaned in to whisper in her ear.

"Once everyone feels they've had their moment with me, they'll all chill out and we can have some proper fun. You just wait," he told her with a grin and she couldn't help but smile back. After all the pomp and ceremony, it was nice imagining the upcoming frivolity.

"Your highness," said a familiar voice from over Tilly's shoulder, bursting their bubble. It was Lilith, and she had Lucas and their children with her. She looked Tilly up and down, somewhat taken aback seeing the two of them whispering and smiling at each other so intimately, but regained her composure again almost immediately. "You remember my husband?" she said, bowing as she ushered towards him with her hand.

"Yes, of course. Hello again, Lucas," Blake said, shaking his hand and then looking over to the three boys beside the pair of them, who also bowed to him. Brent didn't dare look at Tilly, who continued following her orders to stay quiet, and she simply smiled across at Lilith while she spoke with Blake. Before long, it was Lucas who broke the strange silence; pulling Tilly out of her submissive, quiet state.

"How are you?" he asked, much to Lilith's obvious distaste, but neither she nor Blake stopped them from talking freely. Lucas smiled across at her, the same warm smile that'd always made her feel safe and loved in his company, and she couldn't help the affectionate pang that shot through her heart for him.

"Wonderful, thank you for asking. Things couldn't be better," Tilly replied, but then saw Blake gulp down the last bit of his whisky and eye her cautiously. It would've been nicer to have had longer to chat, but she guessed this was Blake's way of telling her he wasn't keen on her getting too close to Lucas or his boys, and she could understand his reasons why. "Would you please excuse me for just a moment?" she asked, ducking away and almost running to the bar to grab another whisky for her master. She returned just in time to see Blake deposit the empty glass onto a passing waiter's tray, and handed him the new one with a smile, while he winked down at her in thanks.

Lilith was going on about some new plans for the circus, having pulled Lucas into their conversation now, but their sons all stood in silence staring anxiously at their feet. She chanced a glance at them and could immediately sense something different about Jackson. Tilly realised that he must now be fully initiated into Lilith's following. He had to be; otherwise he wouldn't be here with them tonight. She was happy for him and smiled over at Lucas again when he caught her watching his youngest son.

Later, once everyone had bent Blake's ear and Tilly had bought him his twentieth glass of whisky, the mood began to lighten and the strong alcoholic drinks started to work their magic on the partygoers. Blake handed Tilly a glass of champagne at last—her first drink of the evening—allowing her a moment to relax while the crowd bustled around them.

"You can have something stronger later, but this will do for now. Can't have you getting drunk now," he told her and she nodded, taking the glass from him with a smile.

"Anything you say, thank you," she replied with a bow, making him beam again. She loved it when he did that, and relished in his warmth towards her, finding her cheeks flushing red when her thoughts gave her away. Blake listened in, and then pulled her to a dark corner where he planted a soft kiss on her lips, his hands cupping her still burning cheeks. Tilly's heart fluttered wildly in her chest, the anticipation of what might be in store for her after the party driving her on. She could taste the whisky on him though, so looked up at her master questioningly, hoping he wouldn't be the one getting too drunk.

"Don't worry, it takes a lot more than this much to get me drunk," he informed her with a cheeky grin, his green eyes alight and his handsome features playful.

"It's true. I once saw him go through an entire crate of that posh whisky before he even started slurring," came a voice from behind them. It was Beelzebub, and he had Gwen on his arm, dressed all in black with an elegant gold chain around her neck. This new look really suited her, and while Tilly felt guilty for having brought her into this world, she was glad to have her here. She could also sense Beelzebub's mark on her and smiled at her friend. "Gwen, this is Blake, the Black Prince, and Tilly's master. Remember what I told you?" he asked, and she nodded and quickly fell to her knees before him. Tilly could see that Blake was reading her, and she saw the telltale inverted red cross come to the surface of the skin inside Gwen's right wrist when he called to the power that now commanded her soul.

"Hello again, Gwen," Blake said, ushering for her to stand. "It seems you've picked up the formalities much quicker than Tilly did, but I'll let her tell you that story later," he told her with a laugh, putting Gwen at ease a little, although she was trembling before him, having obviously been informed by Beelzebub of his status. Renee soon joined them too, following the demon's orders and bowing before Blake immediately as well, who smiled and read her quickly, before he ushered for her to stand beside her master. "Tilly, you may go and speak with your friends for a few minutes while I make some arrangements with Beelzebub here. I'll get my own drinks from here onwards," he told her, releasing her from both his order and his side, for now. She smiled and thanked him, and then made her way over to the bar area with her friends, where she ordered a whisky on the rocks, for herself this time.

"Well, are you gonna tell me what the fuck happened to you, Tilly?" demanded Renee, her hands on her hips. Despite her annoyance, she looked great in her black dress. Her blonde hair was pinned up in a messy knot and she gave off her usual, effortless sex appeal even in these strange new surroundings. Tilly knew she'd be fine once she got the hang of things though, so didn't fret over her pout or the hard stare Renee was fixing her with.

"I'm sure you know everything by now. I'm marked by the Black Prince, and you two belong to Beelzebub. That's it, we just need to live our lives and figure out where to go from here," she answered impatiently, not sure what kind of explanation Renee had wanted from her.

"I think what she means is, how did you even get here, Tilly?" Gwen asked, reaching over and taking her hand for a moment before giving it a gentle squeeze. She always was the calm, sensitive one of the group, and Tilly was glad to see the understanding and affection in her deep brown eyes as Gwen stared at her.

"I know, it's just I'm still getting used to it all myself and I don't need you telling me off, Renee," Tilly grumbled before telling them her story. "Okay, you all know Brent," she said, and both girls smirked and nodded. "Well, his stepmother we met, Lily. She's a demon, and her real name is Lilith. She marked me that first night we stayed at the circus, but then wiped my memory so I didn't even know she'd done it. When I went up to Scotland on Halloween after she asked me, it was for a Satanic ritual, not their anniversary party. She invited me to surprise Brent, to let him know that I'd been marked. I think she'd intended to initiate me into her following, but things went very differently than she had planned," Tilly told them quietly but quickly, and felt eyes on her. She looked over her shoulder to see Blake watching her from the other side of the room.

Tilly smiled at him, and knew he was reading her, so she was eager to get to her point quickly in order to satisfy the other girls' need for information, and to let him know she wasn't dwelling on that part of the story. The three young women went and sat down at the huge dining table and Tilly continued her tale, her friends silent and eager to hear the rest. "Lilith made a kind of speech about him, about the Black Prince, and she said his name. I didn't know I wasn't allowed to, so I just said it. I didn't even think about it until he was stood before me with a face like thunder. The rest of the crowd then bowed before him as well, while I just stood there like an idiot because I had no bloody idea," she said, laughing at her foolishness now, while her friends gasped in horror, having been warned against saying the royal names by their new master, and told about the consequences for accidentally doing it. "He was lenient on me though, and in that moment of stupidity saw something about me that intrigued him or something, because next thing I knew, I belonged to him instead of Lilith," she said with a smile, finishing off her drink and placing the empty glass on the table before her.

"And him alone," said a voice from behind her, and she knew without looking that it was Blake. Tilly hadn't even realised that he'd made his way back over to her, but she was happy to hear his voice and feel him near her again. He placed a fresh glass of whisky before her on the table and plopped in an ice cube, licking the stray drop of water from his fingertip as he peered down into her eyes. "I thought you might like a new one. I don't want you going empty after all," he said, and she thanked him before he headed back off towards his friends. She laughed to herself, thinking that they were developing quite a few inside jokes now, and she liked it.

"Whoa," Gwen said, looking at Tilly as she sipped the fresh drink. "You two are intense together. So, last night at the club, that was that the first time you'd seen him since Halloween?"

"Yeah, I didn't even know he was in there until I saw him at the bar. Then he brought me here," she told them, indicating the penthouse and blushing as she thought of their first night together.

Brent, David, and Jackson then appeared and plonked down a tray of shots on the table, joining Tilly and the other girls.

"Hey ladies, who's up for some fun?" David asked, and Renee grabbed one of the shots and tossed it back without even checking what was in it.

"Oh yes!" she replied, grinning from ear to ear.

"Hell yeah!" David cried, smiling at her and grabbing a tequila shot, which he then knocked back in one gulp. They all helped themselves, Gwen taking a milder shot of liqueur while Jackson opted for the rum, leaving Tilly and Brent to fight over the last couple of drinks, a shot of either vodka or whisky.

"I'll take the vodka," he said, pushing her the other one, even though she knew it was his first choice of drink, too.

"Cheers," she said, supping it back in one go.

"So, are you two still friends then?" asked Renee, breaking the awkward silence that'd descended around the table.

"Of course," replied Tilly, and then mentally added, *'and only ever that,'* just for her master to listen in on.

CHAPTER TWENTY-THREE

"You girls do realise you can't celebrate Christmas from now on, don't you?" Brent asked them later that night, following their third round of shots. He grinned down at the pouting Renee as she swooned drunkenly beside him, but frowned. She was all over him and had been teasing and flirting wildly with him all night. Tilly still couldn't decide if she thought her friend was trying to make her jealous or if she was just after a thrill of her own now that he was a free man, but either way, she decided that she was just going to leave her to it. He wasn't on her mind that way anymore and never would be.

"Oh no!" Gwen cried, looking sad. "That's always been my favourite time of year."

"Sorry. We have a gathering every year instead, run by our stepmother. Speak to your masters, you never know they might have something similar planned for you, too," offered Jackson with a bemused smile. They hadn't celebrated the holiday since he was tiny and he didn't care for the garish, colourful and strange tradition of it at all now. In all honesty, he couldn't see what Gwen was so upset about.

"Either way I'll have to get away. My parents will make me celebrate it if I'm there. It's always been a big deal in our house," murmured Tilly, mentally trying to figure out when the next full moon was. She hoped it fell over the festive period so she would at least have Blake's visit to look forward to.

"Look Tilly. Just say, hey Mum, hey Dad, I worship the Devil now so I do not want any of your stupid presents, okay?" Renee blurted out, her slurs making them all laugh thanks to her clearly drunken state. "What, it's the truth isn't it? Oh, and do you think Beelzebub will let me wear normal clothes again? I can't believe I have to wear black all the time, when have you ever known me to wear black?" she rambled on, only adding fuel to their laughter as she went.

"No, Renee," Beelzebub's voice said authoritatively from the crowd, and he appeared behind her and Gwen a second later. "You absolutely cannot wear colourful clothes again. Any colour is a sign of disrespect to our Dark Queen, so watch your mouth or else I will punish you," he told her sternly, silencing her—and their laughter—immediately. Tilly thought about the red underwear she was wearing beneath her dress, and a lump rose in her throat at the thought that she could be deemed as disrespecting the Dark Queen by wearing even that tiny splash of colour beneath her black gown. "Time to go," Beelzebub then told them, taking Gwen's hand to help her up and then grabbing Renee's arm to steady her. He rolled his eyes at the state she had gotten herself in to, and Tilly could tell she'd have to be careful to keep from being disciplined. She made a mental note to have a serious word with her friend soon.

Tilly began thinking it might be best if she went to find her master now that the other girls had gone. She hadn't seen Blake in a while, and was starting to wonder where he had gotten to, but also felt like he might not appreciate finding her sat drinking alone with the three men, regardless of their friendship.

"Tilly?" called a voice from behind her as she finished her drink. She'd been careful not to drink too much, but the strong whisky was still working its magic on her and it took her a moment to find where the voice had come from. A smiling face then appeared from the crowd behind her.

"Sapphire?" she asked, and the girl she'd met at college just a couple of weeks before nodded and hugged her tightly once she'd made her way over to them.

"Yeah, how are you? I didn't know you'd be here tonight!" she squealed excitedly. "Where's your master, and are you ever gonna tell me his name?" Sapphire asked, joking with Tilly as she joined her and the boys at the table and introduced herself. The three brothers welcomed her and laughed, realising that this girl really had no idea who Tilly's master was, but they sat back, letting her be the one to try and tell her without actually being able to.

"I'm great, thanks Sapphire," she replied. "My master's here somewhere, but I still can't tell you his name, I'm sorry," she added, with an awkward expression that just made the boys laugh harder.

"Why?" Sapphire asked her, looking upset now thanks to the laughter that was obviously directed at her.

"Because she would be in serious trouble for doing so," boomed Blake's voice when he appeared, as if out of nowhere from the crowd. Sapphire then practically fell off her seat in order to kneel before him when she realised who it was that'd spoken to her. He sat down next to Tilly, smiling and taking her hand in his as he peered down at the crumpled heap that was Sapphire, and then nodded to the three brothers in greeting, his calm and casual demeanour taking them all by surprise. "You can get up," he told the still kneeling girl after a few seconds, and she climbed back up to her seat in a flustered mess.

"Thank you, your highness," she mumbled, and tossed back a

shot—clearly not caring what was in it.

"So, what were you talking about?" he asked them, knowing of course that the answer was him. Tilly smirked and gave him a wink, but squeezed his hand and couldn't help but feel her heart beating faster in her chest thanks to his touch.

"Come with me?" Blake asked Tilly a few minutes later, leaning in to whisper seductively into her ear. "I want to do a lap of the crowd again with you on my arm," he told her as he stood and took her hand in his.

"Of course," she replied, and Sapphire swooned as she watched the two of them. Tilly bid the group farewell and followed Blake's lead, his hand never letting go of hers. The gorgeous pair made their way towards the centre of the crowd, where most of the people there were drinking, talking, or dancing to the thrum of the rock music that played from speakers somewhere that Tilly couldn't see. When they reached the centre of the throng, the track changed and the familiar rifts from the night before filled her ears. It was the same song Blake had played for her in the bedroom, and she smiled to herself, instantly thinking of their wonderful first night together.

He then turned and pulled her into his arms. They danced slowly together for a moment before the entire crowd around them then came to a halt. Tilly knew Blake had magically frozen them, just like he'd done to the crowd at Lucas' trial on Halloween. She peered up into his eyes and smiled, kissing her master deeply as he held her close and they moved gracefully together while the rest of the song played just for them. Their closeness and ease surprised her, and Tilly tried not to let herself fall head over heels for her self-proclaimed unlovable rogue. It was no use, and she swooned uncontrollably thanks to his effortless command over her.

"What am I going to do with you?" he asked as the song finished and he let Tilly go, while the partygoers began to unfreeze around them.

"I have a few ideas," she whispered to him with a sly grin.

CHAPTER TWENTY-FOUR

Without another word, Blake pulled Tilly off to a dark corner and pinned her against the wall like he'd done earlier in the hall, but this time much more gently and without his hands around her neck. They kissed feverishly, Blake delving inside her mouth with an urgency she hadn't felt from him before.

"All I can think about are those little red panties, and how I want to rip them off you," he whispered in her ear once he pulled away, planting kisses on her neck and collarbones as he pressed her even harder into the wall. She felt dizzy and giddy in his passionate embrace, and then happily followed him through the doors and back to the master bedroom just moments later, without him even saying goodbye to any of his guests.

Blake locked the door behind them and quickly unzipped her dress, which tumbled to the floor and revealed Tilly's half naked body, and her somehow now black lacy underwear. She looked up at him, puzzled, but he just smiled and laughed to himself. "My mother works in mysterious ways," he told her with a deep sigh, and Tilly couldn't help but panic again that she might be in trouble for having dared to wear the red underwear he'd given her earlier. "Don't worry, she won't punish you. It was my idea remember?" he added, putting Tilly at ease instantly.

"Oh yeah, you're the naughty one. I remember now. A real

life bad-boy," she told him, a cheeky grin curling at her red lips, and his eyes sparkled in the dim light as he took her in, completely mesmerised by her yet again.

Blake grinned and took off his suit, one beautiful piece of clothing at a time while Tilly stood before him awaiting her next order, watching him strip for her. When he was finally naked, she dropped to her knees before her master without needing to be told and took the tip of his rock-hard cock in her mouth. Blake gasped, relishing in her unexpected yet breath-taking move. She sucked for a few minutes, taking his long shaft as far back as she could before he then commanded her to lie on the bed. Tilly quickly did as she was told, and unclipped her bra as she climbed up onto the huge bed, removing it and then throwing it down onto the floor before lying back and relishing in Blake's gaze as his eyes swept over every inch of her almost naked body.

He then climbed up on top of her and gripped the lace panties in his hand while he planted kisses on her stomach, suddenly pulling the material taught. He ripped them off her hips without even trying, and then pulled her up to meet his ready cock, slipping inside her wet opening with ease. Tilly cried out as he pushed hard and fast inside of her, gripping his shoulders tightly and staring up into Blake's stunning green eyes while he moved so expertly. It wasn't long before her first orgasm claimed her body, weakening her for a moment, but also delivering her the wonderful response to his fantastic thrusts that she craved so much. He pulled her up onto his lap and lifted her with his strong arms up and down onto him as she cried out, feeling the next climax building already from her inner nerve-endings. She came again and again for him as he unrelentingly carried on, delighting in her pleasure as well as needing to find his own release.

Tilly weakened again before him after a while, begging him to slow down, and mumbling that she couldn't bear to have another orgasm. She felt so weak and feeble compared to his almighty strength, and almost didn't feel as though she could carry on. She hated it, and vowed to be stronger for him next time. He kissed her, listening to her exhausted thoughts and slowed, but didn't stop, knowing she could still handle more. Blake held her tight in his arms and kept her there, slowly dipping his thick length in and out of her wet, hot opening before a final, intense orgasm claimed her as he too reached his glorious, earth-shattering end.

Tilly couldn't help but fall into a deep, shattered sleep following their epic lovemaking session, her body and mind both wonderfully exhausted from having spent the past two days mostly in his bed.

Blake held her as she slept, watching her, and listening in on her thoughts and dreams. The usually so closed-off Black Prince even allowed Tilly to snuggle into him while she rested.

He knew it wouldn't be long until the moon waned, but for some reason this time he wasn't happy about leaving. There seemed nothing back home to go to other than an inevitable row with Luna and a potential telling off from his mother about the red underwear. Although he still tried to fight accepting Tilly's feelings for him, he knew that the reason for his regret at leaving was the one thing he had kept telling himself meant nothing to him—his enigmatic new lover.

CHAPTER TWENTY-FIVE

They said their goodbyes the next morning and Blake teleported back to Hell, leaving Tilly at the penthouse to rest. Beelzebub had agreed to stay with Renee and Gwen for a while with her, and promised he would teleport them all back home later that afternoon.

Blake went to his chambers and lay on his bed, immediately sensing Luna calling to him through their strong psychic link. He gave her his silent acceptance to join him and she immediately appeared in his chambers, sitting on the bed next to her twin with a sorrowful look on her face.

"I'm so sorry," she said, peering down at him with tears in her eyes while her brother remained cold, his face void of any emotion—as always. "I don't know what came over me. Saying those things, going about it that way. But, please believe me, and read my thoughts. You'll see for yourself that what I said was true," she implored him earnestly. "I know you miss him, I do at times, too. But these memories I've been shown...I can't deny that he was a monster. It helps me accept his fate, and trust in mother's decision to banish him."

Blake looked up at her, sensing just how true her words were, and he decided to do as she asked. He softened at last, taking Luna's hand in his and then opening himself up to her memories as she lay down next to him. She snuggled into her brother's embrace on the dark sheets, glad that he'd forgiven her foolishness.

She focussed her mind and showed him the memory Alma had shared with her. It was of their mother as a younger woman, so frail, innocent, and completely broken. The memory was in the days following the torture Cate had suffered in the fiery pit, whipping chamber, and torture cage at the behest of her would-be-lover. Alma had told Luna how the demons and witches involved were tasked with breaking her will, and by any means necessary, or else suffer themselves. This one vision showed the twins just what Lucifer had put Cate through to make her compliant to his dark desires at last, despite her clear resistance. She barely even looked like the same person they now knew so well, and they watched via Alma's memory as she lay in the black goo bath with a blank stare, while the witches fussed around her, staving off the death that Lucifer had almost let claim his lover rather than admit defeat in this matter of the heart.

They continued to watch as the image then changed slightly before them. Blake gasped as Alma had then shown Luna the sight of Cate, healed now but stripped naked and shaking with fear at the prospect of being in Lucifer's bedchambers that first time. He remained calm, but was grateful when Luna changed the vision again, his anger towards his father burning brighter in the depths of his soul.

Dylan's memory was next, showing them the torture she'd suffered at his command for trying to contact her friend while she was still a white witch. Her awful ordeal disgusted and dismayed Blake. He'd only ever known Dylan as a dark witch and closest ally to Cate. Even when Lucifer was still with them, she'd served him without any question of her loyalty, and the twins knew they'd never realised just what awful past their father shared with her.

Devin's memory then followed Dylan's, which was a rarely shared vision of himself and Cate together, back when they were young. They were living in the same penthouse Blake had just been in with his own lover, but then she was taken away from him with barely a word of explanation. Next, he'd shown Luna the moment he first saw Cate again. It was many years later, and she was a cold shell of herself, broken and manipulated by their master, but there had been nothing he could do about it.

Berith's memory was the final image, showing them the scene in the council chamber the day that Cate had finally taken the throne from Lucifer. Blake shuddered when he saw his father command that the ever-loyal demon was to kill Lottie and Harry. He then watched in both horror and awe as Cate snapped, and saw the transition as she summoned her full power at last. His father had cowered before her, yet still mocked his wife's new found omnipotence right until the end.

It was more than Blake could handle, and he finally pulled away from Luna, coming back from her thoughts as quickly as he could. Despite his cold nature, the visions couldn't help but bring him pain, the truth of his family's history finally unravelling in his mind. Blake's green eyes speckled with black spots thanks to the anger that spiked from within, as was usual for all the dark royal family during times in which their ancient power rose from within. They all experienced the uncontrollable show of darkness at times, whether through pain, anger, or even the overwhelming surge thanks to using their dark powers when marking a soul as theirs or performing primeval rituals.

"Okay, I get it," he told her, his voice a harsh, pained whisper. "But it doesn't change me, what I did, and who I've become because of it, Luna. You need to accept that I won't ever change, and move on," Blake said, rising and teleporting away from his chambers without another word to his sister. He had business with Lena to take care of, and teleported into the prison where he'd delivered her broken body to the night before within a few seconds.

She immediately pleaded with her master for forgiveness, bowing to him and promising him never to be so careless again. Luckily for Lena, he wasn't interested in punishing her further this time. She'd already been on the receiving end of his rage at the penthouse and had learned her lesson, but he didn't mask his distaste with her.

"Don't step out of line again, Lena. You're on your last warning," he ordered, looking down at her darkly.

"Yes, master," she promised as he released her, and they both teleported back to the castle.

CHAPTER TWENTY-SIX

Tilly went home that night after spending a lazy day in the quiet penthouse with her friends and their new master, Beelzebub. They'd chatted for hours, and she'd learned more about the royal family from the warm and friendly demon she'd never have pegged for an evil servant of Satan if she'd met him in other circumstances. She was exhausted and weak, but still buzzed from the amazing couple of days she'd just spent with Blake, and thought back to their intimate moments with a shy smile. The dark and scary few minutes from the hallway after Luna's visit still played on her mind, but she endeavoured to try and understand her master's pain as much as he would let her, even with his usually cold nature towards his emotions always keeping her at arm's length. Tilly thought back to that moment and actually couldn't be happier that Blake had chosen to use her to calm him, rather than her having been the one to cause him more anger during his overflowing and seemingly uncontrollable dark rage.

She couldn't help but feel sorry for Lena, wishing that the witch had just listened to her warning rather than barge into the bedroom unannounced, and yet she was also glad that Lena had been the one to take the full brunt of his rage instead of her. The powerful witch was undoubtedly able to withstand the punishment in that moment thanks to her magic powers, whereas Tilly knew that she could've been really hurt if Blake had turned his black gaze on her frail human body instead.

She returned to college the next morning, still tender, but she didn't care. He was worth it. Tilly studied hard, working tirelessly on recipes and perfecting her cooking and preparation methods, wowing her mentors. She soon became the top student in her class, her passion and skill becoming apparent very quickly.

Later that week, she got a letter telling her that she'd received a much-coveted spot in a young chef's internship program starting in the new year. She'd been invited to re-locate to London and cook under a highly decorated and famed chef named Andre Baxter for the next stage of her career development. Andre had received many prestigious awards over the years, and had a fantastic reputation in the food industry for excellence and impeccable taste. He would be the perfect mentor for her budding career. Tilly was overjoyed, and felt excited to start the next phase of her life under his expert tutelage, so said yes immediately.

As the days passed, Tilly found she missed Blake terribly and cursed the tiny sliver of moon in the sky above for keeping him away from her. He made small appearances in her dreams here and there, sometimes just coming through as a set of deep green eyes that watched her from afar while her subconscious took over the scene around them, but other times she would find herself stood before the large mirror in her room again, dressed in that beautiful black gown as he peered over her shoulder, his arms wrapped around her in that same way she now loved so much. She'd always been independent and strong-willed, but knew now that she was willingly submitting to him. She actually relished in his possession of her, and would find herself leaning back into his embrace while he held her tighter and kissed her neck softly, wanting to be dominated.

The following week, Beelzebub came to sit with her in the college lunchroom with Gwen on his arm. Renee wasn't with them this time; she was in trouble with her demonic master again and so was being punished. While Tilly felt bad that her friend was learning her lessons the hard way, she couldn't deny that Renee most probably needed the stricter approach. She hadn't been at college for the last few days, and Tilly didn't dare ask what she was going through in order to appease her new master, but just hoped he was being fair. Despite his ancient dark prowess, Beelzebub seemed to be the least scary demon she'd come across as yet, and Tilly already considered him a friend. She trusted him and his judgement, believing that he wouldn't harm her friend unnecessarily.

Tilly bought coffee and then opened a plastic box from inside her bag, serving up some lemon and poppy-seed cupcakes she'd just made in class while the three of them sat chatting at the plastic table for a few minutes before the bell rang.

"Gwen, Renee and I are going to spend the holidays at a lodge in the Swiss Alps with Lilith and some of the other demons, along with their followers," Beelzebub told her. "Tilly, you're invited to come along, of course. Blake will join us there during the full moon around halfway through the break." He then looked at them both with a serious expression. "You can tell your parents whatever you want, but are both expected to come, is that understood?" he asked, more of an order than a request.

"Yes, master," Gwen replied, and Tilly nodded.

"Yes, sir," she said, addressing him playfully, and the demon smiled across at her. Beelzebub gave her the thumbs up as he took a large bite of his cake and groaned appreciatively, letting her know how tasty it was. "How are we getting there?" she then asked, trying to figure out if she had the money for airplane tickets.

"You'll teleport with me, as per your master's wishes," he answered once he'd finished his mouthful, and she laughed to herself.

"Of course," she said, but was glad that they now had a plan in place for the dreaded holiday season. Their non-Satanic friends were already going on about their plans for Christmas and what presents they were buying for their families, whereas Tilly and her marked friends actively had to avoid the subject at all costs.

After college finished for the day, Tilly went straight over to the main house to speak with her parents. She told them how she'd decided to go skiing with her friends for Christmas this year rather than spending it at home with them, which was the only plausible excuse she could think of for being away over the entire festive period. It would be the first time she'd ever spent the holidays without them, and she knew they wouldn't be happy about it. Her quiet-natured father, Robert, stayed silent, but her mother was disappointed and angry, immediately chastising Tilly for her cold, closed-off attitude recently.

"It doesn't matter if I'm here or not. I don't want any presents anyway so just let me do what I want. I'm not a child," she cried, eager for them not to question her on it further. Bianca had already tried having words with her about her new dress code and rude behaviour following her disappearance to the penthouse. Tilly wanted to be honest, and hated lying to them, but she simply couldn't talk to her about any of it until Blake gave her permission to, and so pretended that she wasn't interested in her mother's opinion of her dress sense or attitude.

She stormed out the house and stomped over to her small nook, feeling grateful for the solace. In all honesty, Tilly knew that she'd been closed-off with them recently, but her only care other than her career was Blake, and knew she'd spent most of her time thinking of him and how best to please her master. Tilly had even been working out in the college gym, hoping to be stronger and more ready for him the next time they were together. She desperately wanted to keep up with him better the next time they made love, and sizzled inside at the sheer anticipation of it.

CHAPTER TWENTY-SEVEN

Tilly packed her bags and made her way over to Beelzebub's flat on the night that she, Gwen, and Renee had broken up from college for the two-week Christmas break, ready to head off to the mysterious lodge where they'd all be staying for the holidays. It was reported to be completely snowed in, access impossible by both car and foot, so they could all go and have lots of fun, safe in the knowledge that they wouldn't be bothered by any outsiders. They all took each other's hands and teleported away, arriving within seconds outside a huge, snow-covered building that looked as if it was quite possibly used as a hotel, or perhaps even be a tourist landmark during the summer months. Tilly whistled when she saw it, and knew for sure how money was absolutely no object for these beings and their followers. The place was more than impressive, it was monumental.

It was absolutely freezing outside, despite all of Tilly's prepared layers, and she was glad once they got inside the warm and colossal building that'd been completely under-sold to them by Beelzebub. It was enormous, and had been completely modernised inside, with over one hundred rooms and a number of fully stocked bars and restaurants. There was also a vast hall, cinema, gym and a spa for them all to use as much as they wanted during their stay. The girls jaws all dropped as they made their way inside, taking in the lavishly furnished main hallway that led to the huge ballroom. Tilly was lucky enough to have been allocated a master suite, complete with private Jacuzzi and terrace, and she couldn't help but think how she could quickly get used to all this preferential treatment thanks to her black mark and royal master.

Blake hadn't visited her dreams again in the last couple of weeks, but Tilly felt his presence around her somehow, somewhere deep within herself, and she knew he was keeping an eye on her from afar. Beelzebub was still being very helpful and kind; always making sure that she was happy, comfortable and well taken care of in Blake's absence. She assumed it was all at the behest of their Black Prince, but in all honesty, she didn't mind. She was much happier with Beelzebub as her interim demonic guardian rather than having to deal with Lilith too often, and he seemed to sense her preference. Tilly presumed that Blake was more as ease with him watching over her, too. After all, the change in demonic caretaker kept her away from Brent at the same time.

The rest of the demons and their groups of followers soon joined them at the lodge, and then the partying and promised fun well and truly started the next evening, when everyone was invited down to the main hall for the welcoming party. It was a night planned for initiating the new followers into the mixture of human acolytes, as well as welcoming back the demons that were now returning to Earth for their malevolent tours of duty. Some of the partygoers celebrated by participating in all sorts of depraved and sinful acts with one another, and nothing seemed off limits to those who were without prior orders from their demonic masters. Tilly knew without having to ask that she was to stay well away from those groups, but didn't want to anyway. She was far from ready to participate in those kinds of acts, and while she knew she was surrendering to Blake's dominance, whips and chains weren't on the agenda along with her submission.

Most of the other followers relaxed together while chatting and getting drunk, having fun rather than getting into anything too intense, and Tilly joined in with that group along with her friends. She only drank a few whiskies that night, having fun but being careful not to go too crazy or get involved in anything that she knew Blake wouldn't be happy with. Her new follower friends and the demons she met didn't push her or make any advances in their drunken hazes either, knowing all too well that she was spoken for by one of their highest and most feared leaders.

As the first week passed by, she spent her days relaxing, working out in the gym, and watching movies with her friends—staying warm rather than going out in the snow. The cold never really was her thing. Tilly eventually tried her hand at both skiing and snowboarding after Renee's constant pleas for her to participate in the outdoor activities, but after having fallen on her arse more times than she cared to admit, she quickly crossed them off her list of things to do for the rest of their stay in Switzerland. Her master certainly wouldn't be happy with her if he came and found her sore and bruised instead of ready and waiting.

Lilith and her large group of followers took up almost an entire wing of the huge lodge and Tilly had found herself genuinely happy to see them all when they arrived. She hugged Lucas with a cheerful smile before she greeted each of the circus members she'd grown to know so well over the years. She openly enjoyed the three brothers' company too, and they had a lot of fun together. Their time was spent swimming lengths with Jackson in the pool, helping David and Brent to practice their routines in the gym, or settling down together in the warm cinema-style room, propped up on cushions and blankets while they watched movies on the big screen and ate vast amounts of popcorn and ice-cream. Tilly had worked hard to find her way with Brent again, feeling like she could finally put aside all the emotions she'd once had for him, and in those relaxed few days they both understood how they could remain friends as long as neither of them ever brought up any reminders of the past. It was still there—they both felt it—but somehow they each effectively pushed away their history in their efforts to remain friends. Tilly knew that Blake would never let her even be around Brent if he posed a threat, so trusted that his thoughts and memories of his relationship with her must be safely locked away in his mind, and she hoped, for both of their sake's, that they would stay there.

CHAPTER TWENTY-EIGHT

A few days after Christmas, the full moon rose overhead and Blake arrived at the hotel, teleporting straight into Tilly's room to bypass the crowds that might try to take away his attention. After all, he wasn't interested in them, all he wanted was her. He'd decided to stay out of her head while in Hell because he couldn't stop thinking of her, much to his surprise and annoyance. The temptation to visit her dreams had been incredibly strong, but he knew he wouldn't be satisfied until he saw her properly and had physical contact again. Blake knew he was opening up his soul to her more and more as each full moon bought him to Earth, but he still fought his feelings. As usual, he closed himself off to his aching heart each time the turmoil from his past tried to creep in with the love he felt brooding from within. He wasn't ready to deal with it all just yet, and he was certainly not equipped to feel and to love. Blake wasn't sure if he ever would be.

Tilly was ready for him, sitting naked in an armchair by the fire, eagerly awaiting Blake's arrival in their suite. When he appeared before her, she felt the instant flutter of her heart as it sped up, and the immediate moistening of her cleft as it ached for him. He too was overcome with desire, and in just a few seconds had stripped off. Blake then wasted no time in gathering Tilly up and into his strong arms and sliding his hard length inside her whilst pinning her against the wall beside the huge fireplace. His kisses were powerful, eager and deeply passionate, and she willingly gave in to his every desire, wanting every inch of his body against hers. Blake didn't hold this part of his desire back one little bit. He pummelled her with his body, while snaking his mind through hers, and he was more than pleased to discover she'd missed him so tremendously.

Tilly was lost in him, delighting in the delicious taste, touch and smell of the lover she had missed so very much these last few weeks. They then moved down onto the thick rug that lay in front of the roaring fire after a few minutes, both of them thrusting hard together before finally enjoying a shared climax and then falling into one another's arms as they revelled in their joint highs.

"You can greet me like that any time, Tilly," Blake told her, leaning over her as they lay on the warm rug and kissing her neck while he whispered into her ear. She smiled up at her master, taking in his gorgeous face and smouldering, sexy green eyes. He was so strong, so beautiful, and even though she somehow knew he was damaged and broken, she was still so drawn to him, like a moth to a flame.

She didn't care how much she could get hurt in the process, wearing his mark meant everything to her now and she wanted things to stay like this forever. "I have a surprise for you," he told her, climbing up off the rug and wandering over to grab something out of his jacket pocket. He looked perfect in the dark shadows, his naked, muscular body catching the light from the fire at just the right angles and she enjoyed the view very much. Blake quickly returned, and bought with him a small box. He had a huge smile on his face as he looked at his stunning, innocent, yet dirty girl in the flickering light from the bright flames, and couldn't deny he enjoyed his view as well.

Despite his doubts, he'd been trying to open up more over the last month, and had been attempting to let the emotions sink back. He needed to change, and knew it was time after the dust had settled following his educating experience with Luna and the memories she'd shared with him. His twin hadn't left his side, having sensed the change in him, and they'd talked for hours almost every day. She'd opened up more about the information she'd pieced together, and had shown him some more of the old memories that she'd coaxed from their owners, all of them loyal servants and friends of theirs, and so Blake knew that their shared visions could be trusted. "It's a little something to make you think of me when we're apart," he told her, and an almost shy look crossed his gorgeous face.

Tilly sat up on the rug and folded her legs underneath her, completely taken aback by this unusual display of affection from her usually cool master.

"Thank you, your highness. I didn't expect to get a gift from you, and didn't get anything to give you in return," she told him, leaning forward to give him a soft kiss before accepting the present.

"You're welcome," he said, eyeing her with a boyish smile. "It's not a Christmas present if that's what you were wondering, so there's no need to get me anything in return. I have everything I need," he added, stroking her cheek with his index finger and Tilly swooned.

"Can I open it now?" she asked eagerly, and he nodded.

"Of course."

Tilly pulled the lid off the small, black velvet box to reveal a stunning thick, black metal ring with a dark green stone set in the centre that just so happened to be the exact same shade of his gorgeous eyes. She immediately put it on, grinning up at Blake as she stared back and forth from his eyes to the green gemstone.

"It's absolutely perfect, thank you so much," she said, feeling like a lovesick teenager as she stared down at his wonderful gift.

Blake shrugged nonchalantly and said nothing more; he simply pulled her closer and planted a deep, eager kiss on her lips. Tilly immediately climbed onto his lap, keen to have him again despite her tenderness from their first lovemaking session. He slipped inside her naturally again, hard for her at once and just as ready. She moved up and down on him gently, her eyes on his as she rode him and opened herself fully, both physically and mentally. She planted kisses on his mouth and neck as she continued her pursuit, leaning back and crying out as her first orgasm claimed her, feeling grateful for the hours spent at the gym and her new found vigour and strength.

Blake then let Tilly fall back onto the warm rug, climbing between her legs as he pushed himself even deeper inside her delicate tenderness, the soft strokes of his hard cock urging her to continue, and she peered up at him, her hands running through his dark curls as she succumbed to him entirely, willingly. Blake groaned, smiling down at her and basking in her clear submission to his dominant side. He plunged himself hard inside her welcoming cleft at first and then began slowing his thrusts after a few minutes, and the two of them stared into one another's eyes as they kept up the softer, more passionate pace.

When he'd found his release, the pair lay side-by-side on the thick rug, satiated and satisfied beyond anything either of them had felt before. She curled into his embrace, enjoying the warmth of him, his scent, and the gentle buzz she still felt from his touch. Her body was tired but her mind was alive, awakened thanks to the pleasurable hormones released during their lovemaking.

As she lay there in his arms, Tilly suddenly had an urge to say the words, those three little words she knew she felt so strongly but had to fight, knowing he wasn't ready. She tried to push the thoughts away before Blake realised what'd just welled up inside of her, but felt him tense beside her and knew he'd read her thoughts before she'd been able to push them away.

"Please don't," Tilly begged in a whisper, desperate not to lose the closeness they'd just shared. He smiled down at her, but the smile didn't reach his eyes, and she could feel him already pulling away, growing colder thanks to those unconquerable high walls.

"I'm not worthy of those words, Tilly. Don't ever say them to me," he said, looking forlorn yet decisive as he uttered his terrible admission. She couldn't help but feel both angry and sad at his depressive statement, and her response came pouring out of her before she could control her tongue.

"Don't you do that, not to me," she cried, leaning up on her elbow to look at him. "You are more worthy of love than anyone I've ever known. You're warm, kind, merciful and even a little shy underneath that hard exterior, but all you have to do is let me in. Just let me love you, Blake," she begged, and then covered her mouth in shock, trying to take back both her daring words and the name she'd accidentally just spoken, but it was already too late.

CHAPTER TWENTY-NINE

Tears welled in Tilly's eyes and she gazed fearfully at her master, not sure what he might do to punish her for the lapse in etiquette and her presumptuous outburst. When he leaned down, she flinched and pulled back, but Blake gripped her tight. He then stared down at Tilly with eyes that began to churn with black specks, and she trembled in fear. She could sense his anger and venomous rage as it began to boil over uncontrollably, and she flinched when he leaned in close, whispering into her ear.

"Don't ever say anything like that to me again, Tilly. I've given you sufficient warnings, and yet you still think you can treat me like your little pussy-whipped boyfriend? Trust me, your cunt isn't that sweet," he murmured, his tone deadly and full of rage, while his face mashed into a sinister, truly scary mask. Every inch of Tilly's body shuddered in fear and tears began sliding from her eyes. "You'll learn to keep your mouth shut Tilly, not to say a fucking word, and don't say I never warned you," he commanded, and she could hear his powerful voice inside her head as well as in her ears. She knew she had to follow the order, but still tried calling out anyway, to beg his forgiveness, and she quickly realised that she couldn't talk. More than that, she was somehow unable to even open her mouth.

Instinctively, Tilly reached up and touched her lips, finding them magically sealed closed, her body adhering to his command even if her mind wanted to disobey. An evil smile spread across Blake's face, his eyes still black as he watched her begin to panic, finding vile satisfaction in her fear. Tilly sent him pleading thoughts, begging him to calm down, desperate for forgiveness. However, she had the heart-wrenching suspicion he wasn't listening. He was lost to her. Shrouded in an angry haze.

Blake said nothing more as he climbed up and kneeled over her, still staring angrily into her eyes. He then reached his hands up to her neck, grabbing her tight with both hands when he wrapped them around Tilly's vulnerable windpipe, and she could do nothing but peer up at her master regretfully. She didn't grab at his hands or try to fight his hold over her, she knew she deserved to be punished and closed her eyes, ready to take whatever terrible lesson he chose to teach her.

After a few moments she opened her eyes again, and found that he still hadn't moved. His hands were still firmly wrapped around her throat, but he hadn't gone any further in his punishment, and Tilly hoped he was fighting his urges. She wondered if deep down, he didn't want to taint this wonderful day, but she couldn't be sure.

She shuddered beneath him uncontrollably with fear, suddenly feeling cold despite the warm fire beside her, and Blake jumped as though she'd interrupted him from a daydream. He pinned her tighter into the floor with his body, staring into her eyes as he reached across and placed one of his hands directly into the burning fire beside them. The flames didn't hurt him, of course, but when Blake pulled it back out again Tilly could see that his fingertip was now glowing red-hot thanks to the heat. She stared up at him in fear and tried to cry out, her voice getting held captive behind her sealed lips, her pleas unheard.

Blake then lifted her left wrist with his free hand and he quickly drew an inverted cross on the soft flesh inside Tilly's forearm with his burning fingertip, giving her a matching mark to the one that Lilith had first drawn on her opposite wrist. This one, however, was going to remain permanently visible thanks to the instant searing of her flesh as Blake traced his finger along in two perfect lines. Tilly cried out in pain as he branded her, the screams muffled by her closed lips and tears fell instantly from her eyes while the skin burned and singed painfully beneath his touch. She tried to pull away from him, but he held her still, staring down at her with black, unforgiving eyes and watching as she could do nothing but cry.

"I told you I'd hurt you, didn't I?" he then asked her coldly, climbing up from the rug and getting dressed quickly. "Perhaps you might want to rethink your last statement about how kind and merciful I am now," he added, before going out into the main living area of the suite where he made himself a large glass of whisky in silence.

Blake's eyes still burned black while he struggled to lull his rage, and his body continued to tremble with anger despite his efforts, and he down glass after glass of the amber liquid in an attempt to numb them both. The commandment sealing Tilly's lips was lifted as soon as Blake had left the bedroom, and she lay on the rug for a moment, writhing in pain, and sobbing silently as her wrist continued to burn. She then screamed into the fur beneath her, grabbing her arm and pulling it close to her body protectively, but there was nothing she could do to soothe it and the warmth from the fire only made it sting harder. Tilly climbed up off the floor and ran into the en-suite, holding the wound under the cold water, her tears still flowing down her red-hot cheeks. She fell to her knees weakly, holding her arm up in the sink to ensure the cool water still flowed over her burn, easing it just the tiniest bit. She was grateful for the slight respite from the scalding pain, and desperately needed the soothing coolness from the thankfully ice-cold water. Tilly sat there on the bathroom floor and cried as she continued to hold her arm under the faucet, the sobs escaping from her uncontrollably for almost an hour, while Blake stood out on the icy terrace drinking one large dram of whisky after another, desperately trying to calm his temper.

He knew he'd acted rashly, and realised he was no less a monster than his father, but there was no going back now. Blake had actually been considering asking his mother if he could give Tilly permission to use his name when they were alone together, and yet he'd still reacted so strongly to her saying it tonight. He'd been enraged by both her audacity and by the fact that she'd dared speak to him of love, despite his many warnings on the subject during their previous conversations. Blake wondered if perhaps it was the very insinuation that he was such a good man underneath his cold, devilish shell that'd made him punish her so much harder. He hated that he'd felt an overwhelming urge in that moment to prove to Tilly just why she should never love him, that he was still a heartless monster despite her high hopes for him. His instincts had taken over, teaching her a terrible lesson on autopilot. He guessed was as much a slave to his darkness as any of them, and oh how he'd let it take over him in that awful moment.

Blake could feel Tilly's pain, and could hear her scared and hurt thoughts coming to him via their bonded minds right now, but he knew he had to see it through. He couldn't show her any weakness. The Black Prince, no matter his affection for her, didn't trust himself to let down his walls around Tilly, and despite his regret, he was sure that this punishment would finally prove to her that he'd never lied about his unwavering dark nature.

CHAPTER THIRTY

Once she'd calmed down, Tilly got herself showered and dressed, and then wrapped her wrist with a wet cloth to soothe it and keep it cool. She sat on the bed, looking at herself in the large mirror. She looked like she felt—absolutely terrible—but applied some makeup to hide the dark circles beneath her eyes and brushed her dark-blonde hair before pulling it into a high ponytail. She was angry, hurt, scared, and full of regret, but she thought back to the words she'd spoken, and still meant them despite the awful punishment that'd followed afterwards. She also couldn't help but think back to what she'd said before about Blake hurting her, and she endeavoured to keep that promise to him regardless of what'd just happened. Tilly looked down at the bandage on her swollen arm, vowing to shed no more tears over the wound, and she headed out into the living room area where she poured herself a large glass of whisky and joined Blake on the terrace.

Neither of them said a word as they both stared out at the beautiful scenery before them. The snow covered mountains and huge forests all around the lodge were breath-taking and she downed her strong drink with trembling hands before placing the empty glass down on the frozen table.

She went to him, moving round to stand before her master before falling to his feet to kneel before him and then bowed her head, feeling ashamed and embarrassed. She stayed there for a few minutes, Blake standing over her, his expression still cold and distant, and his eyes black as night. Tilly kept her head low, too scared to look up at her master, waiting for him to make the next move.

After a few minutes he unexpectedly turned on his heel, and sent the glass in his hand hurtling to the wall next to the patio door, shattering it instantly. Blake then reached down and grabbed Tilly by the arm, dragging her back inside with him before effortlessly throwing her onto the huge bed. He then climbed up on top of her, pushing her arms up over her head forcibly while he pressed down on her with his strong body. Tilly winced as he brushed against her sore forearm, but said nothing to try and stop him, keeping the promise she'd just made to herself. She then felt cold metal in her hands, and Blake closed her grip around the thick bars of the bed frame.

"Don't let go, not even for a second," he ordered her, turning Tilly over onto her stomach and then pulling down her skirt and knickers. Blake undressed and hovered over her, his face buried in her hair, breathing in her smell in an attempt to stop himself taking this too far, but it was no use. He didn't want to hurt her, and yet a carnal need within him demanded he teach her a lesson, and what better way than owning her body with his own?

"Do it," Tilly whispered, lifting her hips up off the bed in an oddly inviting way. She braced herself for what she knew would be his unfeeling, unloving thrusts, but silently reminded her master that she was ready to keep her promises, and he pushed himself inside her hard and deep. Blake pulled her hips higher, pushing her thighs closed tight as he did, and he took her harder than she'd ever been taken before. She gripped the metal frame as tight as she could with her throbbing hands while he pressed her firmly into the mattress, his relentless thrusts delivering Tilly both pleasure and pain as he continued his animalistic punishment.

He came quickly, pulling out of her without another word, and then headed off for a shower, leaving Tilly trembling and sore in his wake, feeling used and more than ever like she was a possession rather than his lover. She continued to grip the bed frame while he showered, realising that he hadn't yet released her from that order, and so she lay there, sobbing quietly into the pillow. He emerged from the bathroom looking just like his normal self again a few minutes later, his eyes green, but he couldn't hide the sadness in them. He ordered her to take a bath and then left Tilly alone in the bedroom, still trembling and screaming her emotional torment into the pillows beneath her.

"Stay here, I'll be back later," Blake called from the living room a little while later as he grabbed his jacket and left their suite. Tilly didn't respond, she was already laying in the warm bath, resting her sore body and nursing her bruised ego. She couldn't understand where all this had come from, and Blake was so closed-off and distant towards her now that she knew there was no point in trying to talk to him about it. He'd punished her far more than she'd ever thought he would, and over such a tiny mistake, too. She suspected his anger was probably more down to her foolish words of love rather than her saying his name, but Tilly had certainly learned her lesson and knew never to take their relationship for granted again.

She lay in the deep, soapy water and stared at the ring on her finger, the beautiful present that Blake had given her to remind Tilly of him during their weeks apart between the moon's full days. It really was the perfect match for his eyes, and she had to take it off and place it to one side—she couldn't bring herself to look at it any longer. Tilly glanced down instead at her sore wrist, it'd started to heal already, but she was sure it would scar and then undoubtedly show the burned inverted cross clearly against her pale skin once the redness had gone. It'd be her very own brand, and permanent reminder of this awful day.

***

Blake left for Hell the next day with hardly having said another word to Tilly, but she was sulking so didn't care. She tried not to be too obvious about it, but was glad when he'd gone. Gwen came to her room, checking if she was okay, and Tilly lied, saying that she was just exhausted so needed some rest and would re-join the fun the next day. Gwen didn't believe her for an instant, but left her friend to it, Beelzebub having ordered her to keep her nose out. Blake's business was none of hers despite it involving her good friend.

It was actually three more days before Tilly eventually emerged from the huge suite. The despair that'd overpowered her had been awful. She'd cried, slept feverishly, screamed bloody murder, and even smashed up some of the crystal tumblers and vases from the room in a bid to rid herself of the terrible, overwhelming emotions that would burst out of her uncontrollably as she processed the events from that awful few hours. Tilly had cried herself to sleep each night, barely resting as the nightmares crept in, and she would soon wake again, weeping uncontrollably into her pillow. Eventually, her hunger got the better of her though, and she made her way out to the dining room to join the others, remaining silent and sombre while she devoured her huge mound of hot chicken curry and fragrant rice.

She then did her best to take her mind off everything for the duration of their stay, grateful now for the cold weather so she could wear long jumpers and cardigans for the rest of their time at the lodge in a bid to cover the new mark Blake had left on her.

Despite Tilly's melancholy, Gwen remained her usual cheery self, eager to perk up her grumpy friend. However, Tilly noticed Beelzebub watching her with a sad look every now and then, especially when he caught her scratching her arm gently when the scab began to clear a few days later. She suspected that Blake's old friend must know what'd happened, and that perhaps her master had gone to the demon for advice following her punishment that day, but she couldn't know for sure and wouldn't ever ask him. She quickly turned away from his warm gaze, feeling the tears well up in her eyes, so she took herself off for a walk in the snow covered gardens instead. Tilly didn't feel the cold this time. In fact, she felt nothing but numb and emotionless. She could see the appeal, and understood Blake's preference to the iciness, rather than having to deal with her fraught emotions any longer.

She was glad when it was time to go home again a few days later, and hid herself away once she got there, nursing both her still sore arm and her wounded heart for a few more days before setting about making plans for her move to London, intent on focussing on the happier elements of her new life.

CHAPTER THIRTY-ONE

The new year brought with it lots of changes for Tilly, and she quickly immersed herself in keeping busy with perfecting her recipes and organising her move to the big city. It was insisted upon her that she move into the penthouse rather than find her own flat in London, and as much as it annoyed Tilly to have to accept Blake's hospitality while she was still sulking, it was a welcome gift. Living there stopped her having to worry about finding the money for rent or needing to procure furniture and appliances for a place of her own, and she couldn't turn it down.

She left the farm with tears in her eyes, having wanted to feel grown up and independent, but she couldn't help feeling so unsure of herself and her place in the world instead. Tilly would never tell a soul, not even Gwen or Renee, but she was terrified of going it alone with all the changes she now needed to come to terms with, and hated not being able to talk to her mother about any of those fears. She was still angry and upset with Blake, but there was also a part of her that missed him terribly. Her body ached for his touch and if she stopped and let herself think about him too long, her anger quickly waned and was soon replaced by the love she still fought hard to try and suppress for him, but she refused to let it get the better of her.

After a couple of days getting settled into the penthouse and learning her way around, Tilly felt much more like her usual, happy, and confident self again. She made a conscious decision to leave the terrible day in Switzerland behind her and she focussed instead on the future, pushing on towards her selfish goals of fame and fortune as a chef. She was eager to start doing what she wanted to do from now on, and also what would help get her closer to that shallow dream she'd shown Blake in the dream mirror just a few months before.

She worked hard in Andre's kitchen and learned many new skills, while welcoming every challenge he set her. Tilly loved being in both the kitchens and out in the main dining area of the contemporarily designed, critically acclaimed, 'Innov-ate restaurant' near the centre of London. It was modern and incredibly posh, with new and impressive takes on classic dishes that'd won over their clients and earned Andre a reputation as a truly inspired chef and teacher. Tilly soon settled into her role as an entry level commis chef with relative ease, and where Andre had been impressed with her portfolio, he was even more amazed with her fantastic recipes and skilled hands as she worked tirelessly in the kitchen for ten or twelve hours a day with no complaints.

The next full moon came around very quickly thanks to her busy days, but Blake didn't come to her during it. Tilly had stopped sulking now and was eager to sort things out with her master, and she hated not knowing what he was doing, or what his intentions were for her after their fight. His absence brought her nothing but dread and anxious butterflies to her stomach. Despite this terrible bump in their road, Tilly still cared for Blake and hated the fact that she'd not seen or heard from him since their time at the Swiss mountain lodge, not even in her dreams.

Tilly pressed on, regardless of her fear of being tossed aside by the man who'd stolen her heart so savagely it now hurt her just thinking about him and his indifference. She made lots of new friends at Innov-ate, and another chef at the restaurant, Trey, had taken an obvious liking to her. He was a sweet man, and kept on asking Tilly out for a drink or for coffee with him, but as much as she wanted to enjoy the attention, it made her feel uncomfortable. He was cute and friendly, but his advances only served to remind her how lonely she felt in Blake's absence. She kept telling Trey that she was unavailable, and lied, saying that she had a boyfriend who worked overseas and she didn't see him very much, but that they were completely faithful to one another. Tilly would never be honest with her new colleague about the real life she led away from her internship, and she also didn't want to admit that she was unsure what was happening between them right now, not wanting to even admit it to herself.

"All the more reason to come and fill your quiet times with me," Trey had answered with a wink over the salad preparation one lunchtime after his fifth attempt to woo her. She couldn't deny that he was handsome, though. Tall and slim, with black skin and deep brown eyes that were warm and kind, but she was just not interested. In fact, there was actually no part of her right now that wanted anything to do with the hassle of entertaining his advances at all. Tilly was sure it must be that she was still getting over that exhausting and scary day with Blake, and her plate was well and truly full anyway, so she finally put her foot down, telling Trey once and for all to stop pestering her.

"No, Trey, and I've told you more than enough times. Please don't make this uncomfortable, okay?" she asked him with a stern look, and he conceded, nodding his head and holding up his hands in defeat before reaching over for another pack of tomatoes to chop from the centre of the table between them.

The next few weeks passed by in a blur again thanks to her incredibly busy days, and before she knew it, the full moon lit up the skyline over London again. Tilly stood on the penthouse's huge terrace wrapped in a heavy coat with a large glass of whisky in her hand, enjoying the cold night air while looking up at the bright moon overhead thoughtfully. This was the second night of its fullness, and she was now convinced that Blake wasn't coming to see her again.

She couldn't help but feel sad, lonely, and angry that they'd not sorted things out. In all honesty she was pissed off more than still hurt, feeling as if he couldn't even be bothered to fight for her. Tilly rubbed her arm instinctively as she thought of her master, it'd healed a while ago and the scar wasn't as bad as she'd first thought it might be, but she still hated the constant reminder of that awful day. Her mark was still noticeable, and she had to wear either jewellery or long sleeves to cover it, but it was manageable, and she was slowly getting used to seeing it there now. Tilly had also started wearing her beautiful green ring again too, and her hand instinctively moved down to it as she absentmindedly ran her fingers over the soft gem.

Tilly finished off her whisky, placing the tumbler down on the cold stone before her as she peered up at the stars, wondering what to do with the rest of her lonely evening.

"Care for another one?" asked a voice from behind her, and Tilly spun around to see Blake standing in the terrace doorway. His body language was playful and he had a smile on his lips, looking just like he had that first night they'd shared together in this same penthouse. Tilly walked over to him slowly, taking him in in the darkness. Blake wore black jeans and a jumper, looking casual and relaxed rather than in his usual formal gear, and his green eyes twinkled sexily at her in the dim light. He was gorgeous, she still couldn't deny that, but there was an awkwardness that hovered between them now, the elephant in the room that shuffled around them awkwardly and left them both on edge. Tilly nodded and handed him her glass, bowing low as she reached him, never forgetting the formalities that would still be expected of her.

"Yes please, master," she said, and he turned, wandering off to the bar without another word. She followed him inside and closed the glass doors behind her before discarding her coat and shoes. Tilly then flopped down on the sofa next to the fire, watching Blake as he walked over to her with two large whiskies in his hands. He joined her on the sofa, eyeing her intensely, his eyes boring into hers as he read her thoughts for a moment, a knowing grin curling at his lips. *Go to hell,* she couldn't help but think, hating that he could access her forgiving thoughts so easily, and Blake laughed, but said nothing in response.

After a long, tense silence, he smiled across at her, rapidly causing Tilly's cold demeanour to thaw a little piece at a time. He could melt her mood in a second and they both knew it, but she was determined to make him work for it just a little bit, and he didn't mind at all. He admired her strength and would play her game if it made Tilly feel better. He didn't expect to earn her forgiveness easily, and if anything, he wanted her to make it hard on him. He deserved nothing less.

"Firstly, I need to tell you that I am truly, truly sorry. I tried to stop myself, I really did, but sometimes the power utterly consumes me and I'm no longer in control," he eventually said, staring into her beautiful blue eyes earnestly as he spoke. "But, I promise you now that I will *never* do anything like that again," he added, taking her hand in his and removing the large silver cuff bracelet that she'd worn to cover her burn mark. He looked down at the brand for a moment, his eyes speckling with black spots, but he said nothing else, placing the cuff back around her forearm and stroking his hand up to her neck where he left it there, staring at her thoughtfully.

Tilly trembled before him, fear and anguish seeping out of every inch of her, despite every one of her senses going crazy for him. Blake sensed her fear, but continued his apology; eager to regain the closeness he'd so foolishly destroyed during his last visit. "You deserve so much better than how I have treated you, and I should never have lashed out like I did. I'll remember everything about that day for the rest of my sorry life," he said, cupping her cheek with his hand gently. "And I'll spend every day making it up to you."

A small sob escaped from Tilly's chest uncontrollably and she peered up into his eyes, while he wiped away a tear that'd rolled down her cheek and onto her top lip.

"I thought you were here to tell me we were finished," she admitted, not hiding how lost she'd felt during his absence.

"Not a chance in Hell," Blake replied, smiling down at her. "I'm trying to control my emotions better, and I've been letting them back in, learning to handle how they make me feel. All of it, I've done for you," he told her and Tilly let go of all the tension she'd been holding so tightly in her stomach. The butterflies in her abdomen fluttered wildly at his strong words, while her battered heart suddenly beat again in the hope that she and Blake could still have a future together. Perhaps all was not lost after all.

Tilly smiled up at her master, desperately wanting to regain some of their strong bond again, but in that same moment, she quickly came to realise that it'd never left them at all. Yes, their connection had been dulled by the raw emotions neither of them had seemed able to control following their last bit of time together, but it was still as strong as ever.

"You hurt me," she whispered. "But I'm still here, just like I promised. I won't leave you or hate you because of your pain, but I'll learn to understand it. Understand you."

"Forgive me?" Blake asked, his face full of regret.

"Of course, yes." Tilly replied, her pain numbing with every moment that passed.

The pair of them spent the rest of the night sitting on the sofa together, chatting and drinking the last bottle of Blake's expensive whisky while they found their way back to each other again. Blake didn't ask her to join him in the bedroom or make any move towards her sexually this time, remaining understanding to Tilly's unspoken pain. This visit was all about rekindling their emotional relationship anyway, not their sexual chemistry, as both of them knew how that wasn't the problem.

His heartfelt explanations worked, and by the time he left for Hell again the next morning, she was smitten with her Black Prince all over again. Right before he went, each of them vowed to one another that they'd get over all the tough emotions and move past the terrible day at the lodge before the next full moon, and Tilly knew she was almost there already.

CHAPTER THIRTY-TWO

Working under Andre continued to keep Tilly incredibly busy, but when her working day was done she would finally have some time to think, to work through the last of her fraught emotions, and she moved on from Blake's snowy visit at last. He would come into her dreams most nights, eager to show her his much more open emotions thanks to his twin sister Luna's help, and she quickly became far more willing to have an early night than ever before, eager for the sexy, dark god of her dreams to visit. They soon found themselves opening up more and more to each other during their nightly exploits, feeling as though they really were there together in whatever scene Blake had put together for the pair of them in her mind. Miles apart they grew closer, and she loved him all the more for it, even if she couldn't say so.

The full moon that followed brought with it the chance for the pair of them to be together properly again at last, and Tilly was anxious but excited to see Blake. She was also ready to give herself to him entirely, just like before. He arrived at the penthouse almost as soon as the full moon rose in the sky over London, and was greeted by Tilly waiting patiently with her hip resting against the arm of the sofa. She had her arms folded, going for her best dominative look, and was wearing her sexiest black negligee, fishnet stockings and some killer stiletto heels.

"Good evening, Miss Mayfair," he whispered, taking in the stunning sight of her with a smile. "I take it you're giving the orders tonight?" he teased.

"Strip," she ordered him, but in a playful tone, and he grinned. Blake relished in her confident prowess, and obliged her command while watching her through hooded eyes, removing his black shirt and chinos without another word. Tilly took him in with a smile, the beautiful, dark, and dangerous being that she was still figuring out how to be with, figuring out how to love. She knew it was a one step at a time kind of thing, but also knew she was ready to give herself to him again, and needed it, feeling desperate to be closer to him.

She kicked off the heels and walked towards her gorgeous, untamed demon, and looked up into eyes with a satisfied smile while he gathered her up in his strong arms and wrapped her legs around his hips. He then kissed her deeply as he held her there, craving Tilly just as much as she did him. Blake carried her to the bedroom and laid her down on the huge bed, his mouth never once leaving hers and he pinned his lover there with his powerful body. She relaxed into his embrace, breathing him in, desperately wanting to touch and kiss every inch of his muscular body.

Blake then rolled sideways, and she followed his lead. Tilly climbed up onto his lap, straddling her lover as she ran her hands down to his chest and perfectly rippled abs for a moment, savouring the sight. She then stood up on the bed, towering over him while Blake lay back against the pillows, watching her every move. He bit his lip expectantly, thoroughly enjoying the show. Tilly took off her lace camisole and then slipped down her panties, moving slowly and sexily before throwing them to the floor, but she left on the netted stockings and then climbed back down onto his lap, sliding Blake's rock-hard shaft inside her very ready cleft as she did. He sat back, allowing her to be in full control as she slid up and down over her dark lover, taking him deeper while she thrust into his powerful hips. When she came, Blake sat up to kiss her, pulling Tilly down harder onto him so that he could press himself against her wonderfully pulsating muscles.

As she came down from her high, he turned her, lying on top of Tilly before he then began driving into her again, slow and softly at first, and then harder as she opened up for him. His mouth never left hers and his heart began to open up as her wonderful thoughts flooded through him. He might not agree with her adoration, but he didn't fight her either. The tumultuous war within him still raged, but instead of ignoring it, he used the turmoil to empower him. She'd done this to him. She'd forced him to learn to love by refusing to give up on him. Instead of feeling weakened by the emotion within, Blake felt stronger than ever before, and adored her even more because of it.

They continued to make-love for hours, staring into one another's eyes and kissing each other intensely as they moved together so effortlessly. Just before the sun began to rise on the horizon, Blake leaned over her and held Tilly close while he cupped her face in his hands. He stared down at her in the bed, his intense green eyes warm and full of emotion for the first time in his long, cold life.

"I love you," he told her, looking into Tilly's eyes through the dim morning light. She gasped and kissed him, gripping Blake tightly with her thighs when she then began to feel the bed shake beneath them as he reached his climactic end, emptying into her forcefully before slowing down and sinking into her loving arms.

"I love you, too," she told him as he held her tightly in his strong embrace, but knew he'd already known it for a long time.

CHAPTER THIRTY-THREE

The next day, Tilly had arranged to take Blake across the city to Andre's restaurant for lunch. Her boss had heard all about her infamous, long-distance boyfriend, and had agreed to give her the day off while he was visiting as long as she promised to stop by so that he could meet him at long last.

"Blake Rose," he said, introducing himself and reaching out his hand to shake Andre's with a warm smile. He seemed so formal, so refined, and even Andre was taken aback by the young yet so commanding man before him. Luckily, Blake hadn't taken too much convincing to go with Tilly to meet her boss. As well as being interested to meet the mentor she spoke and thought so highly of, Blake also knew just how important Andre and her career were to Tilly. He was mindful to be friendly, courteous, and warm with him, making every effort to come across as a normal, friendly guy, and the two of them seemed to get on well, much to Tilly's happiness. She'd also loved hearing him say his full name aloud as well, and hadn't really considered him having a surname before now.

Blake took the chance to charm Andre while they were chatting, luring him in with a mesmerising gaze and then planting a harmless little seed in the back of his mind. It was only a small, dark spell that would ensure in the future Andre would either instinctively give Tilly the days off during his monthly visits or plan her shifts around the moon without even realising he'd done it. Andre had no idea what Blake had done, but the Black Prince was glad to know that going forward he wouldn't have to sacrifice any of his precious time with Tilly. He didn't care about being selfish with this order, and her work was too important to always have to take a sick day or beg to take holiday hours. At least this way he could be sure that the restaurant wouldn't be getting in the way of his time with his lover again.

After devouring the delicious meal Andre had cooked especially for them, the two lovers then took a walk around the centre of London. They saw the sights for a while before Blake then treated Tilly to a shopping spree in one of the posh boutique's they found along the way. The entire day was wonderful. They walked hand-in-hand as they wandered, and Tilly felt nothing but love and happiness pass back and forth between them as they spent what would seem like a very normal day together if she wasn't walking along with the Prince of Hell, not that any of the humans around them knew that dark truth, of course.

They returned to the penthouse later that afternoon, and were greeted by Beelzebub and his followers that'd let themselves in while they waited for Blake and Tilly to come home. The demon had now recruited three more humans into his following, and much to Tilly's happiness, Renee had found her place with the group at last, evidently no longer questioning her master or his rules, and Tilly guessed that his punishments had worked on her after all. She noticed Renee was holding hands with a new follower in Bob's group, a dark haired boy with a grungy style and a cheeky smile named Jared. Tilly learned from Gwen that the pair had fallen quickly in love over the last few weeks, and that they were absolutely smitten with one another. She had to smile at them as they kissed and swooned over each other while snuggled together on the sofa, but couldn't deny that it was good seeing her friend happy again.

Beelzebub and Gwen had officially become an item now, and seemed great together. Gwen's genuine smile and affectionate glances towards the ancient and very powerful demon proved more than enough to Tilly, and she was thrilled that her friends had found their place in this new life alongside her. They completed their circle of couples nicely, and Tilly thoroughly enjoyed spending her time with them. Both her and Blake enjoyed their company as they all relaxed together and had fun, feeling natural and just like any other group of friends as they chatted for hours.

That evening, they ordered in some Chinese food and popped open some champagne while they all relaxed together happily. Tilly kept catching Blake watching her with a sly grin when she giggled excitedly with Renee and Gwen about their amazing weekend, and she couldn't help but smile back at him, fluttering her eyelashes coyly while enjoying his attention.

He genuinely enjoyed seeing as she chatted away with her friends animatedly in the kitchen, and listening in on her happy thoughts was a welcome treat, far nicer than the ones he'd had to endure hearing not so long ago. Tilly then effortlessly showed off her cooking skills for them all, whipping up some puddings and cocktails for them to enjoy, much to her friends delight and praise.

Tilly also caught Beelzebub watching her a couple of times over the evening, and he eventually plucked up the courage to talk with her quietly after Blake had taken himself off to another room to sort out some music.

"Are you two okay now?" he asked as he helped her clean up in the kitchen, looking slightly uncomfortable and maybe out of his depth asking her such a personal question, but he still had a smile behind his warm brown eyes.

"Yeah we're good, really good actually," Tilly told him with a grin, and she patted him on the shoulder, truly grateful to have someone around to keep an eye on her, someone that she knew she could trust to have her best interests at heart as well as his Black Prince's.

"Good, because I know he's made a really big effort to try and sort out those sides of himself that he's kept locked away for far too long, Tilly. You've made him question everything he thought he knew. It takes a huge adjustment, so promise me you'll be patient with him, okay?" Beelzebub replied, taking Tilly aback, but she was glad he could be so honest with her.

"I will. There's nothing I want more than to carry on this way. I will be everything he wants, and needs me to be," she told him honestly.

"Good," boomed a voice from the doorway. It was Blake, and Tilly wondered for a moment if they might be in trouble for talking about him, but he wasn't angry with them at all. He was still exuding his relaxed, easy attitude and playful nature, so neither Tilly or Beelzebub panicked that they'd been caught discussing their master.

"Speak of the devil," she whispered playfully, and relished in the cunning grin he shot her in return.

"I'll leave you guys to it," Beelzebub said, slipping past Blake with a bow, and he headed back out to re-join the group. Tilly looked up at her lover with a smile, rising up on her tiptoes when he came closer in order to kiss him. Blake grabbed her waist, lifting her onto the counter as he deepened the kiss and pulled her closer. She could feel his hardness through his black jeans and instinctively reached down to unbutton his fly, knowing he could command the others to give them some privacy.

"No," he told her, breaking their embrace and stepping back with a grin.

"No?" she asked playfully, climbing down from the kitchen side with a pout.

"No," he reiterated more forcibly, but still with his wicked, sexy grin in place before he grabbed her hand and pulled Tilly back into the living room. Their friends were all sat on the sofas as they approached, and Beelzebub's other two new followers quickly moved from the couch onto the floor so the pair of them could sit in their favourite spot.

Once she was safely cocooned between his legs, Blake then grabbed a small remote control from the coffee table and hit play. The acoustic rock song that Tilly had not so long ago dubbed as their song then began playing through the unseen speakers. She snuggled into him, smiling and leaning her head up to kiss her lover gently as the song played. It bought back wonderful memories of both their first time in the penthouse together and the moment they'd stolen while the partygoers froze in place around them during the last party. She hummed along, knowing every word by heart now.

Blake let himself enjoy their closeness rather than pushing it away, and had chosen this song purposely. It was a symbol of their blossoming love, and he felt the same way about this one melody that both haunted and comforted him as he relished in her thoughts. He smiled and cupped her face with his palm, pulling her chin back up to his for another kiss before he then leaned forward and poured her a glass of their favourite whisky.

CHAPTER THIRTY-FOUR

Bright sunshine poured in through the huge bedroom window the next morning as Tilly and Blake made love one more time before he had to go back to Hell. The waning moon was treacherously close, but he didn't care, and was eager to stay with her for as long as he could.

The early sunrise brought with it the promise of warmer, spring days, and the weather had already begun to turn for the better. As well as the days getting longer, Tilly couldn't wait for the summer to come—she'd always loved the heat. She thought back to the night of her dream when she'd shown him her deepest desires through the mirror's image, and looked up at Blake as he held her in his strong arms, wondering just how it'd all come true despite his many warnings. She kissed him, allowing her master to pull her up onto his lap with his strong arms as he thrust harder into her pulsating muscles.

"I love you," he told her, reading Tilly's thoughts, and she smiled, laughing quietly to herself before she said it back to him, and then gripped his shoulders tightly as a shared climax claimed them both.

***

The next week of work at the restaurant was a hectic schedule of planning and playing with recipes in preparation for the following weekend. Andre had been asked to provide an elegant banquet for a charity event, complete with fine dining services and some of the more unusual, bespoke requests from their fussy clients. He'd agreed to cater it, but quickly informed Tilly and the other chefs that they'd better get used to not sleeping until it was all over and done with. He worked them hard, encouraging them to give it their full attention and then praising the chefs for their good work before choosing from his protégés' best dishes to serve the guests on the night. Tilly was lucky enough to be chosen to make both a starter and dessert for the elaborate event, and she was over the moon. She thanked Andre for the opportunity, and then quickly got to work on putting together her plans for the dishes to ensure she was more than ready to wow both her colleagues and the banquet attendees with her decadent food.

When Saturday came around, she was well organised and raring to go, eager for her first opportunity to properly shine as an accomplished chef. Trey helped her with the preparations, plating up the starters for her while she checked each piece of her signature first dish, a seafood medley with beautiful mixtures of fresh shellfish and sea vegetables combined with perfectly balanced spices and herbs. Every one of the guests' plates came back clean, and Trey gave her a high-five when they celebrated for a moment before getting to work on the pudding.

The rest of the evening continued to be a huge success, and ended with Andre being given a standing ovation following the last cleared plate of delicious food. He then insisted that the other chefs join him in the hall, ushering for them to bow to the crowd while letting the guests all know that he couldn't have done it without his team.

"Get cleaned up, and then I'm taking you all out for drinks!" Andre shouted to them as the many chefs returned to the kitchen and quickly set about clearing up their workstations. Tilly breathed a sigh of relief and smiled over at her other new friend, another young intern named Jessica, and they did a little happy dance, wiggling their bums as Trey laughed from behind them and shook his head. The girls then got straight to work, hurrying so they could get out of there and have their well-earned alcoholic rewards.

"Why do you always wear black clothes, Tilly?" Jessica asked her absentmindedly as they finished cleaning, catching her off guard. She looked back across the bench at her friend. Jessica was a chatty, friendly girl. Short and skinny with black, bobbed hair and grey-blue eyes. She was a genuinely kind girl and Tilly knew she was only asking out of intrigue rather than to pry into her personal choices.

"Because I'm a Goth, didn't you already know that?" she replied, playfully teasing her friend as she wiped the counter top and cleaned the oven.

"Oh. You don't really look like a proper Goth to me though? Well, apart from your black clothes. And, you don't seem the type of person to hang out in graveyards and dance naked under the full moon?" Jessica replied, laughing as Tilly shot her the best attempt at a menacing look she could manage.

"Well, for one, that's witch's, dur. And how do you know I *don't* hang around in graveyards, are you my stalker?" she joked, but was glad when Jessica just shook her head and laughed to herself before changing the subject.

"You up to anything tomorrow?" she asked, and Tilly shook her head.

"Sleeping all day sounds good, I think I've only had about ten hours' sleep all week," she replied.

"Me too. It'll be good having a well deserved drink tonight first, though," Jessica told her with a wide smile, and Tilly nodded in response.

They soon finished up and got changed out of their work clothes, Tilly quickly changing into black skinny jeans and a sparkly top, pinning up her dark-blonde hair and then applying a little red lipstick before joining her colleagues outside the banquet hall. The group then made their way to a nearby bar, their spirits high as they celebrated their success. Andre went straight to the bar to buy the drinks while the rest of them slipped into the booths and tables, chatting away and revelling in the comments received from the evening's guests.

Tilly had just three glasses of whisky and cola, careful as ever not to get too drunk, but more so because she was with her work friends who didn't know about her secret life outside of the kitchen, and she didn't want to inadvertently say something she might later regret. Trey came over to join Tilly at the table, sliding her another drink before he congratulated her again on her tremendous pudding.

"Oh my God, you were amazing tonight, Tilly!" he exclaimed, waving his hands around animatedly, making her laugh. She blushed, but performed a small bow, complete with twirling hand gestures, and was proud of herself for having done so well with her dishes, too. She thanked him and then clinked her glass with his before she took a big sip. Jessica joined them a few minutes later, polishing off her own drink as she plonked herself down in the chair next to Tilly.

"I've just pulled," she told them excitedly, indicating over to the bar where a handsome man sat looking over at them with a smile. "You don't mind if I head off do you? He's invited me to go to a nightclub that his friend owns for some cocktails, cool or what? Unless you want to come with us?" she asked, her voice a high-pitched squeal. Jessica was obviously excited by her handsome prize, but Tilly was feeling tired, ready for her bed, and so shook her head.

"No thanks, Jess, but you go ahead. Just be careful, okay?" she replied, giving Jessica a hug before her friend took off towards her hot new friend and waved them goodbye from the doorway. Tilly took another swig of her drink then stood up, determined to head off home for some much needed sleep, but then fell back in her seat as a woozy head rush hit her. "Whoa, I don't feel too great," she told Trey, who helped her up and took her arm. Tilly hadn't thought she'd even had that much to drink, but put it down to her tiredness, and took Trey's arm gratefully as he helped her stand, keeping a tight hold of him while she swayed unsteadily on her feet.

"Come on, let's go and get you in a taxi," he told her, rolling his eyes at Andre as they left, the look telling their boss he was happy to help her get home, and Andre smiled and waved them goodbye from the bar.

Trey hailed a cab, slipping Tilly inside and then giving his address to the driver. She heard him and tried to say no, she wanted to go to the penthouse, but no words escaped her lips. Tilly was quickly starting to lose consciousness so wasn't able to tell Trey to take her straight home. Her arms and legs grew incredibly heavy somehow as well, and her eyelids began to droop within seconds of the taxi setting off from the bar. She was in a deep, dreamless sleep almost instantly, and tried to wake herself up, not feeling comfortable sleeping in the back of a taxi, but it was no use.

After the short car ride, Tilly was vaguely aware of being carried down some steps towards a dark basement flat, and she knew for sure that she was not at her penthouse. She tried to move, but her body was still too heavy and unresponsive, so she slumped back into the strong arms that held her, feeling nauseous and worried.

"Home…need to go…" she mumbled.

"It's okay. I've got you," she heard Trey say quietly, and then she felt herself being placed down onto a comfortable, flat surface that she assumed must be a bed before she dozed off uncontrollably again for a few more minutes. She hated feeling so powerless, but hoped a good sleep would sort out her foolish drunkenness, and then she would head home in the morning.

Tilly stirred again a short while later when she heard a strange clicking noise by her ear. She opened her eyes to find Trey leaning over her, his dark-skinned face close to hers as he fiddled with something above her head, his expression calm but focussed. She was much more lucid this time and managed to figure out her surroundings a little better. He'd laid her down on a small bed, just like she'd thought, but her arms were pulled up above her head for some reason. She tried to move, but quickly realised that the clicking sound she'd heard had been Trey locking a pair of handcuffs closed over her left wrist, restraining her arm above her against the metal bed frame. He was now securing a second pair over her other wrist, ensuring that it too was firmly held in place on the top right-hand corner of the bed frame.

"No," she tried to plead, but her voice came out as nothing more than a mumbled sigh.

"Why would you do that to yourself, Tilly?" Trey wondered aloud as he stroked his hand over her burn mark, shaking his head as though disappointed in her for some strange reason. "You could've been so perfect," he added, murmuring to himself.

Tilly looked up at him in surprise. She feared the worst and suspected he didn't have the most honourable of intentions towards her, bile rising in her throat as she contemplated what to do next.

"Trey, what are you doing?" she asked, her speech slurring in her haze as she tried to question him.

"Ah, good, you're finally awake," he replied with a smile, sitting beside her as he leered over at her. "I hope you're comfortable?" Trey then asked with a sly grin.

"You drugged me," Tilly replied, suddenly remembering the drink he'd bought her from the bar.

"Yeah, sorry about that," he replied unashamedly—clearly not sorry at all. He then leaned closer, stroking her cheek as he continued to smile down at her. She shuddered, his touch making her want to wretch. "You really are a very beautiful woman, Tilly. I can tell you make yourself out to be such a good girl, but underneath that seemingly normal exterior there's a bad, dirty girl just dying to come out and play. You hide it well, but I know you can give me what I crave, what I need, and have always looked for in a woman. I've been watching you for a while, coveting you, but I'm a patient man, so I've just been waiting for the opportune moment to take you. And here we are at long last," he told her, and Tilly flinched, both scared and angered by his disturbing little speech.

She had no idea how, or if, she might get away. One thing she did know for sure though, was that things were about to get ugly.

CHAPTER THIRTY-FIVE

Tilly tried focussing every ounce of energy she had on Blake, calling to him via her thoughts. She knew the full moon was still two weeks away and he wouldn't be able to come and save her himself tonight, but she hoped and prayed that perhaps he could get an order to one of the other demons who might be able to come and help her. She closed her eyes and prayed to her master, desperate for a saviour.

When nothing happened, Tilly looked up at the man she'd thought she knew so well, the man she'd believed was her friend, and decided to try a different approach.

"I wouldn't do this if I were you, Trey," she told him, coming around a little more as the drug he'd given her continued to wear off. "You don't know who you're messing with. Let me go now before something bad happens to you," she said, looking up at him with determination and her most threatening stare.

"Oh really?" he asked, laughing off her threat with a genuinely amused look on his face. "What? Do you think you can kick my arse, Tilly, or have you got a secret I need to find out? Don't tell me, I'll find out for myself just how sweet you taste, and I don't mind if you wanna try fighting me off. I get much more of a kick out of it anyway if you struggle," he joked, sliding one hand down her body and cupping Tilly between the thighs, his palm lingering over her mound as a delighted smile spread across his face. She squirmed away, groaning with disgust, while he just laughed harder from beside her.

Trey then reached into his pocket and pulled out a small vial of clear liquid, which he held up for Tilly to see. "Don't worry darling, you'll be nice and relaxed again in a minute, and then I'll have my fun," he told her, and she shuddered. After peering up at the vial in his hands for a moment, Tilly then let a laugh escape her lips, coming up from deep inside of her, and Trey looked down at his captive in surprise.

"Fucking try it," she warned, still laughing. "My master is gonna make your life a living hell, your afterlife, too. You have absolutely no fucking clue. You think you like it bad and dirty now, just wait and see what's in store for you, Trey."

He seemed genuinely confused by her strange threat, but carried on regardless and leaned over her, grabbing her chin and then dribbling some of the sour liquid into Tilly's mouth. She immediately spat it back at him, and Trey slapped her across the face, hard. She cried out as her cheek burned red-hot. He grinned, seeming to have enjoyed that, and poured more of the drug into her mouth, before then holding it closed along with her nose until he was happy that she'd swallowed it. Tilly gasped for breath once he released her, and tried to make herself sick, but it was no use. The medicine worked quickly, and she drifted back off into a forced sleep, the dark haze bearing down on her uncontrollably despite her efforts to fight it.

Trey stood from the bed and wiped his face clean before he made his way over to a chest of drawers to the side of the room. He pulled out a large, sharp knife from the top drawer, lifting it to his eye to check the blade before he placed it on the top of the unit and headed off to the en-suite to freshen up. He was looking forward to taking Tilly in every way his sinister mind could fathom, and then his final act would be to use that blade to end her miserable life, but not before torturing her with it. She would be a bloody, unrecognisable mess by the time he was done, but oh-so beautiful in a gloriously gory way.

He didn't notice Tilly's unconscious body twitch ever so slightly as he wandered off, nor did he see as she opened her eyes and looked around the room, taking it all in for a moment with a strange, powerful stare. Instead of her usual blue colour, she somehow had deep green eyes now, and a dark hue settled in the air around her on the bed, the shadows seeming to cling to Tilly as though drawn towards her.

Blake had possessed his lover from his home in the underworld, his dark power now coursing within her human body as her own consciousness slept on thanks to the drug Trey had forced into her. He could not be thwarted by the drugs coursing through her system though, and grinned as he contemplated how best to take care of the foolish human who dared try to defile his lover.

There were two loud snaps of bone as Blake broke Tilly's thumbs in order to slide her hands out of the cuffs. He didn't feel the pain of the break, but knew Tilly would suffer for it when she woke up. However, there was no other choice right now and he knew she would be grateful for his help in the long run. Her possessed body creaked and snapped, moving slowly while Blake got used to his new role as puppeteer. He then made her stand and walk over towards the wooden unit, moving slowly and carefully before grabbing the knife, just as Trey emerged from the bathroom.

"What the fuck?" he blurted out in surprise as he took in the sight of her. "What happened to your eyes?" he asked, staring into them in shocked bewilderment for a moment while he watched her weak hands tighten around the handle of the blade.

A deep voice that was not Tilly's answered him, sending chills down Trey's spine.

"I'm going to enjoy this," she said with a wicked grin. "And then you'll be mine to torture for all eternity you foolish little shit. You should've just listened to her warnings, Trey," she told him, and his eyes opened wide in shock.

"Who are you?" he asked, his voice a trembling whisper as he peered fearfully into the eyes that did not belong to Tilly.

"You do not know me now, or what I can do to you, but you will know—soon enough. When you reach the gates of Hell my friend, be sure to tell them that your soul belongs the Black Prince," Blake told him as he stepped forward, using Tilly as his conduit.

Trey tried to run towards the doorway, but one final step forward and a slash from her possessed body slit his throat with the knife in her hands with one swing. Blake hoped to feel the satisfying squelch of muscle as he tore his flesh open, but was denied the gratification of the kill. He couldn't feel the way his own hands would feel, but he could see well enough, and enjoyed the view tremendously.

Blood spurted forwards, covering Tilly from head to toe while Trey fell onto his knees before her and then bled out in seconds. Blake watched for a moment, sensing the angel of death as it claimed Trey's soul, but he soon felt himself begin to weaken. He couldn't hold on, and although he hated to, he knew he had to leave Tilly behind. His consciousness slipped away and she fell to the floor next to the dead body of her would-be rapist and murderer, fast asleep like she'd meant to be the entire time.

CHAPTER THIRTY-SIX

Tilly came to a few hours later, and the agony of her hands brought her round in record time. It still took her a few moments to properly wake up though, however her panting breath and trembling body let her know she was in shock. She held up her throbbing hands and inspected them, finding her thumbs completely immovable, hanging limply in their sockets. Tilly stifled a gag when the pain then flooded her system, and she tried to remember what'd happened, but the agony reverberated through her again, the shooting pain travelling up and down her entire body before the realisation finally kicked in.

Fear then added to her adrenaline-fuelled state, giving her strength. It made the pain subside suddenly, and the memory of what Trey had done came crashing back to her. Tilly blinked, clearing her blurred eyes and she ran one of her hands down to her hips, discovering that her clothes were thankfully still on and that her jeans hadn't been removed after all. She quickly and gratefully realised that she hadn't been sexually abused, in spite of what Trey had been promising to do to her before she'd drifted away again thanks to his foul tasting drug.

Tilly sat up, looking down at herself. Her clothes were clinging to her skin, seemingly soaked in blood. She could see it everywhere and even taste it, so she spat on to the floor to her left, which was when she finally saw Trey's dead eyes boring into her from a foot or so away, and she screamed.

Only when she was hoarse from screaming and exhausted, could Tilly finally calm herself down long enough to take in the bloody scene around her, still confused and scared, but she somehow knew she was safe. She'd been lying in the pool of blood that'd seemingly come from Trey's neck wound, and was covered in it from head to toe. A thick spray had also covered her torso and face, and then the pool of blackness had surrounded her while she'd lay next to him unconscious. But she didn't know how on earth she'd gotten there.

Tilly shivered with both shock and the cold. The wet blood had already started to dry on her skin, and the thought of it made her shudder even harder. She looked down at her hands again, realising that they were now thankfully free from the cuffs he'd put her in, but that they still throbbed painfully and were swelling more and more thanks to her attempts at movement. She was still utterly confused, unsure how she'd managed to stop him, but was also relieved that he'd not succeeded in abusing or killing her—or all the terrible things between. Tilly was positive that Blake must be to thank for her safety, and wondered if perhaps he'd heard her prayers after all.

She crawled over to her handbag where Trey had left it by the door the night before and searched for her mobile phone, her broken thumbs making it very difficult to dig around in it properly. She eventually found it, covering the screen in blood as she tried to unlock the handset, her hands completely refusing to work. Tilly eventually dialled the police, managing to say to the call handler that she'd been attacked and needed help right away, and she was grateful for the GPS tracking function when she then felt herself fading again. She fell backwards onto the cold ground, her phone skating across the floor beside her, but it thankfully stayed connected to the concerned woman on the other end, who already had a patrol on the way.

***

When she finally came to again, it was two days later and Tilly was laid in a hospital bed. Both of her thumbs had been operated on, and each hand was now encased in a large, heavy plaster cast. She opened her eyes and listened to Gwen and Renee while they sat beside her, chatting quietly to one another in two armchairs. Renee screamed when she saw Tilly watching them, and then jumped up from her seat excitedly. Gwen grinned and grabbed a glass of water for her along with a straw, which Tilly gulped down, eager and grateful for the nourishment. She then peered up at her friends, enjoying the feeling of being safe and happy for a moment, before she then laid her head back and cried uncontrollably, the tears flowing from her in hot currents. Their arms then enveloped her, both of them crying, too.

Later, once she'd calmed down, Beelzebub came to see her. He smiled down at Tilly while he sat down beside her, but couldn't hide his pain at seeing her this way. She'd been cleaned up by the nurses so was no longer covered in blood, but Tilly was sure she could still taste it in her mouth, or maybe that was just in her mind. He held her thickly plastered hand and tugged at her white hospital gown with a smirk, remaining playful as ever, desperately trying to cheer her up.

"I'm pretty sure you're going to be in trouble for wearing this," he joked, making her smile. She had wondered the same thing herself, but vaguely remembered Blake coming to her in a hazy dream to tell her he loved her and not to worry about anything, he'd handle it.

"Well, I'm assuming that my master is somehow to blame for my broken thumbs, so I think he'll have to let me off this once," she replied with a grin and Beelzebub nodded, confirming her suspicions, but then looked down at her seriously again.

"The police are going to need to talk to you, Tilly. Just say you don't remember anything, okay?" he told her. "We've got friends on the inside that'll brush this all under the carpet, not that you'd be in trouble for finishing that guy off anyway," he said, looking down at the hand he still held, seeming thoughtful.

"So it was me who did it then. I killed him? Surely *he* must have helped with that somehow?" she asked the demon and he nodded, looking back into her blue eyes, his dark-brown ones soft and warm, yet protective and fierce.

"Yeah, he possessed you. It really took it out of him, and that's why he had to leave you there like he did, but he knew he had to do something. There was no other choice, no matter it took. None of us could track you down, and we realise now that Trey lives, well lived, next door to a fucking white church, that'll be why our radars were scrambled. Fucker," he added and Tilly nodded in understanding, figuring the church's threshold probably covered the flat, effectively cloaking her from the dark beings. "They found videos of him with other women, raping and then killing them. There was a camera recording you, too…" he tailed off, as though he felt like he'd said too much.

Tilly slunk back onto her pillow, disgusted and annoyed at herself that she'd never had a clue, never realised what Trey was up to. She'd had no idea, and had trusted him as both a colleague and a friend. She felt like such a fool.

"Why is it I'm nearly always surrounded by demons and yet it's the humans who are the most evil?" she wondered aloud, and

Beelzebub shook his head, unsure how to answer that.

The next day, the police came to talk with her, but they were very understanding and didn't actually question her too much. All they needed from her was an official statement.

"The only thing I remember is falling asleep on the bed after Trey handcuffed and drugged me, and then I woke up in a pool of his blood on the floor," she said, which really was the truth. They nodded, wrote in their notebooks, and then left, one of them giving a nod to Beelzebub as he went. Tilly knew she wouldn't have to worry about the backlash, but was surprised when she put on the television her face was plastered all over it, and she winced. Reporters had picked up on her terrible story and were camped out at both her parents' house and at the hospital. Luckily, they couldn't get to her room though, or into the penthouse, so when she was discharged later that day, Beelzebub teleported them straight there. The reporters would find another story to tell soon enough, and in the meantime, Tilly desperately needed her privacy and rest.

She rang her mum, and after a frenzied explanation to Bianca about it all, quickly set about giving her an update on how she was doing. She also told her not to come to London, to stay put at home and she would call them every day to check in. Her parents weren't happy but agreed, knowing that Tilly was a headstrong girl and that she'd become even more independent during the past few months.

Jessica also rang her, having been refused entry to both her hospital room and the penthouse by her demonic guards. Tilly answered, but was too tired to chat, and just told her not to worry. She said she'd be in touch soon but could do with some space right now, which was actually very true.

CHAPTER THIRTY-SEVEN

Tilly tried to rest, but her fretful dreams kept waking her up, dripping with sweat and shaking uncontrollably in fear, no matter how hard she tried to reason with herself that Trey was gone. Blake tried to come into them at times, attempting to control her nightmares and calm her down, but he couldn't keep the awful visions at bay, and Tilly soon began forcing herself to stay awake instead of letting herself drift off for her much needed rest. She would watch television all night or jog for miles on the treadmill in the penthouse's gym in an attempt to keep herself awake. Her friends stayed there with her, never leaving her alone because they knew she needed the company as well as some help to dress and wash herself, but even with them there by her side, she still could not rest easy.

Blake came to Earth as soon as the moon was full again, finding Tilly locked away in the penthouse bedroom, fear and lack of sleep almost driving her crazy. She jumped on him, attempting to seduce her lover the instant he arrived. She wanted nothing more than for him to take her mind away from all the terrible memories and thoughts that she just couldn't shake. While happy that she wanted him so desperately, Blake refused her advances.

He immediately helped Tilly get washed and changed, and then he teleported her to a tall office building somewhere in the city without an explanation. The night guard led them straight into the dark foyer, and the exhausted young woman followed despite her confusion. Blake placed a strong hand on her back, leading Tilly up to a small room without a word. He then stopped at the doorway, letting her enter alone. But she hesitated, not wanting to be without his strong, reassuring hold on her.

"This is where I leave you, for now. I'll be here when you're finished," he said, guiding her forward with a gentle push on her back.

A kind-faced woman had been sat waiting for her inside the room, and she stood and bowed to Blake formally before addressing Tilly directly, ushering for her to sit down on the sofa opposite. He stepped back and shut the door behind him, leaving the two women alone.

"Hello Tilly, my name's Daisy," the woman said, her voice soft and calm. "Your master cannot enter this room, nor can he hear your thoughts while you're in here. This is a private and safe place, and you can be truly open and honest without having to worry about anyone listening in. He's asked me to help you to get through your fears and worries, and to help you overcome the terrible incident that recently happened to you."

Tilly felt herself instantly relax in the comfortable armchair, taking the woman in silently for a moment. She must've been around forty years old, with long brown hair and soft brown eyes, and she seemed genuine enough.

"So, are you a witch or something?" Tilly asked, and Daisy shook her head.

"No, I'm human. But, I have been marked by the demon Astaroth for almost twenty years, and in that time I've learned a lot about the Satanic world. I'm a psychiatrist by day, so I can help you to deal with everything that has happened to you with insight, knowledge of the human psyche, and the simple fact that you can be open and honest with me about the demonic areas of our world." Daisy gave her another soft smile, and Tilly already felt calmer. She nodded in understanding, but let her new acquaintance continue rather than speak up yet. "You can talk to me without worrying or hiding the details like you must've had to with your human friends and family. I have warded this office with talismans and runes to ensure we have privacy, and your master has agreed to my terms," she added, reassuring Tilly and putting her even more at ease. She looked at Daisy, surprised but glad that this woman was sitting before her right now, and guessed she hadn't realised just how much she needed to talk with someone about it all.

Tilly was already grateful that Blake had bought her here and was soon ready to get started. "So," Daisy continued, sensing her new client relax even more. "Here's what I already know about you. I know that your name is Matilda Mayfair, that your master is the Black Prince, and that you recently suffered a traumatic experience that has stopped you from being able to function properly, both mentally and physically," she said, waving a hand to indicate she meant her broken thumbs and Tilly nodded. "I'd like you to tell me about it, Tilly, but I'm going to need all of it. Let's start with the first moment you became aware of our world," she said, smiling over at her as she grabbed her notepad and readied her pen over it.

They spent a little while talking about the night she'd first met Brent, and the feelings she'd had for him. Tilly started to tell Daisy that she no longer felt the same way about him, but she shushed her, telling her that there was no need to feel like she had to explain. That she had nothing to prove, and Tilly knew she was right.

They soon moved on, discussing the strange night she'd been marked by Lilith, and the big reveal on Halloween, along with Blake's reaction to her that night before he'd then replaced Lilith's mark with his own. Tilly also opened up about her feelings for him and how they'd grown stronger until the day in the Alps. She told her about his punishment that day and the distance she'd felt afterwards before Blake finally had let himself show his true feelings for her.

Tilly was completely honest with Daisy, and it was a weight off her shoulders to talk about his mood swings and the harsh punishment he'd put her through with someone at last. She hadn't been able to talk things through with anyone before, not even Gwen or Renee, and it was really very cleansing. Daisy let her do most of the talking, asking Tilly questions along the way to help her open up further, but not taking over the outpouring of her thoughts and memories at all.

She finally caught up with the most recent events, and talking about her night in Trey's flat was tough. The scars were still fresh, but Daisy helped her understand the strange night a little better, explaining the possession and helping Tilly sort through her scrambled thoughts. By the time she came away from Daisy's office she felt drained but much more level headed, and was more than glad she'd opened up to someone at last.

Blake was waiting for her when she left the small room, and Tilly sensed it as her last few hours lock away in her mind, shielded from him magically, and she was glad. Despite having nothing to hide from her master, she still appreciated the chance to have some privacy. She and Daisy had arranged to meet again in a few days and would keep on doing so until she felt she no longer wanted or needed her help, and Tilly was looking forward to it.

Blake thanked Daisy for her assistance and then quickly teleported Tilly back to the master bedroom of the penthouse without another word. He kissed her deeply, sensing the calmness in his beautiful, yet damaged lover now thanks to her session with the counsellor and was glad he'd taken her. She smiled up at him and Blake knew she was glad to be in his warm and protective embrace again at last, and he adored how having him close soothed her so much.

"Bed," Blake told her with a sly grin, but then walked over to the chest of drawers and pulled out some black cotton pyjama trousers, which he changed into and then climbed under the thin sheets rather than instigating anything sexual with her. Tilly smiled, she wanted more than just sleep thanks to the closeness and deep kisses that'd stirred her hormones wonderfully, but knew better than to disobey even his more playful orders. She could understand why he wanted her to rest, and she could already feel the fatigue starting to well up inside of her again.

She moved over to the drawers and pulled open one of hers before sliding into a black nightdress and climbing into bed with him, snuggling next to Blake who pulled her closer, pressing her into him while he turned and faced Tilly as he lay on his side. One arm went under her neck to support her head and then cradled her around the shoulders, while he slid the other around Tilly's ribs to her back, and cuddled her into him even more. He also pulled his top leg up and placed it over hers to cocoon her, pulling his lover closer, wanting nothing more than to keep her safe and make Tilly feel warm, protected, and snug in his tight grip.

There was no fighting him, not that she even tried. She fell asleep almost instantly, relaxing at last, and feeling safe as she drifted off into a blissful slumber.

CHAPTER THIRTY-EIGHT

Tilly stood at the door to Trey's flat, looking in at the bloody scene before her. She trembled—scared stiff, and desperately wanted to run away, yet felt as though a mysterious and powerful force was pulling her inside uncontrollably.

"No," said a voice from behind her, breaking her panicked silence, and Tilly turned to see Blake looking down at her from the top of the steps which led down to Trey's basement flat from the street. He put his hand out, looking her in the eye, and urging Tilly to take it. He was her beacon now, not the carnage behind, and she pushed herself towards him. Up she climbed, towards salvation rather than anguish. She reached the top step and took his outstretched hand in hers, noticing that her hands were healed in her dream, which felt wonderful. "Good girl," he said, squeezing her hand as he pulled her up the final step. "Now, where do you want to go?" Blake then asked her, seemingly happy to follow her lead.

The view before them changed from the busy London street to a black, blank canvas for Tilly's subconscious imagination to imbue. She wasn't actually sure where she wanted to go, so just tried to think back to her times of having fun with her friends, focussing her mind back to before the permanent sense of fear had become all too familiar inside of her.

The Diablo Circus suddenly came into view before them, lit up brightly against the night's sky, and music was blaring from inside the tent. She looked down at her feet, embarrassed by her choice, but Blake took her chin in his hand and lifted it, looking into her blue eyes once she raised them to meet his. "I don't mind, but I assume there won't be any memories of your private time with Brent?" he asked, only half joking, but remaining playful as he peered down at her, his eyes full of warmth.

She nodded and led him inside, linking her healed fingers through his as they moved through the crowd. They took two seats near the front and watched as her memories of the amazing and death-defying feats by the performers flashed by. Brent to the stage and wowed them with his fast paced and exciting juggling show, and then Jackson's fire breathing and David's acrobatics entertained them before Lucas and the others took to the stage and performed various other tantalising routines for their private, fantasy show. Tilly gasped and laughed along with the other imaginary people in the crowd throughout, a huge smile on her face as she focussed all of her energy on the performance, relaxing more with each passing moment. Blake set aside his jealousy and enjoyed watching her, glad that she was having a nice dream again at last. He was glad to give her this, Tilly could tell, and watched the show alongside her without a word of disapproval or to steer her away from the past.

Tilly slept for half a day, finally waking up when the bright sunshine streamed in through the huge window and hit her face, making her flinch. The pressure she then felt on her bladder forced her even quicker into consciousness and she blinked awake, surprised to find that Blake was still exactly where he'd been when she'd fallen asleep in his protective embrace the night before. He hadn't left, and more than that—he was fast asleep in front of her, his arms and legs still wrapped around her tightly. Blake never slept, not on Earth anyway, and she was shocked to see him there, snoring quietly and seemingly dreaming as he rested.

His handsome, relaxed features were soft, and he actually looked the age he portrayed himself to be—young and almost human-like. Tilly gazed at him for a few moments before pulling out of his grasp and heading into the bathroom, and was surprised that he didn't wake up when she moved away. But, she was glad to have a few quiet minutes to herself as she used the toilet, brushed her teeth, and then ran a hot bath. She checked the bedroom again, finding him still snoozing in the bed, so she stripped off and slipped into the hot, soapy water, having quickly put plastic bags over the casts on her wrists to ensure they didn't get wet.

She lay there for a few minutes, smiling as she relaxed and enjoyed her clear mind at last, remembering their fun dream together as she rested her aching muscles.

"Ha-hum," came a fake cough from the doorway, making her jump, and Tilly looked back to see a smiling but bleary eyed Blake looking down at her.

"What? I needed to pee," she told him with a small laugh.

"So you ran a bath? Strange girl," he replied with a smirk, laughing and shaking his head. He came into the bathroom and leaned against the sink, watching her intently.

"Mind if I join you?" Blake then asked, while slipping off his pyjama trousers and sliding behind Tilly in the wonderfully hot water. She didn't mind at all, and lay back against his warm chest as he cradled her in his strong arms, making sure to hold her waist and let her arms stay on the bath's sides while she lay in between his open legs. "Feeling better?" he asked, and she groaned an almost inaudible confirmation in reply. "Rested?"

"Yes," she answered, more clearly this time.

"Happy?"

"Yes."

"Hungry?"

"No."

"No? Hmm, how about, horny?" he asked finally, reaching down to cup between her thighs with the palm of his hand.

"Yes," she replied, and gasped when he quickly opened her legs and slid his own closed beneath her so that Tilly straddled him backwardly. Blake then lifted her up and onto his ready cock in one quick move, and her breath hitched in her throat.

She leaned into him, arching her back to welcome him deeper and letting her master move her up and down in the hot suds on top of him. It wasn't long until Tilly groaned and stiffened as her first climax swept over her and Blake gripped her tighter to him, pushing deeper while her muscles clenched over his hardness. He continued to move her like that until he neared his own glorious release, cradling Tilly in his strong arms as she revelled in her intense climaxes over and over again until the tub shook around them and he finally came.

The pair then hopped out of the bath and straight into a hot shower, Blake helping Tilly to wash her hair and still trembling body, before dropping to his knees before her and taking her swollen clit in his mouth. She cried out as she came for him again, the wonderfully intense release sending her over the edge one more time.

CHAPTER THIRTY-NINE

The pair relaxed on the sofa together later that afternoon after devouring a huge pizza and an entire tub of ice cream. They were each wearing baggy tracksuit trousers and t-shirts while they lazed and just enjoyed one another's company, all formality blissfully out the window. Blake was sat upright with his back against the thick sofa cushions and Tilly was laid lengthways, her back on the arm of the sofa and her feet in his lap as they chatted. She adored their downtime, and loved how naturally comfortable they could be in one another's company.

"I was wondering—if you don't mind—what do you do while you're in Hell?" she asked him, feeling eager to know more about her lover. Blake smiled, and was more than happy to answer her questions. In all honesty, he was glad that she'd still been thinking of him during their times apart. Her question had caught him slightly off guard at first though, and thinking back, he was sure that she was the first person ever to have actually asked him about himself. Tilly was the first person he'd known in his long life that didn't just automatically know all about him, and yet he loved that she wanted to know, how she was genuinely interested in him and his dark life.

"Well, there are loads of things I have to do on an official basis. Boring stuff really, like council meetings and helping to initiate the demons and welcome new souls," he told her, rubbing her feet absentmindedly.

She laughed, unable to help but think that those responsibilities sounded anything but boring to her. "My main role is simply being the Black Prince. All of our orders come from my mother and I'm next in line. Luna, Lottie and I pass her decrees down the chain of command, and at least one of us are with or near to her at all times. I also have my own dark council, and it's our responsibility to give the demons their classifications. It can be a long process at times because we have a set of tasks the demons have to complete in order to progress higher up the chain. If they want to move up the levels, they have to come through me and succeed under my council's watchful eyes. We oversee the trials for humans who want to become new demons too, like I did with Lucas, not that there have actually been many," he told her, and Tilly's mind was racing, trying to imagine him sat at an altar beside the Dark Queen, issuing orders and ruling by her side. He smiled over at her, his green eyes ablaze as he read her thoughts, enjoying her intrigue and imagination.

Tilly realised after a few seconds that he'd mentioned another name, Lottie, and as she pondered over whom that might be, her mind was suddenly drawn back to the first night that they'd met. She remembered Brent's explanation of Blake's royal family, and his other sister, the Unholy Princess. She opened her mouth to ask him, but he'd read her mind already and shook his head sternly, stopping her in her tracks. "You don't need to know, Tilly. Forget I ever said anything, I should never have said her name up here," Blake said, looking worried at his accidental slip up.

"I won't tell a soul," she promised him, smiling gently. "Please, carry on," she insisted and he took a deep breath and shook off his unease. He knew she meant it, and that he could trust her.

"Okay. Well, I have my coven as you know, they do my bidding and assist me with pretty much everything, so they need me there to give them orders and instructions, too," he added, making Tilly think of Lena and the way she'd looked at him so lovingly that day at the penthouse.

"And what do you do for fun?" she then asked him, hoping that he was not going to say, *Lena*.

"If I'm being honest, I sometimes used to spend my quiet hours teleporting to one of their chambers for a quick fuck," he said, having read her jealous thoughts, and Tilly squirmed. "But not anymore," he added, looking over to her solemnly as he spoke. "I would fulfil my urges and then pull out and teleport away, never giving a shit about staying for cuddles and romance. But I haven't been with anyone else since I marked you, Tilly. I want you to know that," he said, and she smiled, taken aback slightly, but completely reassured.

"I'm glad to hear it," she answered honestly.

"There's another side to my duties though, and it isn't pretty. I sometimes have to deliver punishments, but only if it's someone from my own coven or one of my followers, otherwise there are others who are required to take care of it. Demons with, how should I say it? *Specialities*, in certain areas," he said, looking back down at her feet thoughtfully.

Tilly detected a note of sadness in him then, like a hard truth that was trying to surface, but she didn't dare ask any more of him. She knew he might be thinking of the day he'd punished her at the lodge, and didn't want to talk about it now either. If anything, she wanted to push away that awful memory forever.

He looked over into her eyes, reading her reluctance to talk about the subject, but he needed her to know, and Tilly could sense that he wanted to open up about it despite it being painful for him as well. "I am never going to let myself lose control of my anger with you again, Tilly," Blake promised, needing her to hear it. "I will just teleport away next time, if ever, I feel that way. The burn I gave you was too much, let alone the way I treated you like a cheap fuck afterwards. I couldn't control myself that day, but there's no excuse." Blake took a deep breath and sighed. "I've been working on it. Luna's been helping me, but my cold nature is just too easy to keep hold of. I'm comfortable with my darkness, I don't fear it, but I've feared change for so long simply because I knew that I'd have a lot to deal with once I let myself open up. I'm slowly letting down my walls, but it's not easy for me. I've been this way for a very long time, and it's all I know. This jet-black heart of mine needs time to change," he told her, massaging her feet and calves as he spoke, finding comfort in the contact.

Tilly appreciated his honesty and smiled softly across at him, but said nothing. She didn't want to interrupt his thoughtful admissions, but was glad he felt as though he could finally open up to her. "I know how it feels to be punished severely, and I never, *ever* wanted that for you. Being controlled by someone that way can be so lonely, and trying to be what they expect you to be does nothing but diminish the real you, until you cannot be sure who that person even is any more," he continued, looking across at her again and Tilly nodded, trying to understand. She couldn't help wonder when or how he'd been punished or had suffered so much in the past though, thinking to herself that surely his mother would've never allowed him such a torturous upbringing?

Blake read her quizzical thoughts and stared at her with pure fear in his gaze. He then took a deep breath, as though steadying himself in preparation for his hardest admission yet. Tilly opened her mouth to speak, wanting to tell him to stop, wanting him to know he didn't need to tell her if it was too hard, but he raised a hand to quieten her and shook his head.

He might not fear his darkness, but he'd been afraid once, and that terror had consumed him so entirely the repercussions still affected him now. Blake felt a sudden need to let go of it at long last, to keep on going with his hard confessions, and carried on regardless of the ache in his chest. "Many years ago when Luna and I were children, just four years old, I did something foolish and terrible. I was a stubborn child, headstrong, disobedient, and strong willed. My mother was half human then, and she'd come to Earth for a while because she was getting sick." Blake paused. "You must never tell anyone this story, okay Tilly?" he asked, and she understood that what he was about to tell her wasn't information that'd be given out to just anybody. She felt honoured to hear his story, and nodded.

"I promise, you can trust me," she told him, and wholeheartedly meant it.

"I know. Okay, well…the moon bound our father, Luna and I even then, and we were strengthened by our time in Hell, but she wasn't. Her human side suffered and my mother became ill. She had to stay here on Earth until she was strong again, so we came to visit her each time the moon was full. We had to stay within the Satanic church's protective threshold for our safety. But, I couldn't ever understand why. I was blind to the truth, and didn't want to hear it or care for their explanations why," Blake continued, looking sad. "My all-powerful father was somehow scared to set foot outside, to take me out into the big wide world I so craved to see, and I felt as though he was a fool, as if I knew better—and I pitied him for his weakness. I repeatedly sneaked out, despite their warnings, and even persuaded Luna to come along one night," he said, and then stopped dead, his eyes blackening slightly.

Blake then took another deep breath, as though the memory was hard for him to think about, let alone actually say aloud. "We were cornered, trapped by a coven of white witches, and then kidnapped. I soon realised that my parents had been right all along, but by then it was too late. It quickly became apparent that the witches didn't actually want us though, they only wanted her."

"Your mother?" Tilly whispered, and Blake nodded, his eyes swirling with more black specks as he peered over at her, but he remained calm and in control, and she trusted him to regulate those emotions like he'd just promised.

"She came to rescue us, not that she could even do anything as she was vastly outnumbered, but she left the safety of the church to find us anyway. They used her motherly love to lure her out of hiding, knowing we were the only things she would sacrifice herself for. It was a trap and she knew it, but came anyway." Blake paused for a moment, thinking back to the witches in the park and his and Luna's awful imprisonment in their own bodies all that time before. Regardless of the years that'd now passed, the memory of that night still festered like a deep well of regret that he somehow couldn't stop adding to. It haunted him. Tilly was the only being that'd made him feel as though that pool might slowly diminish, and strangely even his mother's forgiveness hadn't lessened the pain.

"Blake..." Tilly began, but he wasn't done. He had to carry on, and cut her off before she could try and tell him he shouldn't blame himself for what'd happened. He'd been told that by every being who'd been part of his upbringing in an attempt to soothe him, and it'd never once helped ease his guilt.

"It *was* my fault. We were taken away and they used us to blackmail her. I was sent back to our church not long before the moon waned, and my father took me straight back to Hell with him, questioning me about it for hours. He wanted to know every detail of where she was and who'd taken her, but I was just a boy, I had no idea. When I didn't give him good enough answers to satisfy his frenzied mind, he hit me across the face, hard. So hard that I flew across the room and slammed into the wall. I begged for his forgiveness, but he just grabbed me up off the floor, bellowed at me, and beat me over and over again. He screamed how I was to blame for her capture, and that I had to be punished for my insolence. He took out all of his frustration and anger on me, and I was powerless to stop him," Blake told her, his hands still on Tilly's legs, pushing harder and harder into her skin as he massaged them. His touch was so hard it bruised her, but she didn't say anything or try to pull out of his grasp, she was in too much shock at hearing his awful story to feel the bruises yet. "Luna was sent back to Hell soon afterwards too, but she was sick because the moon had begun to wane while she was there, and our high priestess had to take her away to heal her. Our mother, however, didn't come back. Her powerful captor had got what he wanted. We were just the loose ends, the leverage to get her to succumb to him," Blake added, letting go of Tilly at last.

He put his hands up to his face, running his fingers up through his dark hair as the painful memories flooded back to him. "I suffered greatly for my impudence, and for the repercussions of my actions. As punishment, my father sentenced me to endure all kinds of torture in the dungeons and fiery pits of Hell. He gave everyone involved an order of eternal silence—their minds magically forgetting all about what I'd endured. By the time the next full moon came around, my body was broken, along with my resolve, my stubbornness, and my will. I was just a tiny child and he broke me so very easily, I even thanked my father for the lessons he'd taught me, and ever since then I've been that way,

Tilly—cold, closed-off, and emotionless. I was so young when I learned those lessons, and they're hard for me to try and forget now. My father had left for Earth as soon as the moon was full again, while Luna and I stayed behind. He was consumed with finding her, and he never looked back. That was when I learned to focus on my anger instead of my happiness, my rage instead of my love."

"That's terrible, and truly awful that he could do that to you— his son. You were just a child and didn't deserve that no matter what you'd done. Where was she? Did he find her?" Tilly asked, hoping that he wouldn't mind her questions, but she was enthralled and was desperate to find out more. So much of it was hard to hear, but it helped her make sense of the words and actions she'd struggled to understand since meeting her dark and damaged master.

"I cannot tell you where she was, Tilly, but yes—he found her. The aftermath was awful though, and I didn't see either of my parents for another ten years. The ancient powers of dark and light were forced out of balance by a battle between the two, and the portals between the worlds were all closed. We were stuck in Hell while they were stuck on Earth, and we had no idea if or when they'd ever return to us." He took a deep breath and sighed again, and rubbed his eyes.

Tilly was lost in his awful story, but understood it was hard for him to tell her, and urged him on via her supportive thoughts. "Eventually, they did come home, in the interim we'd been raised by my parents most trusted witches, Dylan and Alma. They were my family, along with our Uncle Devin and Aunt Serena, but I was still the same broken, closed-off boy that my father had left behind. I was content in my misery, feeling as if I'd earned and deserved it, and no one but my father and I ever knew the real reasons why. I carried on that way long after she finally returned, refusing to change even then—I didn't feel worthy of her forgiveness. I knew I was to blame and that I could never make amends for my actions, so I didn't bother trying any more. My mother never learned the truth until she took the throne, her full power opening up some of the truths my father had kept hidden from her over their years together. She was a wreck, and disappeared for days. Her rage was truly phenomenal, and I can only assume she went off to dispose of my father once and for all, to make him pay for his many misdemeanours, but I might not ever know for sure," Blake added, reaching down to rub Tilly's feet again, but gently this time.

She let his powerful words sink in for a moment and then jumped up from where she'd been laying on the couch and climbed over to Blake, straddling him and looking down into his gorgeous green eyes tenderly.

"I'm sure she made him sorry for ever having laid a hand on you, and too bloody right. Thank you for telling me, I know it is hard for you to open up, especially over something as intense as this," she said, kissing him deeply as she peered down at him lovingly.

"No, thank you, Tilly. I would still be that dark, broken boy if it weren't for you. My black heart never cared for anything or anyone before you came along, and you've opened up something in me I'd pushed away for so many years," he said, kissing her back and holding her tightly in his arms. "And not just that. I've finally been able to realise just why he punished me so harshly, why he was so scared. When you have something you love so very much, it's like a part of you belongs to them. But, it makes you weak when you lose them, or if you ruin the bit of them they gave you in return. Being in love means that you then suddenly have something—everything—to lose, and you'll do anything to protect it." He kissed her again, and once more for good measure. "You scare the hell out of me. Love was never on my agenda, but somehow you gave yours to me anyway. I'll never break it again. I'll protect your love—protect you—forever, Tilly." Her heart pounded in her chest at his words, and she believed every one of them.

"I'll always be here, ready and willing to do whatever it takes to protect you as well. I won't fight you ever again, but I will fight *for* you—for us. Nothing will ever come between us again, I promise," she said assuredly, and she meant every single word. "You're my very own beautiful tragedy, and I want to be the one person you can truly trust, the only one who can soothe every one of those old wounds, Blake," she told him as she cradled him in her arms, and then jumped, realising what she'd just accidentally said. This time though, he didn't care that she'd spoken his name, and he looked up at her frightened expression with a smile.

"What am I going to do you with you? Naughty girl," he said, without a hint of anger behind his eyes when he laughed quietly to himself and pulled Tilly closer for another deep kiss.

CHAPTER FORTY

The pair of them relaxed on the sofa for a little while longer, neither talking. They simply let each other's deep and powerful words sink in for a while. Tilly couldn't help but imagine Blake as a small boy, being tortured and beaten by his father and she shed tears for that boy. She cradled the man beside her as tightly as she could in the hope that the broken child he once was might be soothed somehow as well. Blake buried his face in her hair, desperate not to fight his feelings. Instead, he let her thoughts spread through him, and he too let a few tears fall, no longer ashamed to admit his past, and wanting to move on at last.

Tilly eventually started to feel her hands throb beneath the casts again, and knew it was time for more medicine. After telling Blake, she climbed up off the sofa to go and grab some painkillers and a cup of water from the kitchen. Tilly needed to numb the pain that, despite her improved mood, continued to serve as a constant reminder of what'd happened, and she couldn't help but start uncontrollably thinking of Trey again while she was alone in the kitchen. She knew she'd done well to push it all aside and overcome the terrible ordeal as much as she had. It was all thanks to Blake's support and Daisy's therapy session, but the memory was still too fresh, and too raw, and it'd often still sneak into her thoughts here and there.

Blake looked up at her as she came back through to the living area, looking thoughtful.

"I have Trey's recording, Tilly," he said, looking over to her with a worried expression when she stopped dead halfway between the kitchen and the sofa. He'd been wondering for a while if she'd want to see it, but didn't know when might be the best time to ask. Blake had the only existing copy of it now, and was more than willing to destroy it if she asked him to, but had to let her decide. He'd read her mind and he knew that she had been thinking of the attack again though, and part of him wanted to get the viewing over with, so he decided to be forward.

"Put it on, I want to see," Tilly replied, stepping forward again, her face pale as she sat back down on the sofa, and he raised the remote to the television screen, clicking it on before selecting the file from the memory stick he'd put in the side of the television while she was in the kitchen.

An image quickly appeared on the huge flat-screen, showing a wide view of Trey's bedroom, empty at first, and then the two of them came inside. She watched as her so-called friend dragged her limply across the room and then laid her down on the bed and began securing her wrists with the handcuffs. Tilly was surprised to hear her own voice as she pleaded with him quietly after a few minutes, scared and trembling at first, and then followed by the strange and disturbing laugh that came shortly after when she'd tried to threaten him. The recording was hard to watch, especially when Trey ran his hand down over her body, his disgusting perversion urging him onwards despite her pleas, and all with that dark and sinister smile on his face that Tilly knew would haunt her forever.

Blake watched her rather than the screen. He'd seen it a couple of times already, and the macabre show had only helped to bring forth his acceptance of his love for her. He remembered every awful moment of how it'd felt thinking he'd lost this girl—his girl. There wasn't a word strong enough for the vengeance he wanted in her honour. He'd imprisoned Trey the moment his soul had arrived in Hell, but that wasn't enough. Blake wasn't against using his arsenal of evil tricks on his soul, and had already made Trey suffer more than any other in the depths of his private dungeon. None had wronged him like he had, and there was no merciful fate in store for him, only pain and degradation.

Blake read Tilly's responses to the video while she continued to watch, making sure it wasn't all too much for her, but he could tell that she was doing fine. If anything, she was actually intrigued more than upset by it, especially when her unconscious body then jerked slightly and opened its eyes on the screen.

"Green eyes," she whispered, looking at herself intently while she watched Blake take control of her unconscious body. She could see the darkness surrounding her on-screen image, a strong blackness that seemed to be drawn to her possessed form in the dim light. Tilly winced when she saw the face that was no longer her own look up at her cuffed wrists before leaning up on the mattress. Her possessed body pulled the metal at first, testing the bed frame for a sign of weakness, but then pushed down hard on first her left, then right thumb before wriggling them free of their restraints. The noise of the crack from each thumb was sickening, but Tilly didn't even flinch. She knew it was the only way that Blake could free her quickly enough.

Tilly's body then climbed up from the bed, moving slowly and jerking peculiarly as she grabbed the knife from atop the unit. She gasped and covered her mouth when she saw Trey emerge from the bathroom, hearing the deep voice that was not her own so clearly as it spoke to him, and then slid the knife over his exposed skin. Her on-screen body then dropped to the floor along with Trey's as he bled out, and then they were both perfectly still, lying side-by-side on the floor, drenched in his blood. "Wow, you weren't kidding about the whole, 'slit their throat and make you bathe in their blood,' threat were you?" she said with a gruff laugh, and Blake couldn't help but snicker, remembering his dark orders the night they first met.

Feeling suddenly overwhelmed, Tilly dropped the façade and looked over wide-eyed at him on the sofa, and stared into his face. She'd thought she knew, but realised she'd had no idea just how dark things had gotten in that bedroom. She sat back against the cushions, trying to make sense of it all, unable to understand just how Blake had managed to possess her all the way from Hell, but at the same time, was eternally grateful that he had.

"It's very difficult to possess someone, Tilly, not at all how they make it out in the movies," he whispered, trying to explain the strange image to her as he switched off the television. "It was only possible because of our strong bond. Without that and the extra power Alma had to summon for me with my mother's permission, you wouldn't have survived his assault. I'm sorry I had to leave you straight away once he was dead. I was too weak and couldn't stay to help you escape the flat, but I knew that you'd wake up once the drugs wore off and was absolutely certain that you would then be safe," Blake told her, seemingly angry with himself for not having been stronger for her. Tilly stayed silent for a few more minutes, letting what she'd just seen and heard sink in.

"Thank you. I guess it was just so weird to watch, and I can't think what else to say, other than that I hope you make him pay, I hope he's gonna suffer?" she finally asked him, not sure how else to respond to seeing the video or what to say to her master about it all, and he nodded.

She was grateful that he'd acted, knowing now how it wasn't easy for him to have done so, and she focussed on his protective urges instead of the strange and sickening scene she'd just witnessed. Tilly then hugged herself, pulling her legs up underneath her protectively, and she was glad when Blake pulled her into his strong arms again. She was so appreciative for what he'd done and used that gratitude to help force away all her questions and fears, knowing he had and would always take care of her, no matter what it took.

"He will do nothing but suffer for all eternity, my love, make no mistake about that. I could've lost you to him and his depraved fetishes, how could I not do something? You are mine, Tilly. My friend, my lover, and my future. No one will ever come between that again," he promised, kissing the top of her head affectionately.

It felt good to belong to another so entirely, and it was freeing to know he'd always be there to care for and protect her. Tilly knew she was more than in love with him now. She was a slave to him and his darkness, but had bound herself willingly, and knew it'd take divine intervention itself to tear her from him.

CHAPTER FORTY-ONE

Tilly stood pouring two fresh glasses of whisky at the kitchen counter a little while later that afternoon. She felt strange and was still thoughtful following having watched the awful recording from Trey's apartment, yet she was still more relaxed than she'd been in weeks thanks to her clearer head and full heart. Blake joined her in the large room, grabbing her from behind and kissing Tilly's neck while he cradled her with his strong arms and pressed his muscular body into her back. She groaned quietly, the small sound a simple yet effective trigger that sent his kisses trailing faster and harder on her skin. He wanted her, and let his hands explore her breasts while she reached her hands behind her to try and run her fingers through his dark curls, being hindered by her casts somewhat.

"Save it for the bedroom, will you?" said a voice from the doorway, making Tilly jump, but Blake turned around immediately to face the voice's owner. He had a broad smile on his face and walked over to greet the visitor, whom Tilly could somehow tell was his mother, Cate—the Devil. She was stood in the doorway, looking every inch the powerful, forceful looking creature that Tilly would've expected her to be, and yet she was warm, beautiful, and so human-like it was a confusing sight. Tilly took another look at the stunning goddess with her long, dark-brown curly hair, blood-red lips, and her intense green eyes, and she fell to her knees, hitting the tiled floor with a loud thud as she did so, and she blushed at her excruciatingly ungraceful reaction to the Dark Queen's presence.

"Hello, mother," Blake said as he kissed her cheek with a warm smile. "To what do we owe the pleasure?" he asked, standing almost a foot taller than she did, and yet seeming somehow smaller and much less powerful than his omnipotent mistress, who effortlessly dominated every inch of space around her.

"I was thinking that it's been far too long since my last visit, darling, and you know I love England in the springtime," Cate told him with a wry smile, and Blake knew there was more to her visit than for just the weather, but didn't press her for more of an answer. "You may stand, Tilly," she then added as she made her way over to the counter, grabbed one of the whisky filled glasses, and took a long swig of the strong drink.

Tilly did as Cate commanded and stood, but didn't dare make eye contact with the alluring Dark Queen. Despite her warm appearance, the human girl was ever so aware that she was in the presence of the all-powerful ruler of Hell, and was scared how to act or what to say. Cate looked misleadingly young, stunning, and elegant despite her many years of existence, and Tilly was already in awe of her. She wore a long, black maxi-dress with sandals, and had a black leather jacket placed casually over her slim shoulders. Tilly admired her casual style, and loved how she had accessorised with lots of silver and gunmetal grey jewellery. Her favourite pieces were the exquisite pair of large diamond earrings that sparkled brightly through her dark hair, and the long necklace Cate wore around her neck, which had a large, ornately engraved locket on the end of it. The pendant was old fashioned but truly stunning, and showed off her figure beautifully, the chain creating a long Vshape between her impressive breasts. Tilly had to tear her gaze away from Cate's body, and flushed. She'd never felt so attracted to a woman before in all her life, and had to hope it wasn't her physical appearance she was drawn to, but the captivating force within—the same force her lover encompassed.

Cate finished off her glass of whisky and placed the now empty tumbler back down, licking her lips and watching Tilly as she peered down at her feet awkwardly. She then moved closer and took the girls face in her soft hands, finally compelling her gaze up to meet hers. Cate stayed like that for just a moment, reading every one of Tilly's thoughts, and taking in her short lifetime's worth of memories as she did so, and Tilly didn't resist her powerful prowess for even the slightest second.

Blake stood to the side, watching the two of them with interest, but he didn't dare say a word as his mother read his lover's mind. He knew far better than to interrupt her, and wasn't the slightest bit worried about what she might discover there. Cate most likely knew everything she needed to about Tilly from his own thoughts already, which he knew she read quite regularly.

"It's a pleasure to meet you, Tilly," Cate eventually said, her voice soft and she smiled warmly at her. "My name's Cate Rose, but of course, you may call me by one of my titles, or address me as your mistress," she added with a grin.

She read Tilly for a moment longer, her thoughtful green eyes boring into hers as she delved a little deeper into her psyche. Cate enjoyed the loving thoughts she found there of her and Blake, and of the mistakes they'd made that'd almost ruined that love she held so dear. Not now, though. Now they were truly a remarkable couple, and it brought Cate a great deal of happiness to discover how strong their bond had become. "You truly love him don't you, Tilly?" she asked her seriously, not releasing her from her grasp or pulling away from her at all.

Cate pinned Tilly to the counter with her tall, strong body, and Tilly found she was actually glad for the support. In all the strange tension, she thought she might fall over if the Queen let her go right now. Her touch was sending powerful waves of sensual emotion and love through every inch of the human girl, making her woozy, and she couldn't fight it, but didn't want to either.

"Yes, your majesty. I love him," Tilly replied quietly. She was uncontrollably trembling in fear before the dark and powerful Queen, and could feel the immense and almighty power in the air all around her, but she was also in awe of this incredible woman, this forceful entity that stood before her. It felt like an honour that she'd graced Tilly with her coveted presence.

"Then say his name to me, now," Cate ordered her with a smile.

"Blake," Tilly said without hesitation, but she was still unsure why the Dark Queen was asking her to do it.

"And again."

"Blake."

"Good, now tell Blake exactly how you feel about him," Cate commanded, stepping back to release her from both her grip and commanding gaze. Tilly looked over to her master, smiling when she made eye contact with him, his green eyes alight and happy as he watched the two of them with intrigue.

"I love you, Blake," she said, still nervous at saying his name aloud, and the Queen's smile widened even more. She walked back over to her son, giving him another kiss before wandering back to the doorway, hesitating for just a moment. Cate turned to watch him again, her eyes sparkling brightly, too.

"Good, that's settled then. Oh, and I've decided we're going to have a gathering here tonight. An orgy, so you two might want to go and get ready," she informed Blake with another impressive smile.

"Really?" he asked, smiling back at his mother. "It's been a very long time. Well, at least it'll be fun now that I have Tilly to participate in it with," he added, looking over to the still pale, trembling girl.

"My sentiments exactly," Cate replied before ducking out into the living area.

CHAPTER FORTY-TWO

"Whoa, your mother really is something else," Tilly managed to say, slowly calming down once Cate had left them alone again in the kitchen. She grabbed the other whisky and took a large gulp, eager to steady her nerves. Blake padded over towards her with a contented smile, immediately gathering Tilly up in his arms for a passionate kiss when he reached her. He then lifted her up onto the kitchen counter and wrapped her legs around his waist, pulling Tilly closer.

"Yep," he said, laughing gruffly when he pulled back from their deep kiss. "She's kind of intense when she wants to be, but did you even realise what she meant by all of that?" he asked, having read her confused thoughts, and he knew that Tilly actually had no idea what his mother had just done to her. She shook her head, one eyebrow raised as she gazed into his gorgeous eyes. "She gave you permission to say my name, Tilly," he informed his lover, a huge smile on his lips, and she couldn't help but grin back.

"Oh of course, and that's a good thing, right?" she asked, wanting to double check with him.

"Yes, it's an incredibly good thing," he told Tilly, cupping her face and leaning forward to give her another deep, passionate kiss.

"Yuk, save it for later will you?" called another new voice from the doorway, but this time, Blake didn't let Tilly go straight away. Instead, he finished his kiss before stepping back and looking over his shoulder to smile at the other new arrival.

"Hi, Dylan," he said, walking over to greet the witch he'd told Tilly about, and he embraced her tightly. Tilly could sense their closeness, and greeted the powerful woman with a warm smile too as she hopped down off the counter top. "Tilly this is Dylan, my mother's right-hand witch, protector, and best friend," he told her, a happy grin on his relaxed face. Dylan laughed at his formal introduction, but smiled over at Tilly once she approached, patting Blake on the shoulder affectionately.

The two women shook hands carefully around Tilly's casts and then chatted for a few minutes about the dark boy they both loved so very much. Dylan was everything Blake had told Tilly she would be—warm, funny, and kind while always maintaining an unwavering loyalty and protectiveness towards her infernal family.

"The party's going to start at nine o'clock tonight, Blake, but you don't need to do anything because the witches are all here to ensure everything is done properly. We don't trust anyone else to do it right," she informed Tilly teasingly, and Blake merely rolled his eyes at her with a knowing smile.

Tilly got the impression that Dylan had become like a sister to him over the years rather than a wise elder to be respected; she seemed far too playful and fun-natured for all of that. "You could do me a favour though and get the guest list together, she wants upper level demons and their choice of partner, plus any new blood you might want to invite along, too. Set me up as well, yeah? One of each, at least," she told him with a wink before she left. Tilly assumed that Dylan must've meant that she wanted both a guy and a girl to have her fun with, and Blake nodded to her with a sly smile.

"Welcome to the family," he told her, laughing as he took

Tilly's hand and led her from the kitchen into the living area of the penthouse. They were greeted by smiles and waves from the witches who'd teleported in with Cate, and who were now busy clearing the furniture from the large main room of the penthouse and setting up some sort of gigantic bed in the centre of the room. It consisted of huge black satin cushions that were spread out across a few square metres of the floor, and it had a thin, floating mesh curtain all around it. Tilly had to wonder just how many people would be sharing it later on during the so called, 'orgy', and at the moment the very thought of it both scared and tantalised her. "Don't worry, it's gonna be fun," Blake told her with a smirk, wrapping his arm around her back protectively and eyeing her as she took it all in.

He then led her over to a corner where a scruffy looking man was messing around with the entertainment system. "Hey, Berith," he said, greeting the man, who then stood and bowed to Blake in respect. Tilly could tell right away that he was a demon and smiled at him, sensing his strong bond with Blake.

"Hello there, Black Prince," he said warmly, embracing Blake and then smiling down at Tilly. "And this must be the infamous Matilda?"

"Tilly's fine, thanks. You're not my mother," she told him playfully and with a huge grin, making them both laugh.

"I like this girl," Berith replied with a wide smile, reaching out his hand to Tilly and she shook it carefully but was then pulled in for a tight hug, too.

"Same here," Blake agreed, grinning happily.

"Well then, Tilly. I'm very pleased to meet you, my name's Berith," the demon told her as he released her again, negating her need to ask him for his name.

"Hey guys," called another voice from behind Blake as a

second man walked toward the three of them in the corner. He was a handsome guy, who looked to be in his late-twenties with brown, slightly curly hair and deep blue eyes. He smiled widely, exuding affection and warmth towards them all as he neared. Tilly could tell that he was a demon too, and she saw Blake's eyes light up when he greeted him, and he immediately hugged the man tightly.

Tilly started to bow as she took in the sight before her, realising that the demon must be Blake's stepfather and Cate's husband, Harry.

"There's no need for that, Tilly," Harry said as he realised what she was doing, reaching out and hugging her after pulling away from his stepson's arms. "I'm just a demon, the name's Harry," he told her with a smile, also saving her the necessity of having to ask for it formally.

"But I thought you…" she started to say, but Blake interrupted her.

"Harry's my stepfather, yes, but unfortunately he isn't worthy of our royal status thanks to his human heritage, and the fact that Berith here sired him demonically," he said, ushering to the two demons who stood shoulder to shoulder, nudging each other like schoolboys and laughing as though they were close friends. "Well, that and the fact that he's as common as muck," Blake then added jokingly, but he'd still made his point clearly enough. Despite him being married to the Queen, Harry was still classed as a level one demon, just as Lilith and the others were. He was part of her council and was afforded many benefits by the Queen and her children for his high demonic status, but he still served her just as any other demon was expected to do so, especially in public where he would always be seen to bow before her and address his wife formally along with his fellow demons.

"Yeah, yeah," Harry replied, smiling at Blake, not having to worry about the formalities while in private without the hordes of other demons around watching their every move. "Hey, aren't you meant to be organising the guests?" he reminded Blake, who jumped and nodded, grateful for Harry's prompt. He immediately summoned Lena to his side, who appeared and bowed, swooning up at her master once she fell under his gaze with a look that made Tilly's gut flare with jealousy.

"Come," he said, ushering the two women away to let the others get on with the arrangements in the living area. Tilly smiled and said a quick goodbye to the two demons before following Blake's lead, glad to have met some more of his family at last, and she was pleased that they seemed to like her.

Cate watched them from out on the terrace where she'd been giving orders to one of the other dark witches, Sara, who took notes and nodded quickly to her mistress as she spoke. The powerful Queen gave the pair of them a smile and a nod as they left the main living room, her warm look making Tilly's butterflies return to her stomach just a little.

As much as being around them all was still nerve-wracking, she wished she could have this life every day—not just the two days a month. Blake's family were amazing, and Tilly already felt part of it.

CHAPTER FORTY-THREE

Tilly followed Blake and Lena into the study, where he quickly began giving his high priestess her orders, along with a list of demons for her to invite to the party. Tilly watched them for a few moments while leaning on the doorframe thoughtfully, enjoying seeing her master in his official role, and glimpsing for the first time this business-like way he had about him when it came to the duties he'd told her about earlier that same day. She checked her watch, it was only six o'clock, so she wasn't going to panic about getting ready just yet, but she started to wonder about the guests, thinking if there was anyone else that she could bring into their world. Gwen and Renee seemed quite happy now that they were fully initiated and committed to their master Beelzebub, and she was sure that new disciples were always appreciated in the dark followings. Just then, her new friend Jessica's face popped into her mind. Tilly felt guilty that she hadn't rang her back since that quick phone call when she'd gotten home from the hospital, and how she'd been quite hermit-like the last couple of weeks so thought she really should make the effort to catch up with her friend now that she was feeling better. Tilly was also thinking of her because she'd always thought Jessica seemed like quite a lonely girl, and she wondered if maybe she would do well in this dark yet close and protective circle of beings, too.

"Good idea, Tilly. Go and get dressed into something a little less casual and I'll teleport you there before I go and deliver my personal invitations to my Earth-based family. Give me five minutes to finish up here," Blake called to Tilly from across the large wooden table, breaking her train of thought, and she smiled back at him.

"Yes, master," she replied automatically as she began backing out of the study.

"Blake," he corrected her with a smile, and Lena glared over at Tilly, seemingly shocked to discover he was allowing his human to call him by his name, a name that she was still forbidden to say despite all her years of service in his coven.

"Yes, Blake," she said, smiling over at him and then she plodded over to their bedroom, were she quickly changed into some black skinny jeans and a figure-hugging vest, opting for easy choices thanks to her casts. She also applied a bit of makeup and pinned her dark-blonde hair up in a high ponytail, making a little extra effort regardless of her impaired dexterity. As much as she adored them, she couldn't help but feel so plain amongst all these beautiful godlike creatures, demons, and witches that were now in her home. Blake loved her, she knew, but a little more confidence definitely helped boost her ego.

A few minutes later, Tilly was teleported across the city to Jessica's doorstep in Blake's arms.

"Just let me know when you're done," he said, tapping her temple to remind her to just think of him. "But don't forget you haven't got long," he added, and she nodded and kissed him goodbye before knocking on the heavy metal door. Jessica answered and squealed in excitement when she saw Tilly standing there. She threw her arms around her and ushered her inside, chatting animatedly giving her updates from the restaurant and telling her how everyone there was thinking about her, and how they were disgusted and appalled at what Trey had done. Tilly followed her in quietly, taking in Jessica's flat as she did. It was small but cosy, and it reminded her of her own small nook on the farm. Jessica was wearing pyjamas, which made Tilly wonder if her friend had even set foot out of her home yet today, but it wasn't any of her business, so she followed her into the living room, smiling to herself as Jessica pulled back her greasy hair and checked her unwashed face in the mirror for blemishes. She was a pretty girl, always smiling, but Tilly knew that she wasn't happy with the lack of social life she had since moving to the city. Despite her seemingly never ending chatting, Jessica seemed as though she was actually a very lonely girl—Tilly could always feel it in the air somehow.

"Where the hell have you been?" she finally demanded, looking Tilly over thoughtfully, but she didn't give her the chance to speak. "Well, I suppose you look like you're okay, apart from the casts. Is it true that you broke both of your thumbs to get out of the handcuffs? Hard-core or what!" she cried, still not actually letting Tilly get a word into the conversation. When she finally quietened down it took Jessica a few deep breaths to stop panting in an attempt to catch her breath. Her chatting, it seemed, had been put before her need to actually breathe. Tilly smiled warmly at her friend though, grateful for the affection she sensed behind her chatty ranting.

"I'm much better thanks, and yes apparently I did break them, but thankfully I have no memory of it. Can we please change the subject now?" she replied, making Jessica jump, and she realised it might all be too raw for Tilly to talk about so she nodded eagerly, her eyes gazing back at her apologetically. "Are you up to anything tonight, Jess?" Tilly then asked her friend and Jessica shook her head no.

The two of them took a seat on the small couch and Tilly looked down at her hands thoughtfully. "Well," she said, an awkward smile on her lips. "I was wondering if you wanted to come to a kind of party at my flat? It is the full moon after all, so it's time to get your Goth on," she told her with a cheeky smile, joking with her friend, but she knew she had to get onto the subject somehow, so she used their old conversation in the restaurant as a way to ease them towards her explanation as quickly as she could. Tilly still had no idea where to start to tell her about the secret life she'd been living, and as it was the first time she'd needed to do this, she struggled with how best to broach the matter.

"Sure, count me in, but you know I was kidding about the witchy stuff yeah, unless are you really a witch?" she asked, her eyes widening as she took in Tilly's serious expression.

"No, I'm not a witch, but I am a Satanist, Jess. Do you know what that means?" she asked, not wanting to scare her, but needing to get to the point. Jessica shook her head, visibly pulling back from Tilly as she stared into her blue eyes. "Well anyone can be one, like any religion, but I'm actually involved in it, properly—as in forever. My boyfriend is very high up the chain of command, and we were wondering if you wanted to come and check it out, to see if it's for you."

"Your boyfriend? As in the guy you always talk about but won't even say his name, and who I've never even met? I actually assumed he didn't really exist in all honesty, Tilly, so he is real?" she asked, ranting again because she was confused as to Tilly's agenda. She even seemed a little standoffish, but Tilly just hoped it was the shock, so she smiled and shrugged, unsure what to say. She opened her mouth to respond anyway, but was cut off.

"Yes, of course I am," Blake said, appearing in Jessica's living room all of a sudden. She jumped, almost out of her seat at the sight of the magnificent man before her, and stared at her open mouthed as Tilly stood and wrapped her arms around his waist and he planted a gentle kiss on the top of her head affectionately.

"Whoa," Jessica said, and Tilly just smiled and shrugged.

"So, are you up for trying something completely different?" she asked and Jessica nodded. Tilly could tell that Blake needed to head back, and she took Jessica's hand, gripping her tightly as he teleported the three of them back to the penthouse's main bedroom.

When they arrived, he took Tilly to the side, asking her to get Jessica cleaned up, into some black clothes, and for Tilly to bring her up to speed on as much as possible, especially his family and their expectations of her in their presence. She nodded and gave him a quick kiss before he headed back off to the living area, his business-like head back on again.

Tilly then proceeded to tell Jessica everything she could in the short time they had while they helped each other get ready. She managed to apply her own makeup, and Jessica helped tie her hair up into a bun. Tilly chatted as they worked, and her explanation wasn't far from the one Brent had given her on Halloween, and just like he'd done with her, she left the finer details for another day.

Jessica seemed pretty happy and surprisingly relaxed when she followed Tilly down the hall towards the busy living area later that evening though, and Tilly was glad. She'd borrowed a short black dress and high heels for the night, and Blake had told them to wear some sexy black underwear, ready to show off when the orgy began.

Tilly couldn't be sure how much Jessica was willing to

participate in, and whether she'd leave the party as a marked follower or if she'd decide his world wasn't for her after all, but either way, she was glad she'd come along. It was also nice to get the chance to catch up, regardless of the evening's outcome.

They wandered through the doorway and into the pre-orgy party. Both girls were nervous but excited, and Jessica scanned the room with anticipation as she took it all in with a happy smile.

"Thank you," she whispered to Tilly, sliding her arm through hers.

"What for?" she replied with a frown.

"For not forgetting about me even though you had all of this to contend with," she answered, indicating to both her cast-covered hands and the demonic party they were about to dive into. "I'm always forgotten in the end," Jessica added with a sad sigh.

"Not here, and certainly not with me. The possibilities are endless, Jess. Don't give up on yourself," Tilly replied, and was glad when she saw her smile again.

CHAPTER FORTY-FOUR

Tilly locked eyes with Blake as soon as she was inside the large living room and he smiled over at her, taking in the stunning, tight black dress and high heels she was wearing. She looked fantastic, and like a dream with her dark makeup, bright red lipstick, and delicately wound bun. He nodded his head in the direction of Berith, giving Tilly her silent order to deliver Jessica to the demon, and she immediately followed her master's unspoken instruction, taking her friend over to Berith's side to introduce her to him.

He was due to move up to Earth again for a little while so was looking for new followers, and seemed quite taken with her somewhat naïve and innocent friend, so Tilly didn't mind leaving them alone together after just a few minutes. The two of them were already comfortable in one another's company, and when Jessica gave her a wide smile, Tilly knew it was safe to leave them to it. She instantly felt a strong pull from somewhere deep inside herself, urging her through the crowd. It was gentle at first, and then more potent after a couple of seconds. Tilly knew it was Blake summoning her to his side, the sensation was unmistakable, and she quickly made her way through the crowd, not even needing to check where he was in the room.

She arrived at Blake's side in less than a minute, and found him chatting with Harry and Beelzebub, so cuddled into him as he gave her a sly grin and kissed her in greeting. She felt as though she was both welcome and wanted at his side now, and it made her so happy to be a part of this strange group. The others smiled and greeted her. Harry beamed at the two of them with almost paternal warmth as he watched them interact so effortlessly, and she loved seeing how Blake's stepfather watched over him, regardless of their lack of blooded connection. The four then chatted for a few minutes before being joined by Gwen, who immediately took Beelzebub's side and smiled over to Tilly, looking relieved and sensing her calm happiness again at last.

"So, are you guys all ready for tonight?" Harry asked the two couples with a cheeky grin, knowing Tilly and Gwen were both very new to all of this. Gwen flushed innocently, and Blake and Beelzebub exchanged knowing looks and laughed. Tilly knew their inexperience showed, but she didn't care, and grinned up at Harry shyly.

"Absolutely," she answered when Gwen remained silent, feeling brave and excited despite her naïveté with their open-minded parties. "I just hope Blake can keep up with me," she joked, making Harry laugh loudly, almost coughing on his beer as he shook his head and peered at her as though genuinely intrigued. He had a soft twinkle in his gorgeous blue eyes, a benevolent spark, and Tilly could see why everyone seemed to adore him so much. Despite being a demon, she knew that he was once just a human—a human who'd fought hard to win the heart of the powerful woman he loved so very much. She couldn't help but hope that someday she would be where he was now—immortal and powerful, and with the hand of her soulmate firmly in hers for all eternity.

Dylan came over after a few minutes and chatted animatedly

with the group, and they all interacted with each other effortlessly. Even Gwen seemed right at home with them all now and joined in the happy, relaxed conversation with a new found confidence that Tilly thought could only have come from the having the love of the demon beside her.

Blake still held her close, his strong hands caressing her shoulders gently and she could feel his whole body shake while he laughed with Dylan as she joked and shared her silly stories with the group. He had an easy, carefree nature to him that Tilly enjoyed being privy to when he chatted with his friends and family, and she loved how the banter flowed between them all so naturally.

The room soon started to fill with eager guests arriving for the event of the decade, and it quickly became apparent to Tilly that Cate really didn't visit Earth very often. It was evident her being here now was already cause for celebration in itself, let alone the added excitement of the promised orgy that would soon commence.

Music started playing after a few minutes, thanks to Berith's earlier expertly set up mixture of small but powerful speakers. They echoed the sound around the room wonderfully while the guests chatted happily, and some even began dancing as the melodic rock music enveloped the crowd. The conversations continued all around them, but Blake soon led Tilly away without a word to the others, following Harry towards the centre of the room. She quickly realised both of them had clearly been given an unspoken summoning order from their Queen.

All the other attendees around them peered at the two powerful men longingly, watching them as though mesmerised when the three of them passed by—no one seeming to even notice Tilly. She watched them with intrigue, and noticed how the other women in the crowd, whether demonic or human, seemed besotted with Harry as much as they were with Blake. She wondered if perhaps that in knowing he had the Queen's heart, it made him the ultimate, unattainable man, and therefore highly desirable to them. She could easily imagine Harry being a coveted, beautiful prize and perhaps also a forbidden craving.

Blake stopped in the centre of the crowd and pulled Tilly around so she was in front of him, where he then cradled her in his strong arms just as he had in that first dream, with one arm across her stomach and the other on her neck as he leaned down and kissed her collarbone softly. They were lost in their moment for just a few seconds before his mother's silent order quietened the crowd, and she stepped into the room from the open terrace doors. Everyone stopped to stare, and Cate took a moment to bask in their adoration, while smiling lovingly at her variety of minions.

Blake then stopped his kisses and took her hand again, urging Tilly forwards through the group, which parted for them and Harry, the three of them stopping only once they'd reached Cate's side.

"Welcome," the Queen then called to the partygoers, and then—with the exception of Blake—every single one of them fell to their knees before her, including Harry. She soon released them from their respectful bows and grinned around at her gathering with a beautiful and ominous gaze, taking in each and every thought from her devoted attendees. Her powerful prowess surrounded each of them somehow, and Tilly could sense herself staring up at Cate dotingly, unable to control herself. She knew it was part of her seductive lure, but she didn't care, and wanted to please her mistress in whatever way she commanded. "We'll be starting in just a few minutes, so everyone, if you'd like to begin undressing and we can get ready to have some fun," she told the crowd with a wide smile, her eyes ablaze. Every one of the adoring faces smiled back at her, sensing the sexual tension and promise of dark pleasures hanging in the air all around them, and none of them could wait.

Tilly looked up at Blake, who was smiling down at her thanks to having already been listening in on her desire-driven thoughts. He licked his lips anticipatively, and then leaned closer in order to whisper into her ear.

"The royals take the lead, meaning my mother and Harry start off the proceedings, followed by us, and then the level one demons can bring in their partners, and so on," he informed her, reaching behind his lover to unzip her tight dress. She couldn't help but gasp at his words, and looked over her shoulder into his eyes nervously.

"So they *watch* us?" she asked, feeling slightly uncomfortable at the prospect of being the centre of attention.

"Yes, but it's not in a dodgy way, and you won't even notice them. I promise to keep you well and truly distracted," he assured her with a quiet laugh as he tugged her dress down her arms and to the floor. She absentmindedly stepped out of it and then reached down to pick it up and place the dress on the back of the armchair beside her, too thoughtful to even care if anyone was looking at her half naked body just yet. Tilly then reached up and slowly unbuttoned Blake's shirt for him, taking some time thanks to her cast, but carefully slid her fingers over the small plastic as she whispered back to him.

"Do other people join us as in, join in?" she had to ask, and was glad when he shook his head firmly.

"No, absolutely not," he replied sternly. "Not unless we invite them to, which of course we won't. In all honesty, most demons aren't faithful to one lover, but those that are monogamous still participate. They simply don't invite others to share their personal space with them and their partner. My mother and Harry will be shrouded, on show but they cannot be touched by anyone else thanks to their sacred union, and our bond will be recognised and respected too. It's one of the strictest rules for the orgy," he told her, pulling off his black trousers and placing them on the chair along with their other discarded clothing before cupping her face in his hands and planting a soft kiss on her lips.

As he pulled back, Tilly took a moment to appreciate his half naked body. This sexy as hell, godlike being that stood before her was about to make love to her under the watchful eye of hundreds of dark beings, but she wasn't scared. Tilly smiled up at him, ready and willing for whatever was to follow.

"I'll follow you forever," she whispered, her voice a soft hum mimicking their song, while their lips remained just inches apart and he still cupped her cheeks affectionately, staring into her hooded eyes lovingly.

"Just say yes," he whispered back, his lip curling as he planted another soft kiss on her lips. Tilly could then feel the air suddenly begin to shift around them even more, darkening, enticing, and exciting her. Blake smiled when he pulled back to watch her, sensing it as she began openly embracing the power all around her. She was succumbing to its pull, belonging to it—to him. A deep, satisfied groan rumbled through his chest. "I'm gonna enjoy his," he told Tilly, while she panted with excited expectation.

This was all part of their fun, the lure—the seduction. Blake couldn't wait for the moment when she begged and pleaded for him to take her. Before the night was over, she'd finally surrender to him under the eyes of his Queen—and for the first time in public, he was more than ready to accept her submission for all to see.

CHAPTER FORTY-FIVE

Cate and Harry climbed into the makeshift bed while Dylan lifted the thick veil that surrounded the huge, black, padded floor area. They reached the top edge, which was slightly higher than the rest of the bed, and kneeled before one another, kissing passionately. The crowd watched on in enthralled silence as a second thin black shroud fell around the pair, encircling them and giving the omniscient couple a tiny bit of privacy in the otherwise open area of the huge bed. Cate slid off her underwear and lay back as Harry leaned over her and nestled himself between his wife's thighs. Their years of love and lust combined to provide the onlookers with a wonderful glimpse into their powerful union—the proverbial forbidden fruit barely hidden so enticingly before the crowd. Tilly couldn't help but stare up at them, mesmerised. She was already enjoying being one of the voyeurs, and could feel herself opening up to the naughty, sexy thrum in the air around them as their Queen commanded all eyes on her, along with their thoughts and desires.

Tilly felt dirty, but she didn't care. It was as though the sight before them was seducing her, rather than her feeling embarrassed to be watching such an intimate moment, and she thrummed inside with a dark desire while eagerly awaiting her chance to join in.

Blake moved forward after a few minutes, breaking Tilly's

reverie when he grasped her arm at the elbow and guided her onto the large bed with him. They shuffled upwards on their knees, moving to their spot just below the Queen, where he gripped Tilly tightly and kissed her before removing his boxers without even a hint of insecurity at showing off his magnificent body. She heard the mumbled words of appreciation for his gorgeously toned muscles and huge erection from the women in the crowd behind her, but didn't care about them. Blake might be a mighty sight, but he was all hers and she wanted him—needed him. Tilly realised at last what he'd meant by her not caring about the others around them, and she quickly zoned out the sounds of the crowd and the sensation of being watched, all of her focus on Blake and no-one or nothing else.

He laid down on the soft floor, pulling her over to him with a smile while leaning up on his elbows and nodding as Tilly leaned down and took the head of his rock-hard length into her mouth. She let herself go, sucking and sliding him back and forth for a few minutes, before he suddenly sat up and grabbed her forcefully, pulling Tilly onto his lap in less than a second thanks to his unadulterated desire and powerful strength. He cupped her face in his hands and stared into her blue eyes with a wry smile before reaching his hands down and grabbing her hips as she straddled him. He kissed his lover fervently before ripping off her black lace panties with ease, and then sliding inside her wet, ready cleft. Tilly's deep muscles gripped him tightly and she gasped, as did a few members of the turned on crowd, and then she moved her hips back and forth on top of her master, relishing in his touch and the still heady air around them while Cate and Harry did the same above them.

The upper level demons and their lovers then joined in, eagerly taking their masters' lead, and there were soon bodies moving all around them. Tilly heard many cries of pleasure and need as they all throbbed together, a collective throng of indulgence and power that reverberated through each and every participant in this darkly erotic experience.

She could hear other women around her crying out in pleasure as they came, along with other men as they groaned their releases and basked in the aftershocks that followed, but her attention remained fully on Blake. Tilly had no need to care or even consider who might be close by on the huge bed, or whether they were watching them. She and the man she loved with all her heart made love so intensely it were as if they were alone, and she knew that even though they had an audience, this wasn't for anyone's benefit but their own.

A couple of hours later, following a second shared orgasm of the evening for the hot, young couple, Tilly knelt before Blake on the bed. Her body was pressed into his while he caressed her, neither one ready to start again, but also not ready to call it a night just yet. As they kissed, Tilly suddenly felt a pair of powerful hands caress her shoulders from behind, and immediately stiffened in shock. Blake had assured her that no one would try to join them on the bed, but when she looked up into his face, she quickly realised that this not an unwelcome presence. His shy smile put Tilly immediately at ease, and she gazed into his gorgeous green eyes. The strong and commanding hands then moved to her chin, gently pulling her head around to face their owner, which, of course, was the Dark Queen. She knelt beside Tilly and Blake, completely naked except for the beautiful locket that still fell sexily between her cleavage, and her body seemed to be reverberating with a combination of her immense power and a calm throb, as well as a glow that could only be the aftermath of the very recent orgasm they had all felt tremble the ground beneath them.

Cate pulled Tilly's face closer to hers, and she leaned towards the beautiful Queen while Blake held her tightly, keeping himself pressed against her while his hands gripped her hips, giving his weak lover some much needed support. Without a word, the powerful Queen then kissed Tilly's red, tender lips with a soft and intoxicating touch that sent an array of spine-tingling, sensuous shockwaves throughout her entire body, and she felt like she might faint. Cate held her there for a few more seconds though; her powerful mouth caressing Tilly's for just a little bit longer before pulling away.

She then climbed back up and ducked under the veil to join her husband, who stared up at her adoringly as she climbed onto his lap and began riding his hard and ready cock again.

Tilly couldn't help but watch them, feeling both confused and mesmerised for a moment, until Blake's mouth on her neck made her turn her attention away from the royal couple and back to her master. He kissed her lips, and then lifted one of her thighs up around his waist before he thrust himself inside her again, laying Tilly down on the satin padding while pulling her hips up to meet his.

She came quickly. It was a drawn-out and intense release that sent her body into overdrive, and her happy heart beating faster in her chest. She felt the telltale shuddering begin as he climaxed again too, and gripped the sheets beneath them with her few exposed fingers as the powerful waves claimed them both. He pulled out, trailing kisses down her breasts and stomach as she lay before him, before taking her swollen nub in his mouth to deliver her one more burst before he pulled her into his arms and kissed Tilly deeply. He tended to her body's need to recover with kisses and gentle touches, while he waited for her to be ready for him again, knowing she could still take a lot more pleasure from him yet.

His treasured love was so ready to be everything he commanded and more, and yet Blake knew he was her slave, too. Her body said go, and they went. It demanded they rest, and they rested. She cried out with desire, and he delivered her everything she craved.

He was hers, just as she was his, and Blake vowed never to let anyone come between them as long as his black heart beat in his chest.

CHAPTER FORTY-SIX

A few hours later, only a few lovers remained on the large bed-like area of the living room. Cate and Harry were still passionately enjoying one another's company, along with the attention they were getting from atop their padded throne, while Blake and Tilly revelled together in their final shared orgasm. Dylan was relishing in a threesome with two male demons below them, her playful smile still firmly in place as she commanded her own little following.

The crowd around them were tired, lusciously exhausted, and many of them had been ducking in and out of the shrouded area between getting drinks and replenishing their energy or swapping partners. Tilly had never been able to carry on for so long with Blake before, but her body responded to his touch so readily, and she had loved every second of it. She hadn't felt tired, thirsty or hungry the entire time, but was now starting to weaken thanks to their wonderfully exhausting and intense session.

"Ready to call it a night?" he asked her, rising from their embrace and pulling Tilly to her feet. He nodded to his mother, who smiled down at her son, watching them while Harry kissed her neck and held her from behind, his hands exploring her body lovingly.

Tilly followed Blake's lead, glad of the strong hand on her

back as they made their way to the bar and slipped on two fresh black robes handed to them by a very sour-faced Lena. Blake ignored the witch completely and handed Tilly a bottle of water, smiling when she drank it all down in one go. She was spent, but had loved every single moment of their publicly displayed affection. Next time an orgy was arranged, she knew she wouldn't hesitate.

Tilly's hands then felt itchy in the casts, and she grabbed a straw from the bar. She slipped it under the tight plaster to scratch at them, wondering if perhaps she might be sweating under there or something, as they didn't normally feel this way. "Let's get rid of these now shall we?" Blake asked her with a knowing smile, leading Tilly to the kitchen.

He grabbed a pair of strong scissors from the utensil holder on the counter top and came towards her. She went to tell him no, that the casts had to stay on until she'd healed, but he insisted and clipped away at the right wrist's protective casing. The cast broke open and she wriggled her hand free of the bandage, suddenly realising that there was no pain there, and no resistance at all from her somehow perfectly healed thumb. She looked up at Blake, who grinned and took her other hand, proceeding to cut off the cast, and he gave her other thumb a wiggle. He then turned her hand over, exposing her inner forearm as he did so, and revealing to them both how the burned inverted cross he'd so foolishly given her was gone too. Her arm was healed, unscarred, and the skin was miraculously soft once again. Tilly stared at it for a moment, completely taken aback by the flawlessness.

"It seems my mother's kiss really does heal all," Blake whispered thoughtfully, running his hand over her forearm as he leaned down to kiss her. Tilly stood on her tiptoes to reach him, throwing her arms around his shoulders and deepening their kiss before finally pulling away.

"I was wondering what that was all about," she told him a few moments later when she stood washing the plaster residue from her hands in the kitchen sink. "I thought she was trying to flirt with me for a minute, but I guessed she didn't know I'm not into girls," she joked.

"You never know," he replied with a wink, but then laughed, letting Tilly know that he wasn't being sincere. "In all seriousness though, she doesn't do that for just any one. Only those that are truly worthy of her powerful gifts are blessed this way. You've received a very rare favour from her Tilly—twice actually," he added, referring to their moment in the kitchen when she'd released her from the ban on saying his name. Even Tilly knew it was a sign that she'd actually been deemed more worthy than any other human Blake had ever known before, as well as many of their demonic and magical beings.

Tilly nodded in understanding and gratitude. There was no doubt she felt darkly blessed by the Queen right now, and by her master who'd also shared a rare favour with her in opening up the way he had.

"I don't doubt it, and I won't forget her belief in me, Blake. I am, however, quite sure that this all has much more to do with the changes in you, than it has to do with me," she said, reaching up to touch his face gently once she'd dried her remarkably healed hands.

"So intuitive aren't you?" he asked, peering down at her, and he kissed each of her thumbs. "Though you're probably right, my love," he admitted, smiling as he leaned in for another kiss.

"Hey, I just thought," she said as they pulled back. "Why didn't you just heal me yourself, like when you gave me your blood before?" she asked, suddenly wondering why he hadn't helped her again.

"Because I wasn't completely honest with you, Tilly. Yes I healed you, but I also found myself asserting my control over you along with my gift of vitality. I couldn't resist, and found myself automatically following the same path of many that came before me, including my father. I couldn't help it, and swayed your choices and put myself in your favour. I realised afterwards just how foolish I was to do it, how I would never be sure of your affection and loyalty while I controlled you, and I vowed never to give you my blood again—at least until you and I can share it equally," Blake said, reminding her of the blood-sharing she'd witnessed between Lilith and Lucas.

Tilly thought back to Brent's explanation of the sharing of power rather than the demon taking control of their lover, and finally understood the concept at last. "How do you think my father got those human women to agree to attempt to give him an heir? They'd all magically forget thanks to his power over them, while the three that managed to bear a successor found themselves with surprise pregnancies, even though they'd unknowingly agreed to it the night they were conceived," he said, adding a tiny bit more to a story she still was very confused about, but didn't dare ask for a better explanation. Tilly wondered about Lucifer's first three heirs, and especially his relationship with them. He'd taken Cate for his bride while betrothing Devin and Serena, and yet Blake and Luna had later come along as his two offspring borne solely in the darkness. His chosen heirs to the coveted hellish throne. She had many questions, but wasn't sure she was ready to know the truth yet.

Shaking it off, Tilly smiled up at Blake, understanding his hesitation at giving her his blood, and she was glad he'd decided against asserting his control over her too much. It would've been so easy for him to sway her to accept his every impulse, but he'd chosen not to, and she loved him even more for it. There was still so much she had to learn about her dangerous Black Prince, but Tilly knew for sure now that she would endeavour to carry on learning these lessons forever. Blake read her thoughts and stroked her now unmarked flesh with his index finger absentmindedly, looking down into Tilly's eyes with an almost shy expression.

"A clean slate," she said, relieving his guilt, and he smiled. Blake leaned down to give her one more kiss before they headed back out to join the last of the party in the living room.

CHAPTER FORTY-SEVEN

The next morning, after everyone had finished their frolicking and had their fill of drink and sex, the partygoers dispersed. The demons headed home with their lovers and followers in tow, while the dark witches took care of the cleaning up.

Blake and Tilly relaxed on the sofa together, her tired body still buzzing thanks to the wonderful and eye-opening night before. She'd managed a few hours sleep in the master bedroom, but hadn't wanted to waste any of their time together. As she sat there, Tilly couldn't help but smile to herself about their amazing and sensuous evening the day before. Both of them had gotten changed back into some comfortable clothes, and Tilly lay wrapped in his arms while the witches bustled around them. They'd both had such an amazing evening, and she curled up lazily on his lap, their hands interlocked with one another's as they chatted with their friends. They didn't have long before he and his mother would have to head off home with the waning moon, and she hated that he had to leave again.

Harry sat with them while his wife was busy, but he was used to it, so he, Berith and Dylan had joined the smitten young couple to relax with them and enjoy the calm afterglow of the incredible night. None of them could deny that they were all quite taken with Tilly now, too. They didn't try to deny it either, and chatted along with her happily, already sensing that she was swiftly becoming a permanent part of their dark family.

When Cate was finally able to join the relaxed and cheerful group, she plonked down in one of the armchairs and took in the sight before her with a contented smile. Her family were all so precious to her, and meant everything to the Dark Queen. Having Tilly around was doing wonders for her son, even if it had taken him a bit of encouragement and a lot of patience to get him here. She'd enjoyed watching them together the night before, and could hear Tilly's happy thoughts running through her mind now as she snuggled in her lover's arms. Blake caught Cate watching him and rewarded his mother with a big, bright smile, which were once so few and far between, but had become a regular occurrence now that this girl was in his life. They'd had their struggles, but seemed to have made it through everything relatively unscathed. There'd been a little push here and there from her of course, but she was more than happy to help if it made him thrive and let himself be happy at long last.

Cate had been busy again that morning, having spent a long time saying goodbye to their guests, but she'd also decided to keep Lilith and her husband back for a moment. Having read both Tilly's fond memories of Lucas, and Blake's excellent report on his capabilities in the demonic trials, Cate had decided to give him his much-desired prize—true and eternal demonic power. He was a more worthy human than she'd seen in a long time, and had been kind and warm to Tilly when she'd needed it most. That act alone had proven to the Queen that there was a place for him in her now far steadier underworld.

She and her family still firmly believed in the idea of a balance for their powers, and had done so for many years following the events that'd brought her to the throne. Her commandments had come from a much more steadfast mind-set ever since the ancient power had chosen to bless her rather than Lucifer all those years ago, and Cate still remained loyal and firm to her faith in that balance, as well as upholding their darker ways of life.

The Dark Queen had watched Lilith and Lucas the night before at the orgy with interest. They were a passionate couple, and very much in love, and Cate knew that they regularly shared one another's blood. She was also aware that it wasn't for Lilith's control over him, but a sign of them as equals, which surprised her. To her knowledge, Lilith had never had a bond with another being as strong as she had with her human lover, not even with Lucifer.

Despite her loyalty to Cate now, she knew that Lilith had struggled more than any other demon with her ex husband's demise. Her fierce loyalty to him had been hard to break through, and so Lilith had been sent to live on Earth because, at the time, Cate hadn't been sure she could be trusted. But, Lilith had found her way, and she'd found a love stronger than any she had felt before in all her years of existence. It was a love that reminded Cate of her beginnings with Harry, and she admired the usually so ruthless demon for letting down her own walls and opening her heart to Lucas so openly. And so, she'd called the couple aside and had given them the news before they left the party. Lilith had bowed her head and thanked the Queen profusely for her promised gift, while Lucas fell to her feet and uttered a silent prayer to her.

"We'll perform the ceremony on All Hallow's Eve," she'd then told them, so that they could make the necessary preparations for the ritual, and the pair had thanked her again and left, huge smiles on both of their faces. Alma came over and deposited a tray piled with mugs, tea bags, milk and sugar on the coffee table before them, along with a hot water urn and a thick glass jug full to the brim with steaming hot and delicious smelling coffee. Harry poured Cate's tea first, of course, and passed her a hot, milky cup along with a handful of biscuits. Tilly couldn't help but watch as the Queen, ever so human-like, dunked her biscuits in the tea and devoured each of them with a satisfied smile. She seemed so normal to Tilly at times, like an everyday wife and mother. Like when she'd seen her fuss over Blake the night before, and how she kissed her husband gently in thanks now, and she found herself growing more and more in awe of her almighty mistress. Cate caught her watching and gave Tilly a wink, making her look away, ashamed to have been caught. But, when she looked up again, Cate was still looking at her, and she had a warm smile on her lips that put Tilly at ease again instantly.

Tilly smiled back at the beautiful Dark Queen and leaned forward to pour Blake a mug of coffee. She handed it to him before making herself a sweet drink, and she grabbed a biscuit from the plate in the centre of the coffee table. She then sat back into Blake's warm arms, careful not to spill either of their drinks as she did so.

"I could do with some air," Cate said after finishing her cup of tea, and then stood from her chair and gave Harry a quick kiss before looking down at Tilly. "Would you care to join me?" she asked.

"Of course, your majesty," Tilly answered, jumping up from Blake's lap and following Cate to the terrace without hesitation. He'd given her hand an encouraging squeeze as she stood, putting her at ease. She had to admit though, she was still a little scared to be alone with Cate in case she accidentally said or thought the wrong thing in her presence—something that Tilly was aware she had a bad habit of doing all too often. Her only hope was that her mistress might be forgiving should she lapse in etiquette.

CHAPTER FORTY-EIGHT

Cate and Tilly stood together on the terrace looking out at the late-morning sunshine. It was a warm and clear day already, and Cate closed her eyes and took in a deep breath of the fresh air. Tilly watched her, mesmerised by her dark beauty as the sunshine hit her skin, but she could tell it wasn't warming the omnipotent woman like she wanted it to. The rays somehow didn't touch her like they did a human, as if they couldn't penetrate the air around the Dark Queen, and Tilly wondered if perhaps her ancient power wouldn't let it. She shook her thoughts away, desperate not to let her quizzical mind lead her into trouble, but she caught the slight smile that curled at Cate's lip before she could chase the question away. It was the exact same way Blake's curled when he was trying to hide a knowing smile from her, and she cursed her wandering thoughts.

"I do miss it up here sometimes, I have to admit that," Cate said, turning to look at Tilly. "It's been a very long time since I was last on Earth. Whenever I come, I cannot just roam where I please—I have to stay where it's safe," she added, looking back towards the sunshine again. Tilly wondered if it was to do with her previous kidnap, but didn't ask. Cate clearly wasn't ready to share her reasons for having to keep her earthly movements limited either so didn't answer her thoughts.

She simply ushered for Tilly to take a seat with her at the patio table. It was a cushioned rattan set that Tilly had moved from one side of the terrace to the other so it was now in the perfect spot in which to enjoy the view over London, and Cate agreed with her decision. The view really was wonderful. They sat down next to one other and Tilly watched Cate for a few moments as she continued to gaze out across the city thoughtfully. The light fell on her face beautifully, and Tilly couldn't help but feel such admiration for the stunning woman, but also so very small in comparison to her. What a tremendous and terrifying gift she'd been fated to possess, if what Blake had told her was true, and she wondered how she managed to remain so grounded. "What do you think of me, Tilly?" Cate asked, stunning her for a moment.

She read her shock and had to laugh, smiling at Tilly, and then she shrugged apologetically. "Hmm, okay, shall I rephrase that? How do I compare to your own mother?" she then asked, letting Tilly see she was actually just as insecure as any parent, and wanted to know she'd done the best by her children as seen through another's eyes.

From what Blake had told her, Tilly knew that his upbringing hadn't gone the way any of them would've wanted, especially as he seemed to have ended up being worse off than any of them thanks to his father's dictatorship. She couldn't help herself from thinking back to Blake's story from the day before, and how he'd become Lucifer's literal, and emotional, punching bag during those dark days, but she also knew that none of that was Cate's fault. "You have my permission to speak freely here," she added, clearly reading her thoughts, and her permission to answer honestly was reassuring.

"Thank you. Well, that's quite hard for me to answer, your majesty. My parents are nice, normal, boring people. They've never thrown wild parties, or lived for hundreds of years, and they most certainly have never been to an orgy," she told Cate with a smile. "I think any comparison of you two would be unfair, simply because of the very different lives you've led." Tilly shuffled in her seat, suddenly uncomfortable, and she forced herself to carry on. "But, I will admit you're not at all what I thought you'd be like," she added, and looked over at the Queen.

She stopped to check that she wasn't talking out of turn, but Cate seemed genuinely relaxed and ready to talk openly, so she carried on. "I understand that I don't know the entire story of Blake's childhood, but it seems to me you had a pretty rough time of it. You've done your very best to love and protect your children every step of the way though—putting them first, and never knowingly letting them come to harm despite your own hardships. Blake talks of you with such devotion and pride, and despite the terrible lessons he was forced to learn, I don't think he ever lost that affection for you. He simply hid it all behind those high walls of his," Tilly said, talking slowly and carefully, desperate not to upset Cate.

Silence descended, serving only to make Tilly more nervous, so she filled the quietness by carrying on. "I never thought I'd actually get to meet you, but I thought if I did, you'd be a truly scary, powerful, and unfeeling being—if I'm completely honest. I assumed the Devil would be that way, and I suppose that was me stereotyping you, rather than actually having any basis for that assumption. When I met you, I learned for myself the way you make me feel—the way you make everyone feel in your presence. I feel loved and protected. It's like I can do anything, *be* anything. Until yesterday, I couldn't fathom a dark world without an evil dictator at the top, but now I see how it might all be down to interpretation." Tilly let out an awkward laugh. "Don't get me wrong, you still scare the shit out of me, but I also think you might just be the strongest and most wonderful person I've ever met," she said, finishing her little speech and staring at her hands self-consciously.

Cate let Tilly's words wash over her, along with her thoughts. She raised an eyebrow, taking it all in with a smile.

"Thank you. Well done for being so brave, I admire that. You've no idea just how strong I've had to be over the years. But, to stay strong that sometimes has had to include an evil deed or two, so don't give me too much credit on that one quite yet," she said, a guilty smile crossing her lips before she continued. "I appreciate your kind words, though. You've an open mind and warm soul. I hope they're never quashed under the many burdens you already carry, and the even darker world you must encompass as your life by my son's side goes on," Cate said, eyeing her seriously now.

"Thank you, your majesty," Tilly replied with a small bow, trembling as she took in Cate's omniscient words. "I've really enjoyed meeting you, and I don't think I can ever show you how much I appreciate the gifts you chose to give me during your visit," she added, looking at her hands again. Cate smiled and reached across, taking Tilly's once burned arm in her hand.

"The pleasure has been all mine," she said, stroking the freshly healed skin with her index finger thoughtfully. "I want the two of you to keep on moving forward, rather than be constantly reminded of the hard path you've had to take to get here. You're the only person he's ever let in, and I want you to continue helping him learn and grow. I promise to keep a closer eye on Blake going forward, and will intervene if I ever see fit, but you'll have to do me a favour first," Cate added, looking into Tilly's eyes seriously.

She went to ask her what the favour was, but Cate quickly

interjected. "Wear my mark. Our bond will make you stronger, and it'll also act as a direct link to me should you ever need my help. You only narrowly escaped that disgusting boy and his perverted plans for you, and I don't ever want things to get so far out of our control again. There are many dangers you might have to face thanks to your chosen allegiance to us, Tilly, and there are many beings that are opposed to our way of life that might try and harm you. Don't be naïve now—question everything and everyone, and don't trust anyone except Blake, his family or our demons," she told her, looking at Tilly with a serious stare, holding her gaze as she continued to hold her arm in her hands. "So, are you ready to make a deal with the Devil?" she then asked, her beautiful green eyes bright in the morning sunshine.

"But, I'm already marked, your majesty. If I made a deal with you, would that mean I'm no longer Blake's?" Tilly asked, and was uncomfortable even contemplating saying no to the all-powerful Queen, but she couldn't even begin to imagine losing her connection with Blake either.

Cate took in her frenzied thoughts and laughed, feeling pleased that Tilly's loyalty to her son was so strong.

"No, of course you'd still be his, my dear," she said with a broad smile, while Tilly still looked uncomfortable under her powerful gaze. "I am, of course, no ordinary demon, nor am I a god. In a way I *am* God—your ruler, Queen, and mistress, Tilly. All of the above. My mark wouldn't come to you as an inverted cross on your forearm, but as a permanent blackening of your very soul itself."

"Whoa," Tilly replied, and was both terrified and intrigued by her fierce explanation. She was also excited at the prospect of being chosen by the Dark Queen to wear her mark—the mark she'd only known her highly respected ministers to bear.

"These crosses," Cate continued, and Tilly watched as her familiar black cross rose to the surface inside her right forearm in response to Cate's summoning. "They're a sign of your dark possession, a mark of your ownership if you will, and nothing more. The symbol itself is an ode to my reign, a powerful talisman, and sign of your allegiance both to me and to whichever master gave you it."

"Oh, I'm so sorry," Tilly said, realising she may have inadvertently offended the Queen.

"You weren't to know," Cate replied, putting her at ease. "You've already completed the first step by performing the commitment ceremony, and this would just be an extension of that. Wearing my mark would bind your soul to me, and in return you'd become stronger, more respected in our world, and you will have a direct link to me. One silent prayer and I could answer your call at any time, in one way or another. There's just one more step we would have to take."

"Let me guess, sell you my soul, right?" Tilly asked, laughing even though there was nothing funny about that prospect. Cate nodded, taking in the girl before her. Tilly really was very intuitive, and the ambitious woman within Cate respected her for it. She could understand just why Blake had chosen to mark her after only knowing her for a few minutes, and she wanted that clever prowess at her full command, too.

Despite Cate's still kind nature, she'd completely embraced the dark power inside of herself and knew she'd lost her human side a long time ago. She was every bit as powerful, commanding, and formidable now as her predecessor had once been, only she chose to use and show that power using very different methods, and so ruled in her own way. However, she still couldn't help herself from admiring, desiring, and demanding every bit of strength and love from her loyal servants in return for the gifts she bestowed on them, and the girl that sat before her now was no exception. Cate knew Tilly just needed a push in the right direction and she'd succumb to her request, they always did.

"Perhaps you might prefer a different approach," Cate said, staring into Tilly's blue eyes with a kind smile. "What do you want from your future with Blake? Will you grow old and live a human life as his follower, only to die and come to Hell where you'll have to suffer at the hands of the lower level demons? Will you be ready to then prove your worth and work your way up to be a demon and then finally—hopefully—make it to level one many years later?" she asked, and Tilly took her words in, honestly not having thought too much about it all before. "Or, do you take this next step now, and then eventually complete your demon trials as a human before joining the demonic ranks and earning your place at Blake's side, just as Harry did with me?" Cate added, clearly intent on selling her the latter option.

"Either way I get to choose Blake?" Tilly asked, making Cate smile again. She nodded.

"Of course, I would never deny my son a thing," she said, leaning closer to her before continuing. "Loving him was never going to be easy, Tilly, but you must choose now. Do you live your life as normal, or do you commit yourself to him entirely and follow the path I just told you about that'll lead you to his side? Only then would you be free to love him for all eternity."

"Then, of course I choose him, and I choose you, my Queen. What do I need to do?" Tilly asked, looking up into Cate's eyes. She had never been so sure of anything in her life as she was of her love for Blake, and knew she would do whatever it took to be with him.

"Just say yes," Cate told her with a smile.

"Yes," Tilly replied, taking a deep breath.

Cate smiled and lifted Tilly's hand up to her face. She inspected her inside forearm for a moment without a word and then slid her finger across the veins at Tilly's wrist, slitting open the skin in an instant. Tilly gasped but didn't pull back, stifling her squeamish gag as Cate pulled her bloody arm closer and started to drink from her.

Tilly could feel herself becoming woozy, unsure just how much blood she was required to give in offering to her Queen, but she remained calm, focussed, and determined. Her prize was firmly rooted in Tilly's mind's eye—Blake. She used her resolve to steady her thoughts, imagining herself as a demon with a place at his side.

Cate finished and pulled away after a few minutes, placing a quick kiss on the wound to close it instantly, and Tilly couldn't help but notice the smile on her crimson lips. She was mesmerised by the gory sight, but strangely unafraid of what she saw. Blood dripped down the powerful Queen's chin and her eyes were black as she looked up into Tilly's wide ones, and yet she regarded her lovingly.

"Do you renounce all others and pledge your soul to me, Tilly?" she asked, licking her lips with a satisfied grin.

"Yes," Tilly replied, and then Cate bought her own index finger to her lips. She bit the tip, drawing a small drop of blood to the surface.

"Then drink of me," she told her, offering Tilly the bloody fingertip to take the bead from. Tilly reached over and held onto her mistress' hand, pulling the finger closer and sucking the tiny drop of blood from Cate's already closed bite wound. She felt her wooziness subside instantly, strength and power resonating inside of her in its place. Tilly panted, looking up into her mistress' still black eyes as she caught her breath and steadied herself.

"Whoa," she said, making Cate smile. Her eyes went back to being the deep green she was so used to staring into on the face of her master, yet Tilly saw the darkness within them now. She could sense the power and the control buried within her human-like exterior, but she didn't care, she wasn't scared anymore and wouldn't ever fight it.

Blake joined the two women on the terrace a few minutes later, watching them with a serious expression, and taking in the sight of his mother's chin as it dripped with Tilly's blood.

"Wow, I leave you two alone for five minutes," he said, producing a handkerchief from his pocket and handing it to her. He sat down opposite Cate at the table next to Tilly, looking between the two of them thoughtfully as his mother wiped at her mouth. "You didn't think to run this by me first then, mother?" he asked her, but Cate just shrugged in response.

Tilly looked from one of them to the other. Their likeness was remarkable. They looked more like brother and sister than mother and son, Cate's young appearance playing tricks on her as she took them both in.

"It makes no difference, my darling," she told him. "Tilly would've come to me eventually, I just thought why not get it over with now. She'll be stronger and more powerful in every way thanks to my many gifts, and it won't be long until she can begin her trials. You should be thanking me," she added with a playful pout.

"Of course. Thank you," he said, bowing to his mother while grinning at her cheekily over the table. "So she has your permission to attempt it?" Blake clarified, and Cate smiled broadly back at her son. She let herself enjoy his playful demeanour and happy nature for one more moment before she decided to give them a few minutes alone.

"Yes. I'll leave you two to talk, but we must go soon my love," Cate told them as she stood up from the patio set, and Blake nodded. The moon would soon wane, and he cursed its hold over him just as he did every month. "Farewell, Tilly, I shall see you again soon," Cate added with a smile.

Tilly bowed to her with a smile in return. She couldn't help but still feel a little strange following their blood-sharing, but was glad she'd gone through with it. Tilly already felt stronger thanks to her Queen's tiny offering, and began to think about her dark new life and how strangely at ease she was with all of it.

Blake then reached over and took her hand, breaking Tilly's reverie and he pulled her up out of her chair and over onto his lap. She straddled him and peered into his gorgeous green eyes, mesmerised in an instant. Blake reached up and brushed her dark-blonde hair behind her ears as he gazed back at her and then kissed her deeply. The sun hit his face as Tilly pulled back and she noticed that the dark barrier she'd sensed around Cate wasn't surrounding him. It was as though the small part of him that was still human allowed the sun's warmth through, and he basked in it the same way his mother had tried to do.

"You continue to surprise me, Tilly," he then told her with a smile. "So strong and courageous. There'll be no stopping you will there?" Blake asked, catching her off guard slightly.

"Is that a bad thing?" she asked him, looking down into his warm face.

"Not at all. It's just that most humans have to wait many years before they're afforded the opportunities you've already been blessed with. Take Lucas McCulloch for example. He and Lilith have been together for twenty years and he's only just completed his trials. He was permitted to pledge his soul to my mother ten years ago, having spent the ten before that proving himself worthy of her blessings," Blake told her.

"Whoa. Well, despite what your mother just said, I'm not in any rush. I don't think the trials are in my near future. If anything, the very thought of going through what Lucas has still scares the hell out of me, so I'm happy to wait," she said, being honest.

"I don't blame you, they're incredibly tough challenges. Has anyone told you about the other two trials?" he asked, and Tilly shook her head.

"Well, the first one is relatively simple, but not easy. It's a signifying step to show the Dark Queen that you're willing to undertake any cunning deed, to lure humans into doing your bidding, and to prove that your conscience is ready to be ignored. You have to de-flower six virgins," he said, a wicked grin on his face as her mouth opened in shock.

"What? No, I couldn't do that. You'd be furious for a start," she said, and couldn't understand how that could even work.

"Exactly," he replied. "For if you simply fucked them yourself, you and I would be over and the poor boy would be dead before he even finished his first time, of course," Blake told her, his face darkening at the sheer idea. "The trick is to find a way to lure, seduce, and force the will of susceptible innocents, but not actually take care of the virginity problem yourself. There's always a way," he told her with a smirk.

"Ah, I see." Tilly said, still feeling highly uneasy even with his explanation, but then she jumped as the realisation dawned on her about her own first time, and the words Lilith had said to her afterwards. She looked down at Blake, hoping not to anger him with her memory, but he read her mind anyway, understanding why she'd suddenly chosen to think of it.

"Yes, you were one of Lucas' de-flowered virgins. You helped him complete his first trial without even knowing it," he told her, his eyes speckling with black spots at the very thought of her and Brent together.

"I'm sorry," Tilly said, cuddling Blake tighter, not wanting him to be angry with her.

"It's okay. I'm the one who raised the issue of the trials so I have to be honest, even if it makes me crazy with jealousy," he said, kissing her gently, his eyes going back to their usual shade.

"Yours and Brent's feelings for each other were real, Lucas simply provided the much needed encouragement for the two of you to go ahead with the deed itself. He made you feel at home in their company, and convinced Brent to take the next step when he had second thoughts because you seemed so sweet and pure," Blake told her, clearly uncomfortable talking about it, but still wanting to put her mind at rest. She nodded and smiled awkwardly at her lover.

"Gross, remind me to give Lucas a slap the next time I see him. Can we change the subject now?" she asked him, eager to get away from this subject. Blake nodded, seeming just as keen to move on with his explanations.

"Yes, absolutely," he replied, the smile returning to his exquisite face. "Your second trial would be one of pure evil. It shows my mother just how much you're willing to do to others in order to cross over into the demonic world. You'd be required to kill six innocent people," Blake said, and Tilly's eyes widened in shock.

"Whoa," she answered him, feeling sick at the sheer thought of taking another person's life. She'd technically killed Trey, but felt like that didn't count because Blake had actually been the one that did it—neither her consciousness nor conscience were involved that time.

"And not just that, you don't have any control over who you kill. A demonic adjudicator would make the decision for you, just like how I was given the choice of deciding how to torture Lucas on that final trial. An unbiased, high-ranking official has to be involved during these trails. If Lilith had done it, she would've no doubt gone easy on her lover in order to help him succeed, and we can't have that," he told her, and Tilly absorbed the information, even more thankful that she was in no rush to complete the trials herself.

"And what if I failed?" she asked him, her own eyes dark at the terrible prospect of her not being deemed worthy of a place at Blake's side.

"There are other choices. Luna's lover Ash became a warlock for her when he wasn't worthy of becoming a demon, which is fine for them and they're happy with the choices they made. They get to be together forever as he's now blessed with immortality, but he is and always will be her servant Tilly, not her equal." Blake told her, and she knew that while it was an option, she didn't want that.

"For now, I think I'll settle for simply being your follower, lover, and human," Tilly told him, kissing his soft lips. "We can figure the rest of this stuff out later."

Blake nodded, wrapping her in his arms for a deep embrace.

"Absolutely. And, I think you can call yourself my girlfriend now, Tilly," he said with a laugh. The once so unusual sound of his laughter sent wonderful tingles throughout her entire body, and she looked over at him again with a wide grin.

"I like the sound of that."

Tilly and Blake had to say their goodbye's a short while later, and then the royal family along with their demonic servants and covens teleported away from the penthouse, leaving Tilly alone for the first time in days and she hated it. Until that morning, she hadn't contemplated the steps involved in becoming a demon herself, but now knew she'd do each of them willingly if they meant she didn't have to tackle this monthly loneliness for the foreseeable future.

CHAPTER FORTY-NINE

The next week passed by slowly, and Tilly threw herself back into cooking, and tested out recipes on her friends when they stopped by to check in on her. She went to see Daisy a few more times too, and felt happier than she'd been in a long time thanks to the woman's help. Her once jumbled thoughts were clear and focussed again at last, and she was ready to tackle everything the future held for her and Blake.

Tilly went to see Andre the following week, having decided she was ready to get back to the restaurant, and not wanting to be left at a disadvantage with her career thanks to Trey's attack.

"Oh my God!" her boss cried as she came into the bustling kitchen. He rushed over to her and ushered Tilly into his office with him after barking orders at one of his sous chefs to take over the kitchen. Andre looked her up and down, checking her over, and looking down at her hands as if he couldn't quite believe she was standing before him. She'd anticipated some attention and had decided to wear thick bandages around each hand so as not to attract too much attention to their incredibly fast healing time.

After a few tense moments under his scrutiny, Andre seemed happy that she looked well enough to be out and about, but couldn't look Tilly in the eye once they were alone. He perched on the edge of his desk staring at the floor as she took a seat in front of him. "I can't believe what he did—or nearly did to you, Tilly. How did I not see what a monster he was? I let him take you home that night thinking you'd be safe, that he was a good guy," he told her, opening up about the burden he carried regarding the night they'd all gone drinking together.

"No one knew, Andre. Don't blame yourself, okay?" Tilly replied, and he finally looked up into her warm blue eyes with tears in his own. "Like you said, he was a monster, and monsters have a way of hiding in plain sight. Look, I was hoping to come back, if you'll have me, of course. I need to get back into a routine," she added, making him smile.

"Of course, I wasn't sure when you'd be ready though. I heard you'd broken your thumbs, how are they?" Andre asked, looking at her hands again.

"Well, it was more of a dislocation than a break really. They're nearly better already," she lied.

"Great, well yes I definitely want you back, however I'm afraid your intern's slot has been filled," Andre said, making Tilly's face drop. "But," he quickly added with a smile, "I do need a new sous chef if you're interested?" he asked and she grinned up at him.

"Absolutely, yes," she said, and then laughed. "That's a little fucked up though don't you think? I don't want to be accused of killing off the competition," she added, taking Andre's breath away with her dark joke.

"No, oh shit. I'm sorry, how inconsiderate of me!" he cried, staring at her wide-eyed. "I was planning on giving you the promotion anyway, everything that happened just got in the way, and you're not filling his spot on the team, I promise."

"Don't worry, I was just joking," she said, realising that her darker humour wasn't necessarily to Andre's taste, and she made a mental note to dial it down a notch in the future.

He smiled, taking her in. She really did seem to be doing better. In fact, she looked happy and stronger than before, as though the attack had made her more determined to succeed than send her running off in fear. Andre shook off his hesitation, deciding to give Tilly the benefit of the doubt.

"Okay, I guess I'm still a little raw on it all and hadn't expected you to be ready to make jokes," he told her, which was true. Andre had always prided himself on being a good judge of character and being intuitive, and it pained him to realise just how grossly mistaken he'd been with Trey.

"I'm still raw, too. I just hide it with jokes, however inappropriate they might be," she replied with a shy laugh. Andre nodded and then reached behind him to grab her a new uniform, instinctively knowing to give her the black outfit rather than the white ones. Tilly grinned as she peered down at the new kit, running her hand over the embroidered restaurant logo with the words, '*Sous Chef*,' underneath it.

"Take the rest of the week though, Tilly. I'll see you on Monday," he told her, and she nodded in thanks.

"See you next week, boss," she said as she left.

Tilly bumped into Jessica on her way out, and hugged her tightly before pulling her over to the corner to talk in private. She could sense her friend's new mark and was glad to have someone at work that she could talk with about all the Satanic side of her life. "So, I gather it went well then?" she asked Jessica, not having had the chance to catch up with her properly since before the party.

"Hell yeah!" Jessica cried, making Tilly laugh. "It was such an amazing night, thanks for the invite. Berith marked me and we fucked for hours on that big bed thing," she said, blushing at the memory.

"Whoa, that's great. I'm sorry, I didn't even realise you had joined in. I was kinda engrossed in other things. Have you been learning about everything in more detail since the party then?" Tilly asked with a grin, wanting to make sure she was up to speed on the etiquette and her demonic master's expectations of her for the future.

"Yep, he gave me a bible before I went home, and I've been researching ever since," Jessica told her. "And anyway, I'm not surprised you didn't realise we were there. You and your gorgeous master were well and truly in the zone, if you know what I mean?" she asked Tilly with a wink.

"Yeah, we were feeling it," she admitted with a sly smile.

"Understatement much? You two were all anyone could talk about, well apart from the Queen obviously. I can't believe I actually was in the same room as her, best night ever!" Jessica said with a smile, making Tilly glad she'd decided to invite her along.

She hugged her friend goodbye, telling her to pop by the penthouse any time with her master. It was fast becoming a centre for the Earth-based demonic social scene, and she didn't mind at all. In fact, she was glad to have everyone around to keep her company. Tilly couldn't help but be envious of her friends for having their masters with them every day though. It was becoming harder and harder only seeing Blake once a month and she missed him so much in between them that it hurt.

.

CHAPTER FIFTY

Tilly decided to go and visit her parents for the rest of her week off before starting back at work, feeling guilty for having been so closed-off the prior few months. She sent a silent prayer to Blake, asking for his permission to leave the safety of the penthouse, and immediately got a knock at the door. It was Beelzebub. He looked casual in his black polo shirt and jeans, but the posh brand names embroidered on them gave away the demon's expensive taste. He smiled at her, his dark-brown eyes warm, and she couldn't help but smile back.

"I'm here to take you to your folks," he told her, as an almost immediate answer from her master, and she smiled, ushering him inside while she packed some bits for her stay.

"That was fast," Tilly replied as she checked her handbag to make sure she had her mobile phone and purse.

"Our Black Prince is not one to hold back when it comes to giving his orders, Tilly, and anyway, you know I'm always more than happy to help. So, what's the plan?" he asked.

"I'm just gonna go up and stay for a few days and then come back for work on Monday," she replied, making him smile even wider.

"Work? That's great, so you feel ready to go back then?" Beelzebub asked, unable to help being cautious and protective of her, and she was glad. He and Tilly had become genuine friends over the last few months, and while he'd promised Blake that he'd keep a closer eye on her in his absence, he also wanted to.

"One hundred per-cent. I got a promotion, too. I'm a sous chef as of next week," she told him with a grin.

"Whoa, that's great, you gonna kill the boss next to take his place, too?" he asked her jokingly and she giggled loudly, struggling to catch her breath thanks to laughing so hard.

"Ha-ha, yeah I know, right? Now I know where I'm getting my new darker sense of humour. I told a similar joke to Andre and he looked at me like I was crazy! I'll keep those kinds of comments for our circle of friends in future," she said, still laughing as she finished getting her things together.

The two of them then teleported to a hidden alcove down the road to her parents' farm a few minutes later. Tilly thanked him, and then popped straight up and into the shop to greet her mother after he left.

Bianca shrieked and threw her arms around her daughter straight away, only pulling back to take her in and check that she looked okay. They'd still been estranged somewhat thanks to the huge amount of secrets between them, but Tilly was glad to be there, and hoped to regain some of their closeness again if they could.

She helped out in the shop for the rest of the afternoon before heading to the main house to cook her parents some dinner, where she elegantly arranged a three-course meal for them, showing off her new-found flair and techniques with ease. In the few days that followed, Tilly and her parents reconnected wonderfully. She told them about her new boyfriend and promised to bring him up to meet them when he was visiting sometime, much to Bianca's delight. Tilly was sad to say goodbye when Sunday came, but also looked forward to getting home, and smiled warmly when Beelzebub came to collect her from the alcove again that afternoon.

***

Once she was back at work again, the time flew by for Tilly. She didn't care at all and was happy working such long days, often falling straight into bed at the end of her exhausting shifts for much needed rest, where she dreamed of her gorgeous boyfriend. The next few full moons brought a more relaxed and intimate time for her and Blake. The pair of them were blissful and content in their little bubble, making love and talking all night long, growing closer and closer every time. She was truly happy, and finally felt settled and safe with him, as though they'd found their way together at last. Her human friends all thrived thanks to their dark lovers' influences too, and still came to the penthouse most nights to keep her company in between Blake's visits. Life was good, and she hoped nothing would change.

When Halloween came around again, Tilly was teleported up to the old castle in Edinburgh with Berith and Jessica. They arrived the day before so they could properly join in on the celebrations for Lucas' final demonic ritual, and she was eager and excited to see Blake the next day. Only those close to the royal family and to Lucas were allowed to be present during the ritual, so it was quiet—private. However, the rest of their friends and the other demons had been invited to join the party that'd then follow Lucas' fantastic transformation.

Tilly was led to her room in the old castle by one of Lilith's darkly dressed followers, and then she immediately got changed into one of her beautiful, figure-hugging black tube dresses that

Blake had bought her when they'd gone shopping in London. Lastly, she accessorised with high-heeled ankle boots and chunky black jewellery before heading downstairs to join the others for dinner.

Lucas and Lilith were buzzing, and chatted excitedly with their guests over numerous whisky shots until just before midnight. They knew that the Queen and Blake would come to Earth just after the clock struck twelve, thanks to their divine loophole on that day each year, and so the small group made their way into the great hall so they could await their arrival. The large clock tolled midnight, and Cate immediately appeared beside the altar that'd been set up for the ritual, just like it'd been the year before when Tilly had first learned about this dark world. Tilly peered up at her with a loving smile. She was genuinely happy to see the Queen again and she revelled in the smile Cate gave her in return.

"Happy anniversary," a deep voice whispered in her ear, and she turned her head towards the sound, finding herself looking directly into Blake's deep green eyes.

"And what a year it's been, my love," she whispered back, leaning in to give him a kiss in greeting. By the time she pulled back from his kiss, Tilly realised how the small crowd around them had fallen to their knees before the royal family, except her— again. She awkwardly fell to her knees too, and was grateful when Blake chose to laugh at her forgetfulness rather than tell her off. A few seconds later, they all climbed back up and he took Tilly's hand, leading her over to the side of the altar where they joined the now quiet Brent, David, and Jackson. He left her there, going up to join his mother beside the altar, who smiled down at Tilly again and then gave her a wink as she kissed her son's cheek.

"Welcome," Blake said, addressing the small crowd who remained silent as he spoke. "We're all here to celebrate the gifts our almighty Dark Queen has agreed to bestow on this human. Kneel."

They all did as he commanded, while Lucas and Lilith moved over to the large pentagram that'd been drawn on the wooden floor and kneeled inside. Lilith lifted her hands, turned them palm side up and bowed before her Queen to indicate that she was ready to begin. One of Cate's dark witches Tilly recognised from the night of the orgy then appeared and came over from the other side of the altar with a large goblet in her small hands. She slit Lilith's offered wrists without a word, pouring a large amount of her blood into the vessel. Tilly watched as the demon wobbled slightly, seemingly woozy from the loss of blood, but steadied herself immediately, eager to continue. Their love meant Lilith was willing to sacrifice her essence for Lucas' transformation, and Tilly felt honoured to be part of this unifying ceremony.

Both of them knew exactly what was expected, and so Lucas then raised his arm to the dark witch as well, which was also slit. He then placed it directly over his wife's mouth, and she quickly sucked on his vein, eager to replenish her lost life force.

Jackson let out a tiny yelp as he watched, doing his best to stay quiet although he was clearly squeamish and worried for his father. He was the most inexperienced in their group thanks to his age, and Tilly knew it must be hard for him to understand it all. Brent immediately reached across and took his brother's hand, offering him as much comfort as he could in the quiet darkness of the old hall, and it made Tilly smile as she watched them.

"Before the almighty Dark Queen, and in the presence of demons and witches, do you renounce all other allegiances and pledge your soul to your mistress, Her Infernal Majesty, Hecate?" the witch, who Tilly remembered was called Alma, asked Lucas.

"Yes, I do," he replied, panting and obviously a little woozy himself now thanks to his demonic wife that still sucked on his bloody wrist. Alma reached down and took his arm away from Lilith before she then held the blood-filled cup to Lucas' lips for him.

"Then drink of your demon, share her blood, and become her progeny," she told him, and Lucas did as he was ordered, gulping down the thick liquid quickly. "So mote it be, hail to the Dark Queen. Hail Satan!" Alma proclaimed, and then turned to bow before Cate as she presided over the ritual silently from the altar. Tilly too looked up at her, taking in her dark expression and the almighty power that resonated all around her in the darkness and they all called out in respect to her, repeating the words Alma had just spoken.

"So mote it be, hail to the Dark Queen. Hail Satan!"

Dark smoke then quickly enveloped Lucas and Lilith in the pentagram, making Tilly's eyes blur as she tried to see what was going on inside, and she soon gave up. Just a few minutes later it was over, and Lucas climbed to his feet, hand-in-hand with his wife. Tilly could sense his power, strength, and darkness, just as she could when in the presence of other demons, and knew that the ritual had worked.

"Wow," she whispered to herself, wondering if one day that would be her and Blake standing there like them. That was when she caught the two sets of deep green eyes that were watching her intently from beside the altar, reading her thoughts, and she looked up to find two matching dark smiles there for her, too.

CHAPTER FIFTY-ONE

It wasn't long before the debris from the ritual was cleared away and the party really started. The other attendees joined them all in the hall and each congratulated the new demon as they entered. Lucas was strong and eager to show off his new abilities, and Lilith was happy to give him his day to celebrate before they had to go to Hell and start his proper training. According to Blake, he had to begin his initiation into the demonic hierarchy, and both of them were eager to get him to the top as soon as possible.

Lucas immediately made himself look younger, around thirty years old, and he exuded a seductive prowess now that drew everyone to him. The whole thing fascinated Tilly more than she'd thought it would, and she was keen to find out how he felt now that he'd made the transition at long last.

Once he had a quite moment, she joined him for a drink at the bar and hugged him tightly. Tilly congratulated Lucas for his successful demonic transformation while Blake continued to watch her from his mother's side with a smile. He had to wait until she released him from his duties before he was allowed to join her, but could still listen in on their thoughts, and enjoyed hearing her curiosity on the subject.

Brent and his brothers then joined the two of them at the bar with drinks in hand, and they too toasted their father's success. All three of his children beamed up at him, genuinely pleased that he'd obtained his desired power and demonic status at long last. Tilly chatted openly with them, absorbing the fun and carefree atmosphere as they all interacted effortlessly, and she was glad the four men had stayed her friends despite all the ups and downs of the past year.

A young girl then approached and joined the brothers, along with two of her friends, and Tilly introduced herself with a smile. The first girl bounced around, giggly and energetic as she stood with them at the bar.

"Are you new?" Tilly asked, although she was pretty sure she already knew the answer.

"Yeah, we were marked by Lilith a couple of weeks ago," she said, and Tilly couldn't help but cringe a little at her bouncy attitude. "I'm Juliet, and these are my friends, Tara and Chloe," she said, indicating to the two other girls she'd appeared with using a wave of her hand. Tilly smiled at them all politely and shook the girls' hands, watching as David then put his arm around Tara and Chloe slid her hand into Jackson's. She then looked up at Brent who smiled back at her and shrugged as Juliet leaned up on her tiptoes and gave him a kiss on the cheek.

"By any chance has your stepmother been matchmaking?" Tilly asked him teasingly, genuinely not bothered by his new arm-candy. If anything, she was glad to discover he'd moved on, and was grateful that he'd gotten over their break-up without resorting to his old womanising ways again.

"Yep, I think she's trying to make sure we stay busy while Dad's away learning and doing his initiations. We've put the circus tour on hold for a while too, so we're gonna settle here in Edinburgh. I might even give college a go," Brent told her with a shy grin.

"Wow, that's fantastic. You should study English literature or something, I'm sure you'd be great at it," Tilly replied with a genuine smile, remembering his love of reading.

"Yeah, and I'm moving in with him," Juliet added with a satisfied smile, eyeing Tilly curiously, and holding Brent tighter as though laying her claim on him. "He's never even had a serious girlfriend before me. Lilith's hoping I'm the one," she added with a romantic sigh.

Tilly couldn't help but feel a little uncomfortable at Juliet's offhand comment, but in a way she was glad that they'd decided not to make a big deal out of their history. In a way, she couldn't blame Juliet for not knowing the truth, as it actually made it easier.

Tilly wouldn't let an awkward silence descend following that last comment. She simply smiled back at the girl and took a sip of her whisky, honestly hoping for the best for the pair of them while Brent just stared at the floor, seemingly eager for the conversation to move on.

A few seconds later, Blake suddenly appeared at her side. Tilly looked up with a wide smile to greet him, but then her face dropped when she quickly realised he was standing eerily still instead of wrapping an arm around her in his usual calm way. He seemed to vibrate with anger and stared down at Brent with cold, black eyes.

The partygoers around them then began to slow down and freeze in their places, their eyes turning blank. Silence descended in seconds, while Blake continued to stare down at the trembling boy before him with a menacing look. Invisible hands then seemed to grip Brent's throat and he fell to his knees, grabbing at his neck and choking, gasping for air. Tilly didn't dare move or say a word, knowing that Blake might punish her if she got in the way, and knew he could inadvertently turn his anger on her and do something that they'd both regret. She couldn't help but stand and stare, helpless and trembling with fear, but she also appreciated that he hadn't frozen her along with the others for a reason. He wanted her to see this.

Blake then reached down and grabbed Brent by the neck with his actual hands. He lifted him off the floor while he trembled and continued to choke—fear in his eyes as he stared into Blake's dark, blank face pleadingly.

"You don't ever think of her," he bellowed loudly at him, although their faces were only a few inches from one another. "You hear me? If I ever catch you remembering her like that again I'll rip your fucking throat out!" he ordered before dropping Brent to his knees and walking away, releasing both his physical and invisible grip on the boy's windpipe. Tilly turned to follow him but caught Cate's eye from across the room as she did. She saw her give a tiny shake of her head, stopping Tilly's approach immediately. Cate then took her son's hand as he reached her and teleported them both away without a word.

The crowd then slowly began to unfreeze, no one even realising what'd just happened except for Tilly and Brent. Everyone around the bar suddenly dropped to their knees to help him, but he shooed them away saying he was fine.

"My drink just caught in my throat," he said to his father, but a quick look at Tilly's pale face told Lucas a different story. He whispered in his son's ear as he helped him up.

"Don't ever be so foolish again," Lucas chastised Brent as they walked away, but he didn't say a word to Tilly. She watched them for a moment and then had to fight back her tears when she then wandered off in a daze too, trying to piece together the events from the last few minutes. She plonked herself down onto an empty stool at the bar, cradling her head in her hands as she fretted over what'd just happened, and she wondered if Blake was okay, hoping that he'd come back to her again.

"Don't worry, Blake will be fine," a voice said from beside her, and she lifted her head to see Luna sat there, smiling sweetly at her. The Black Princess took a long swig from Tilly's drink, finishing it off, and ushered at the waiter for two more. Tilly started to climb out of her seat in order to bow in respect before her, but Luna shook her head. "Don't even think about it," she said kindly, ordering her to stay on her stool.

"Is he coming back, your majesty?" Tilly asked, hoping that their day hadn't been spoiled for them.

"Yes, our mother took him home so he can calm down before heading back up here. She stands by her promises," Luna told her and Tilly smiled, thinking back to the deal she'd made with Cate on the penthouse terrace. She took a long swig of the fresh drink the waiter delivered them and then took in the beautiful Princess before her for a moment. Luna was wearing black skinny jeans and a purposely ripped rock band t-shirt that showed off her black bra and slim stomach underneath; looking cool and relaxed, yet still so powerful and fierce. Her long, dark-brown curls were pulled back into a high ponytail and it cascaded beautifully down her back, accentuating her curves even more. Luna truly was a stunning woman. She looked so much like her mother, but also had that special something about her that made her different. The Black Princess possessed kindness and a loving nature that exuded from her without her even speaking, and her affectionate gaze alone put Tilly immediately at ease. She enjoyed her company immensely and hoped that they might become good friends in the future.

"Thank you," Tilly replied. "I didn't even know what was going on with him at first, but I assume Brent was letting his mind wander, am I right?"

"Got it in one," Luna replied, shaking her head. "Foolish boy. Blake hates it that Brent's been with you, that he was your first. I think he would've killed him if it wasn't for our mother summoning him away."

"Whoa. So she can do that with you guys, too?" she asked, but then shook her head and smiled apologetically. "Of course she can, she's the Devil," Tilly added with an awkward laugh. Luna just smiled sweetly and reached her hand up, taking Tilly's chin in her palm and then sliding her soft thumb over her lips as she took her in.

"You really are very beautiful, Tilly," she said, making her blush. "There's something about you isn't there, something different, has he ever told you that?" Luna asked, and Tilly nodded.

"He says I intrigue him," she replied, unsure if that was what Luna had meant.

"We each have our gifts, Tilly. I can sometimes see things in others that my family cannot, and I see something in you. I don't know what it is yet, but we can all sense it in you. I think it's an energy that's all kinds of ancient, and maybe even lucent. Beautiful. I know he doesn't like to share, but perhaps one day," she mused, tailing off before finishing her thought.

"Would you share Ash?" Tilly asked her, feeling slightly uncomfortable thanks to Luna's affectionate comments, so she tried to bring the conversation around in a different direction—to the Princess' lover that Blake had told her about.

"Hell no," Luna replied with a sly grin. "I suppose it's probably just sibling rivalry, or perhaps it could be mine and Blake's strong twin bond, but I'm drawn to you," she said, planting a soft kiss on Tilly's red-hot cheek.

"Thank you, your highness, but," Tilly began to say.

"But, she belongs to me, as you well know, dear sister," spoke a deep voice from behind them. It was Blake, his eyes the normal deep green, and his expression gentle and calm once again. Tilly jumped, but Luna just smirked at him, a playful glint in her own matching green eyes.

"Took you long enough," she said, standing and giving him a kiss on the cheek before waving to Tilly and teleporting away.

"Ignore her, my love, she was just trying to get me back here quicker, knowing that I'd sense her advances towards you. You'll get to know Luna better in time, and she's ever the playful, yet annoying one of the family," he said, sitting on the stool where his twin had just been. Tilly bowed to him slightly and leaned forward, planting a passionate kiss on his ready lips, and she was grateful to feel his urgent need for her in return.

"Blake, I didn't..." she began to say, wanting to explain that she hadn't led Brent on or thought of him the same way he seemed to have been thinking of her, but he shook his head, stopping her.

"I know Tilly, it's okay. He won't be punished further, but you don't realise what it's like for me. I not only hear the thoughts of others. I can see their memories like some sort of movie that's playing in their mind, like the image you showed me in the mirror that night of your dream. And he was remembering a very intimate time with you, only for a second or two, but it was a time that he absolutely should not have been reminiscing over in my presence," Blake told her, his anger welling up again, but he pushed it away, shaking himself off and then changing the subject. "So my love, what are we going to do with the rest of our day?" he asked her, a seductive smile on his lips.

Tilly grinned back and took her master's hand, and then led him from the party without another word, only stopping when they reached their suite to open the door. Blake grew impatient as she fumbled with the key, so he lifted her up into his arms and pushed Tilly against the closed door. He kissed her deeply and then took the key, slipping it into the lock with ease before then carrying her over the threshold as he began ripping the clothes off her very ready body.

CHAPTER FIFTY-TWO

Blake and Tilly emerged from their room, giddy, happy, and glowing following a few hours of wonderful lovemaking. He lifted her onto his back and playfully carried her back towards the party. There were still a few drunken partygoers going strong, and the castle's staff members were busy laying out breakfast for them and the few early risers, or in Blake and Tilly's case, the ones who had gone to bed but hadn't actually been to sleep. Tilly got stuck into a large plate of bacon and eggs straight away, and refilled her mug of coffee three times, eager to stay fuelled and refreshed. Sleep was not an option for their day together. She'd dressed in a long jumper and leggings, feeling frumpy, but it was the warmest clothing she'd brought along, having forgotten just how cold the old castle could get. Even with her insatiable boyfriend there to keep her warm, the cold Scottish air still chilled her to the bone.

Berith soon joined them with Jessica, who looked exhausted in a good way, and she eagerly helped herself to some coffee and food as well. Tilly noticed that Berith had made himself look younger, more polished and much more presentable than when she'd first met him in the penthouse. His dark-brown hair was shorter and he'd swept it casually to one side in a stylish quiff. He'd even trimmed his beard so that it was shorter and much more flattering on his pale face. She wondered to herself what Berith would do with his time now that he was staying on Earth for a while, but hoped he was going to keep the adorable smile plastered on Jessica's face.

"Berith's first mistress is rock and roll, Tilly," Blake joked with her, reading her thoughts as usual. "But his days of being a dirty scruff are over now. Rock stars are much more polished and preened these days. You're putting a new band together aren't you?" he then asked the demon, who smiled and nodded.

"Yep, and I've already started writing our first record. I'm going back to the acoustic stuff I think," he replied with a grin.

"I didn't even know that you were a musician, Berith," Tilly said, realising she hadn't really had much chance to get to know him better over the last few months due to her being so hectic at the restaurant and him being so busy with Jessica and his other new followers while establishing his presence back on Earth.

"Yeah, I had a few bands when I was back on Earth a couple of hundred years ago. It's kind of in my blood," he replied nonchalantly, as if it was nothing. Tilly laughed, and was honestly impressed. She also hoped that one day a couple of hundred years would mean so little to her, too.

"There's a song of his that you particularly like, Tilly. I've played it for you a couple of times, it's called *follow you forever.'* Do you remember it?" Blake asked her with a cheeky smile, knowing all too well that he was talking about the track she'd dubbed as their song—the song they'd first made love to. She blushed and nodded, grinning over at Berith.

"Wow, I wouldn't have thought you'd have such a soft voice, even without the scruffy exterior. You'll have to sing it for me sometime, if you don't mind, that is?" Tilly asked, and Berith smiled at her, put his hand over his heart, and bowed slightly.

"Of course I don't mind. I tell you what, I'll play it at your demonic rebirth after-party," he promised with a sly grin, clearly expecting her to follow in Lucas' footsteps.

After breakfast, Blake took Tilly's hand and told her to close her eyes.

"Don't open them until we get there," he ordered her, and she nodded with an excited smile. She felt the telltale pull of being teleported away, and then suddenly felt hot sunshine on her skin, the bright light streaming in through her closed eyelids. Tilly was desperate for a peek, but followed her master's orders and waited until he gave her the go-ahead to open them again. "Open up," Blake said after a couple of seconds, and she eagerly did as she was told, taking in the beautiful view around them. They were on their very own private beach. The pure white sand, clear blue ocean, and cloudless sky were more perfect than anything she'd ever seen before.

"Beautiful," she said, taking in the breathless view, stripping off her jumper and boots, suddenly feeling very hot.

"It is now. Don't stop there," Blake commanded, reaching down to grab the waistband of her leggings and he pulled them down, throwing them onto a table next to a large hammock that swung between two huge palm trees. Tilly peeled off the rest of her clothes, basking in the hot sunshine as it warmed her pale skin.

"Where are we?" she asked him, following him to the water's edge and looking up into Blake's sparkling green eyes that shone thanks to the strong, bright rays that reflected off the water into them.

"A small island near Bali," he told her, undressing himself as he spoke. "Don't worry, it's all ours," he assured her as he pulled off the last of her underwear and then his own. He then lifted Tilly up into his arms and carried her into the warm water while she wrapped her legs tightly around him and kissed him passionately. He carried on deeper, taking the two of them straight into the crystal clear waves, where he then slipped his hard length inside her with ease. They made love, thrusting together powerfully with the waves as they bobbed up and down in the deep water, Blake delivering her pleasure eagerly and staring into Tilly's eyes as she came for him over and over again. She gripped his hips with her thighs and locked her ankles behind him, never wanting to let him go.

When he too had reached his own climactic end, Blake lifted Tilly back out of the water and carried her over to the hammock, where he laid her down and the hot sun dried them almost instantly. He climbed on top of her and kissed her deeply while he ran his strong hands down her still trembling body. She groaned loudly, unbelievably ready for him again, and he slid inside her hot cleft. Blake took her hard, and she cried out for him, desperately wanting him to take possession of every inch of her willing body and soul. He graciously accepted, and appreciated every single moment of her desperate submission.

"Well, that was a lovely surprise," Tilly whispered to him a little while later, and was exhausted but still revelled in their last shared climax, while Blake laid with his arms and legs wrapped around hers in the hammock. They were so strong together now, and their connection was so deep that Tilly was surer than ever that she wanted to stay like this forever, to stay with *him* forever.

"Well, I still have a few more things planned for us to do today my love, so you'd better think about getting dressed," Blake told her, grinning down at her as he stood and tossed Tilly her clothes. She scowled and groaned, but did as she was told, eager to find out what the next treat might be. "Close your eyes," Blake told her again when they were ready to go, and Tilly quickly followed his orders. They teleported away again, and this time she felt the icy sting of freezing cold wind on her face when they arrived at their destination and wrapped her arms around herself as she waited for Blake to release her closed lids.

When she was permitted to open them again, Tilly looked around and took in the beautiful sight before her. She could tell right away they were in New York City, overlooking the metropolis from a gorgeous penthouse garden. It really was a beautiful place, and looked exactly like it had in pictures Tilly had seen in books and on television before, a city that she'd always wanted to visit. Blake stood behind her and wrapped her in his arms to warm her up, giving her a few moments to take it all in before leading her inside the huge apartment. It was lavishly decorated in blacks and reds, just like the other flat in London, and was obviously another of their family's many bases for when they visited Earth.

"There are some coats in the closet there," he said, indicating for her to choose one, and Tilly grabbed a warm looking fur-lined coat in black, of course.

"Hungry?" Blake then asked, and Tilly nodded, realising she was famished thanks to their both relaxing and active morning on the island. Without another word, he took her hand in his and, after giving Tilly a kiss, led her out through the main doors towards the elevator. They went down and out through the lobby into the cold, busy street, where a limousine waited at the kerb to take them to their secret destination. She could hardly contain her excitement, and Blake loved watching as Tilly peered out the window, taking in the bustling city while they made their way to his chosen venue. He'd arranged to take her to lunch at a fantastic and very posh restaurant run by one of the world's most famous leading chefs,

Maximilian Dante. He was also a member of the Crimson Brotherhood, a secretive group of dark beings and their followers that was run by Devin Black, Cate's brother. Blake knew Tilly was eager to hear more about the mysterious order, but he still hadn't been granted permission to know more about them yet. There were some elements of his sinister world she didn't need to be privy too, but that didn't stop him using those connections to his advantage.

Tilly stared open-mouthed as they pulled up outside the impressive building, and Blake took her hand, leading the way into the empty restaurant. The entire place had been reserved just for them, and they feasted on a fantastic five-course meal that'd been specially prepared for them by Maximilian himself.

After their meal was complete, he came out to greet his prestigious guests, bowing to Blake formally and then shaking Tilly's hand. She was star-struck at first and could barely find the words to speak with him about her hopes and dreams of becoming a famous chef herself. Blake helped her out, doing most of the talking while she stood awkwardly and laughed embarrassingly at herself, but then Tilly gave herself a mental kick up the bum and found her voice, knowing that these experiences didn't just happen to aspiring chefs in real life. She knew she had to make the most of it, and before long she chatted comfortably with Maximilian about how her career in the food industry was going so far, and how she was getting on working under Andre.

"Andre Baxter is an exceptionally good chef, and will be a fantastic teacher for you, Tilly," Maximilian told her with a gracious smile. "But, should you ever choose to relocate to New York, don't hesitate to contact me. We're always looking for talented young chefs to join us, and if Andre says you're his up and coming protégé, I'll gladly relieve him of you if I get the chance," he added, making Tilly smile and blush timidly as she absorbed his kind words.

They left the restaurant a little while later and walked along the busy avenues together for a while before Blake took Tilly shopping. They then took the limousine around the city to see the sights for their last few hours in the beautiful metropolis, but the time was whizzing past too fast for Tilly's liking. In all honesty, she didn't ever want this wonderful day to end.

"There's still one more surprise," Blake told her with a smile when they'd deposited her shopping in the penthouse ready for one of his witches to collect and teleport back to London for her. He took her hand again and Tilly instinctively closed her eyes, knowing that it would've been his next order anyway, and he teleported the pair of them away for one last treat. When they arrived at the next destination, they were indoors and Tilly felt the warmth of an open fire on her skin. She could smell the logs burning in it, as well as the musty smell of old wood and pine needles.

"Open up," Blake told her one more time, and as she did so, the inside of a beautiful log cabin came into view. It was quaint and beautifully decorated with warm, earthy colours, and had two large, brown leather sofas draped in heavy quilted throws in the middle of the room before the huge fireplace. Beneath her feet was a thick animal-skin rug, making her feel cosy and warm already.

"Wow, where are we?" Tilly asked, looking up at Blake and relishing in his happy smile.

"Greenland," he told her, walking towards Tilly and then turning her around so she was looking out the window behind her at the jaw-dropping scenery outside. The sun was just starting to set and a colourful haze filled the sky above them. It was a truly stunning and beautiful sight that instantly took her breath away.

"Whoa, is that the Northern Lights?" she asked, and he nodded. "Wow," was all she could add, completely mesmerised by the colourful show that played out before her.

Blake watched her rather than the sky. He didn't care about the lights that shimmered above them, Tilly was the only thing in this entire world he wanted to look at. Nothing compared to her. He'd adored reading her mind during their day together, and every happy thought and experience she'd had thanks to his careful planning was a welcome presence in his mind. He'd wanted to give her the perfect day—a lovely mixture of tantalising treats and fantastic experiences to create a wonderful memory of their first anniversary together—and it really had been perfect.

CHAPTER FIFTY-THREE

Blake drew the fur coat down from Tilly's shoulders and tossed it onto a hook near the door before heading over to a small cabinet and pouring them both a drink. She smiled graciously and accepted the shot of whisky over ice, taking a small sip as she continued to watch the breath-taking illuminations in the sky before her.

"Thank you. This really has been the most wonderful day, Blake," she told him honestly, smiling over to him as he wandered over to a set of drawers and pulled out two black bathrobes.

"And it's not over yet, darling," he told her, unbuttoning his shirt. "Strip," he then commanded with a cheeky wink, and Tilly immediately did as she was ordered, delighting in his gorgeous gaze as he watched her undress with a satisfied grin. Blake then stepped forward and handed her the robe and she smiled, unsure what he was up to, but she pulled it on and then followed him out the front door of the cabin. He led her down a set of icy stairs that went around to the back of the frozen hut. They soon reached their destination, a steaming pool of water that was illuminated in the darkness by small spotlights that'd been set into the ground underneath the blue water. Blake untied his belt and deposited the robe, showing off his gloriously muscular naked body in the dim light for a moment before he slipped down into the water, ushering for Tilly to follow his lead. She watched him for a few moments, gliding through the water gracefully, before she threw aside her own robe at the pool's edge too and gasped as the cold air hit her naked skin, making Blake laugh. "Hurry up and get in then," he said and she quickly stepped down into the hot pool, letting out a delighted sigh as she submerged her cold body in the soothing water.

"It's so warm," she said, treading water while he swam over to her.

"Yeah, these are naturally hot springs. Nature at its best," Blake said, wrapping her in his arms before kissing her. The natural saltiness of the water kept them afloat effortlessly, and the pair then laid back and watched the sky for a while, taking in the stunning show above them as they relaxed together, their hands entwined.

Later, when they were back in the cabin, Blake lay Tilly down on the thick rug that was sprawled out in front of the still roaring fire. The rug seemed to absorb the heat from the flames, making her hot and restless. Blake didn't help matters as he expertly caressed her swollen nub with his tongue, and his fingers rubbed the tender spot inside of her cleft as he pursued her next climax.

"Blake!" she cried out uncontrollably, running her hands down through his dark hair as she came, and she could feel her heart pounding in her chest, her body completely at his command. He took her to the edge of madness with his touch, delighting in her cries of pleasure, and yet Tilly never wanted it to end, and he obliged her silent demand to be taken—owned.

When she calmed down again, Blake trailed kisses up her stomach to Tilly's breasts, taking each of her nipples in his mouth in turn and sucking gently on them before moving up to her neck.

She panted, feeling hot and more covetous when his lips pressed into every inch of her skin, delivering her with a sweet and sexy tingling feeling thanks to her heightened sensitivity.

"Are you ready for more?" Blake asked, his voice a husky groan against her neck.

"Yes, always," she whispered back, completely lost in their passionate moment.

He pressed himself into her naked body even harder with his own, his hands coming up to her throat to lift her chin so that he could kiss her deeper, commanding her silently while she willingly surrendered to his every whim. Tilly then felt a burning, hot sensation on her neck as he leaned over her, followed by the strong and powerful lips of her lover when he covered the stinging area with his mouth.

She was confused at first, but soon became aware that Blake was sucking gently on her neck, his tongue flicking over the spot that'd been burning seconds before, and she quickly realised that he must've made a small cut on her skin. Tilly gasped as she felt him draw out a mouthful of her blood and then heard as he swallowed it down, but wasn't scared. She'd promised to give him every part of her self willingly, and she'd meant it.

Blake leaned up over her, a tiny bit of her blood still on his lips, and he bit down on his finger and placed it in Tilly's mouth, giving her a few drops of his blood in return for the small amount that he'd just taken from her. She realised straight away what he was doing, that he was blood-sharing with her, and she smiled as she sucked his fingertip clean. It was just seconds before the wonderful partaking of strength, power, and love washed over her, without there being any hint of control in it at all. She felt amazing, and had never been more alive.

He leaned down to kiss her again and Tilly could taste her

own blood on his lips, but didn't care. The sharing of blood between them had been intense, and they could both feel its power as it strengthened them and their already powerful bond. Tilly reached down and grabbed Blake's hips, cupping his bum-cheeks with her hands and pulling him towards her. She needed to give herself to him, and had to have him inside of her in every way she could imagine, and of course, he obliged.

A couple of hours later, they teleported back to the old castle in Edinburgh, signifying the end of their perfect day together. The pair arrived just in time for Blake to drop Tilly off at her bedroom and kiss her goodbye, unable to stay even a minute longer otherwise he'd quickly react to the harsh restrictions the Earth and moon held over him.

"See you in four days," Blake whispered, checking the clock.

"I can't wait," Tilly told him, leaning up to peck him on the cheek. "Now go," she then ordered him with a smile, and he teleported away just seconds before the clock struck midnight. Tilly did her best not to get upset this time, knowing that she'd see him again in just a few days, so gave into the tiredness that finally hit her once she laid down in the bed, and she drifted off to sleep almost instantly.

***

The next morning, Tilly joined Jessica and Berith for breakfast in the castle dining hall again. Most of the other guests had left the city already, but the pair had stayed to take Tilly home after her day with Blake was over.

"Wow, you look like you had an amazing day. Did he take you somewhere nice?" Jessica asked her when Berith was out of earshot, taking in the bags under Tilly's tired eyes, but also the content, relaxed smile she couldn't help but wear.

"Oh yes," Tilly replied, with a romantic sigh, and she told her friend all about their whirlwind world tour the day before. She couldn't help but exude happiness after the wonderful time she'd shared with her master, and couldn't wait to see him again in a few days time.

"Ready ladies?" Berith asked them when he returned to the girls' side, and they both nodded. Each took one of his hands and felt the familiar pull of the teleportation as they set off towards London.

On their way, Tilly somehow felt as though she'd slammed into a brick wall. An intense rush of pain swept through her, and she felt as though she was being pulled downwards towards Earth. She fell to the ground with a hard thud, which winded her instantly. Tilly coughed and sputtered, trying to catch her breath, while struggling to figure out what on Earth had just happened.

When she could stand, she looked around, trying to take in her surroundings in the hopes of figuring out what was going on. She was in a field—definitely not at the penthouse where they should have landed—but neither Berith nor Jessica were anywhere to be seen.

Tilly stepped forward, trying to head off in search of her friends, but felt some kind of resistance in the air around her. It was reasonably gentle at first, but then a force that felt like a kick to the gut sent her flying backwards onto the floor. The wind was knocked out of her for the second time in just a few minutes, and she was forced to lay there for a while, feeling confused and sore. It wasn't long before a voice called out to her from a few feet away.

"Well, well, well," a woman's voice chimed as she

approached slowly. "Look what we have here. It seems I've caught a rat in my little trap," she said, looking down at Tilly with disgust when she reached the weak human that was still lying on the dirty ground gasping for breath. "I just knew it'd work. I caught you in my invisible net while you teleported overhead, how very clever of me," she added, clearly pleased with herself.

"Who are you and how did you trap me?" Tilly asked, rising to her feet, but standing still this time to avoid being thrown around again by the strange force field.

"I set up my wonderful little trap here that's specifically designed to ensnare dark beings and their followers who might be teleporting overhead. Unfortunately, your friends got away from the lightning-like hands that tried to grab at their ankles, but one out of three isn't bad I suppose," the witch replied, eyeing Tilly thoughtfully. "My name is Beatrice. I'm a white witch and my master is the angel Michael," she then told Tilly. She even added an over-dramatic bow and a swish of her hand as though enjoying herself. "Your turn," she added, staring at Tilly expectantly.

"Go to Hell," she answered, not wanting to give this witch any information about herself or her master. Tilly silently pleaded for guidance, or at least a sign, but couldn't sense any connection to Blake or Cate right now, and had to assumed that the witch must somehow be stopping their links to each other with her white magic.

Beatrice stepped over the invisible circle that entrapped Tilly, unrestricted by the threshold, and slapped her hard across the face. The force sent her flying across the dirt once again. She rolled onto her front and tried to stand, but suddenly felt herself being teleported away from the field, her body unable to move as though invisible ropes had now wrapped themselves around her.

They arrived at an old white church within seconds, and Tilly was thrown straight onto the floor where she lay in a heap before the dusty old altar. Beneath her was a large pentagram, painted with white lines, and she could feel herself growing woozy and weak. She knew it had to be thanks to its light power as it seeped into her, and could tell it was trying to take hold of her senses, as though attempting to force her cooperation. The unseen ropes soon released her body, but it didn't matter, she was already too frail to even try and fight back. Tilly had no idea what was happening, but it felt as if the powers of light and dark were seemingly having a battle of wills inside her own skin. It itched. Burned. She scratched at her skin and clutched her chest; unable to endure the torment another second, but somehow managed to force her body to submit to her mind.

"You feel it already?" Beatrice asked her, staring down at Tilly in amazement while her aching body still lay curled around itself inside the powerful mark. "Who *is* your master?" she asked her again, scowling at her from outside of the pentagram. Tilly laughed, a deep and crazy laugh that reminded her of the same one she'd heard escape her lips just once before—in Trey's sinister embrace.

"You're going to get your throat ripped out, witch, and I cannot wait to see it," Tilly replied, and added as much venom to her weak voice as she could muster when Beatrice approached. She looked young, but Tilly knew that she was more than likely hundreds of years old, and had bright blue eyes and blonde hair that seemed almost white in the dim light of the old building. Beatrice stared down at her, her cold eyes boring into Tilly's as she trembled and started coughing uncontrollably.

She tried to sit up but was thrown backwards onto the floor without another word from the witch. Her body was pressed into the hard wood, while her arms were stretched out to her sides, mirroring the iconic figure that stood on the cross nearby. Beatrice then spoke a quiet spell that Tilly couldn't understand, the words neither English nor any other language she'd ever heard before, and she could do nothing but lie there, powerless to fight back.

The inverted cross on her right arm rose to the surface following Beatrice's incantation, and Tilly tried to twist her arm over. She wanted to cover it, but was unable to move even an inch. "Bingo," Beatrice said when she looked down at the black mark, and a dreadful grin spread across her face as she took in the symbol on Tilly's arm. There was even a knowing twinkle in her eye.

She stepped inside the pentagram and climbed over Tilly, straddling her on the floor and looking down into her wide eyes as she spoke. "So, let me work it out, and you can tell me when I get it right, yeah?" she asked, mocking Tilly's resistance to her questions without a care for her unease. "Luna's followers were all killed, except her warlock boyfriend, so I know you aren't hers," she said, and she began ticking off her fingers as though working through a list. "Blake doesn't have any that we know of and neither does Serena, nor her filthy offspring. So, you must be Devin's, am I right?" she asked, leaning down to cup Tilly's cheeks with her hands.

"Fuck you," she murmured, but Beatrice didn't even bat an eye. Tilly knew she was done for, but that she'd die protecting Blake if she had to, and kept her mouth otherwise closed.

"But then again, you stink of darkness—reek of it even. Your master has fucked you very recently hasn't he, or else you're the coven slut? Hmm, this is a conundrum," Beatrice mused aloud, sitting back upright and tapping her index finger against her chin thoughtfully.

Tilly could see she was enjoying being overdramatic far too

much, and didn't even bother to retaliate with another curse, not giving Beatrice the satisfaction of an answer. "Oh well, I guess I'll just have to let you go then if you aren't gonna tell me," Beatrice then said, tilting backwards on her heels as if she was going to stand. Tilly felt a small glimmer of hope flare up from somewhere deep inside of her, but she pushed it aside instantly, knowing that this witch wouldn't let her go—not just like that.

Beatrice could tell that Tilly didn't believe her, and smiled as she sat herself back down with a hard thump and knocked the air out of Tilly's lungs. "Okay, you got me," she admitted, and then she pulled a long, rune embossed dagger from her boot. "Let's try this instead," she added, and slid it straight into Tilly's abdomen, all the while with a very sickeningly satisfied smile on her face.

Tilly gasped desperately for breath that couldn't come. Pain seared through her instantly as her body fought against the intruding blade, and her mind immediately threatened to lose consciousness. "Don't you go anywhere just yet, little girl. I need you to take a message to your master, whoever it might be, and to your Dark Queen," Beatrice said, leaning down closer to Tilly's face, demanding that she stay conscious, yet pushing the dagger deeper into her body as she did so. "Tell them that the angel Uriel demands that Cate delivers the child she stole from him before the next All Hallow's Eve, along with the fallen angel, Lucifer. Failure to do so will result in the High Council of Angels raining white fire down from Heaven—she'll know what all of that means," Beatrice informed her. She then withdrew the blade and stood over Tilly again, watching with a smile as she finally passed out.

***

Black, complete, and totally engulfing darkness enveloped

Tilly. She was neither falling nor floating, but it was as though it was suffocating her, seeping inside her body uncontrollably. She tried to scream, to shout out, but there was nothing but endless night all around her, and her body was no longer whole or real. She was a mere shell of her human self—a soul—a ball of energy already marked and claimed, and on its way down into the dark abyss below to its master.

She felt a throb from somewhere deep inside of her chest, almost like a pulse that sent her consciousness into overdrive, and two distant lights came into focus from somewhere seemingly very far away. As they grew closer, Tilly realised that they weren't lights, but eyes. Green, gorgeous eyes. She urged them closer, prayed for them to come to her faster, and in a blink she was kneeling inside a black pentagram, surrounded by hooded figures and dark shadows. Before her stood her master, and his beautiful eyes were sad as he took in the sight of his lover before him. This was one time when he was clearly unhappy to see her. She choked, trying to catch her breath, but soon realised that it was useless.

"Master," she managed to cry out, looking up at Blake pleadingly, desperate for answers or an idea of what was going on, but she was already coming to the terrible realisation by herself.

"Leave us," he said, commanding the rest of the demonic greeting party forcefully. He needed to speak with Tilly alone. They did as they were told, and then Blake kneeled down to gather up Tilly's frail form in his arms, kissing the top of her head as he cradled her.

"Am I dead?" she asked, sobbing into his black cloak.

"Not just yet, but almost," he informed her. "I've sent Alma up to help you, and she'll do everything she can, but you need to hold on, Tilly. Do not let yourself linger here. Fight your urges to stay with me now, for if you stay that means you've chosen to die, and I cannot allow that. Fight the darkness, fight me," Blake told her, looking down into her face seriously and forcing her to stay lucid. "If you die now, you'll be nothing more than a weak soul thanks to that fucking witch. You'll have no place at my side," he told her, and she sobbed harder but nodded, understanding his words. Tilly knew she had to go back, to force herself back to her broken body. First though, she had a message to deliver.

"She told me to tell you, to tell the Queen," she managed, eager to pass on the strange yet terrible information, and Blake stiffened.

"What? Tell me everything she said, Tilly," he urged her, pulling her gaze up to meet his.

"She said to tell your mother that the angel Uriel wants the child she stole from him, and he wants Lucif…he wants your father," she said, realising in time not to say his name, but Blake didn't care. His eyes grew wide at her words, and it was the first time she'd ever seen him truly scared. "He wants them before the next All Hallow's Eve otherwise the Council of Angels will rain down white fire from Heaven," she finished. "Does that make sense?"

"Yes, Tilly. It makes sense. She means all-out war," Blake said, his face pale thanks to her dark words, but he didn't say any more. He kissed her gently, and then placed a hand over her chest. With a grimace, he pushed hard over Tilly's heart, and she felt the heavy throb burst out of him and reverberate through her forcibly, and then he did it again, and again until she felt herself pulling away. "Hold on. Don't you die, okay?" he told her as he delivered one final burst into her chest and she lost consciousness again, her soul returning to a body full of nothing but pain and suffering. But, she'd already promised him long ago to take whatever pain Blake thought she could handle, and he was going to hold her to it. Tilly could deal with her agony for him just one last time, he knew it.

Blake then turned and teleported away from the antechamber. He knew that time wasn't on his side, and Tilly was fading fast, but in order to save her he might have to strike a deal with his mother first. For the first time in his long and lonely life, Blake truly knew how it felt to be afraid.

Losing Tilly wasn't an option. He'd do anything—give anything—if it meant saving his lover's life, but the Black Prince was also extremely aware he had a very grave and sinister message to deliver first.

The end of book two in the Black Rose series.

About the author

Laura started her writing career putting together short stories and fan fiction, usually involving her favourite movie characters caught up in steamy situations, and wrote her first full length novel in 2013. A self-confessed computer geek, Laura enjoys both the writing and editing side of her journey, and regularly seeks out the next big gadget on her wish list.

She spends her days looking after her two young children and their cocker spaniel Milo, as well as making the most of her free time by going to concerts with her friends, or else listening to rock music at home while writing (a trend many readers may have picked up on in her stories.)

Laura also loves hearing from her fans, and you can connect with her via the following:

www.facebook.com/lauramorganauthor
www.twitter.com/lauram241

If you enjoyed this book, please take a moment to share your thoughts by leaving a review to help promote Laura's work.

Laura Morgan's novels include:

The Black Rose series:
Embracing the Darkness: book #1 in the Black Rose series
A Slave to the Darkness: book #2 in the Black Rose series
Forever Darkness: book #3 in the Black Rose series
Destined for Darkness: book #4 in the Black Rose series
A Light in the Darkness: book #5 in the Black Rose series
When Darkness Falls: A Short Prequel to the Black Rose series
Don't Pity the Dead, Pity the Immortal: #1 in the Black Rose series
Novellas

And her contemporary romance novels:
Forever Lost
Forever Loved
Rough Love

Laura also writes dystopian Science Fiction under the alias LC Morgans, with her new novels:
Humankind: Book 1 in the Invasion Days series
Autonomy: Book 2 in the Invasion Day series
Resonant: Book 3 in the Invasion Day series
Hereafter: Book 4 in the Invasion Day series

40717619R00177

Printed in Poland
by Amazon Fulfillment
Poland Sp. z o.o., Wrocław